AN INCONVENIENT DUKE

ANNA HARRINGTON

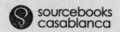

sourcebooks
casablanca

Published by Sourcebooks Casablanca, and imprint of Sourcebooks
P.O. Box 4410, Naperville, Illinois 60567-4410
(630) 961-3900
sourcebooks.com

Printed and bound in the United States of America.
OPM 10 9 8 7 6 5 4 3 2 1

Dedicated to Bruiser
for keeping me company during the long
hours on the porch writing this.

And a very special thank you to
Sarah Younger, Sarah Otterness, and Cat Clyne.

Prologue

April 1814

To General Marcus Braddock
Coldstream Guards, 2nd Battalion,
  Household Division
Bayonne, France

Dear General Braddock,

It is with a grieving heart that I write to you to tell you of the passing of your sister Elise.

There was a terrible accident. She was on her morning ride in the park and was thrown from her horse. The horse guards who found her assured me that she did not suffer. While there is nothing I can write that will lessen your pain, I pray you might find some comfort in that.

I know that your attention must now be fixed on your men and on the fight you are waging against Napoleon, but please be assured that I will do everything I can to support your sister Claudia and Elise's daughter, Penelope, while you are away.

Yours in shared grief—
Danielle Williams

June 1814

To the Honorable Danielle Williams
No. 2 Bedford Square, Mayfair
London, England

Dear Miss Williams,

Although the news was bitter, I thank you for your kind letter. It brings me solace to know that Elise was so dearly loved by you. I am more grateful than I can express to know that you are looking after Claudia and Pippa during this time of mourning.

> *With gratitude—*
> *Marcus Braddock*

January 1816

To the Honorable Danielle Williams
No. 2 Bedford Square, Mayfair
London, England

Dear Miss Williams,

My regiment's work in Paris will be ending soon, and I will be returning to London. I would very much appreciate the opportunity to call on you. I wish to thank you in person for the kindnesses that you and your aunt have shown to my family during my absence.

Yours sincerely,
Marcus Braddock

February 1816

To General Marcus Braddock
British Embassy
Hôtel de Charost, rue du Faubourg Saint-Honoré
Paris, France

Dear General,

Your appreciation is more than enough. Please do not feel obligated to call on us, as I know how busy your homecoming will surely be. I wish you the best with your new endeavors. Please give my love to Claudia and Penelope.

Yours in friendship—
Danielle Williams

April 1816

To the Honorable Danielle Williams
No. 2 Bedford Square, Mayfair
London

Dear Miss Williams,

I have returned home but discovered unsettling information regarding my sister Elise. I must insist on meeting with you. Please reply with the best day and time for me to call upon you.

                             Marcus Braddock

April 1816

To the General His Grace the Duke of Hampton
Charlton Place, Park Lane
London

Dear Duke,

While I wish to congratulate you on your new title, I must decline your offer to receive you. Elise was my dearest friend—in truth, more like a sister. To speak of her death will only refresh our shared grief and remind us of all that we have lost when your return should be met with joy. I could not bear it and wish to grieve for her in peace. Please understand.

                             Sincerely,
                             Danielle Williams

May 1816

To the Right Honorable the Viscountess Bromley
& the Honorable Danielle Williams
No. 2 Bedford Square
Mayfair, London

You are cordially invited to attend a birthday celebration
in honor of the General His Grace the Duke of Hampton,
on Saturday, May 5, at 8 p.m. Please send your acceptance
to Miss Braddock, Charlton Place, Park Lane, London.

And the handwritten note tucked inside with the invitation…

Danielle, please attend. The party will not be the same
without you. And to be honest, I will need your support
to survive the evening. You know how Marcus can be
at events like this. That it is for his own birthday will
most likely make him all the worse. And Pippa misses
you as much as I do.

~ Claudia

Danielle Williams bit her bottom lip as she read the note, dread and guilt pouring through her in equal measure.
God help me.
There was no refusing this invitation.

One

May 1816
Charlton Place, London

MARCUS BRADDOCK STEPPED OUT ONTO THE UPPER terrace of his town house and scanned the party spreading through the torch-lit gardens below.

He grimaced. His home had been invaded.

All of London seemed to be crowded into Charlton Place tonight, with the reception rooms filled to overflowing. The crush of bodies in the ballroom had forced several couples outside to dance on the lawn, and the terraces below were filled with well-dressed dandies flirting with ladies adorned in silks and jewels. Card games played out in the library, men smoked in the music room, the ladies retired to the morning room—the entire house had been turned upside down, the gardens trampled, the horses made uneasy in the mews…

And it wasn't yet midnight.

His sister Claudia had insisted on throwing this party for him, apparently whether he wanted one or not. Not only to mark his birthday tomorrow but also to celebrate his new position as Duke of Hampton, the title given to him for helping Wellington defeat Napoleon. The party would help ease his way back into society, she'd asserted, and give him an opportunity to meet the men he would now be working with in the Lords.

But Marcus hadn't given a damn about society before he'd gone off to war, and he cared even less now.

No. The reason he'd agreed to throw open wide the doors of Charlton Place was a woman.

The Honorable Danielle Williams, daughter of Baron Mondale and his late sister Elise's dearest friend. The woman who had written to inform him that Elise was dead.

The same woman he now knew had lied to him.

His eyes narrowed as they moved deliberately across the crowd. Miss Williams had been avoiding him since his return, refusing to let him call on her and begging off from any social event that might bring them into contact. But she hadn't been able to refuse the invitation for tonight's party, not when he'd also invited her great-aunt, who certainly wouldn't have missed what the society gossips were predicting would be the biggest social event of the season. She couldn't accept and then simply beg off either. To not attend this party would have been a snub to both him and his sister Claudia, as well as to Elise's memory. While Danielle might happily continue to avoid him, she would never intentionally wound Claudia.

She was here somewhere, he knew it. Now he simply had to find her.

He frowned. Easier said than done, because Claudia had apparently invited all of society, most of whom he'd never met and had no idea who they even were. Yet they'd eagerly attended, if only for a glimpse of the newly minted duke's town house. And a glimpse of *him*. Strangers greeted him as if they were old friends, when his true friends—the men he'd served with in the fight against Napoleon—were nowhere to be seen. *Those* men he trusted with his life.

These people made him feel surrounded by the enemy.

The party decorations certainly didn't help put him at ease. Claudia had insisted that the theme be ancient Roman and then set about turning the whole house into Pompeii. Wooden torches lit the garden, lighting the way for the army of toga-clad footmen carrying trays of wine from a replica of a Roman temple in the center of the garden. The whole thing gave him the unsettling feeling that he'd been transported to Italy, unsure of his surroundings and his place in them.

Being unsure was never an option for a general in the heat of battle, and Marcus refused to let it control him now that he was on home soil. Yet he couldn't stop it from haunting him, ever since he'd discovered the letter among Elise's belongings that made him doubt everything he knew about his sister and how she'd died.

He planned to put an end to that doubt tonight, just as soon as he talked to Danielle.

"There he is—the birthday boy!"

Marcus bit back a curse as his two best friends, Brandon Pearce and Merritt Rivers, approached him through the shadows. He'd thought the terrace would be the best place to search for Danielle without being seen.

Apparently not.

"You mean the duke of honor," corrected Merritt, a lawyer turned army captain who had served with him in the Guards.

Marcus frowned. While he was always glad to see them, right then he didn't need their distractions. Nor was he in the mood for their joking.

A former brigadier who now held the title of Earl of Sandhurst, Pearce looped his arm over Merritt's shoulder as both men studied him. "I don't think he's happy to see us."

"Impossible." Merritt gave a sweep of his arm to indicate the festivities around them. The glass of cognac in his hand had most likely been liberated from Marcus's private liquor cabinet in his study. "Surely he wants his two brothers-in-arms nearby to witness every single moment of his big night."

Marcus grumbled, "Every single moment of my humiliation, you mean."

"Details, details," Merritt dismissed, deadpan. But he couldn't hide the gleam of amusement in his eyes.

"What we really want to know about your birthday party is this." Pearce touched his glass to Marcus's chest and leaned toward him, his face deadly serious. "When do the pony rides begin?"

Marcus's gaze narrowed as he glanced between the two men. "Remind me again why I saved your miserable arses at Toulouse."

Pearce placed his hand on Marcus's shoulder in a show of genuine affection. "Because you're a good man and a brilliant general," he said sincerely. "And one of the finest men we could ever call a friend."

Merritt lifted his glass in a heartfelt toast. "Happy birthday, General."

Thirty-five. *Bloody hell.*

"Hear, hear." Pearce seconded the toast. "To the Coldstream Guards!"

A knot tightened in Marcus's gut at the mention of his former regiment that had been so critical to the victory at Waterloo yet also nearly destroyed in the brutal hand-to-hand combat that day. But he managed to echo, "To the Guards."

Not wanting them to see any stray emotion on his face, he turned away. Leaning across the stone balustrade on his forearms, he muttered, "I wish I could still be with them."

While he would never wish to return to the wars, he missed being with his men, especially their friendship and dependability. He missed the respect given to him and the respect he gave each of them in return, no matter if they were an officer or a private. Most of all, he longed for the sense of purpose that the fight against Napoleon had given him. He'd known every morning when he woke up what he was meant to do that day, what higher ideals he served. He hadn't had that since he returned to London, and its absence ate at him.

It bothered him so badly, in fact, that he'd taken to spending time alone at an abandoned armory just north of the City. He'd purchased the old building with the intention of turning it into a warehouse, only to discover that he needed a place to himself more than he needed the additional income. More and more lately, he'd found himself going there at all hours to escape from society and the ghosts that haunted him. Even in his own home.

That was the punishment for surviving when others he'd loved hadn't. The curse of remembrance.

"No, General." Pearce matched his melancholy tone as his friends stepped up to the balustrade, flanking him on each side. "You've left the wars behind and moved on to better things." He frowned as he stared across the crowded garden. "This party notwithstanding."

Merritt pulled a cigar from his breast pocket and lit it on a nearby lamp. "You're exactly where you belong. With your family." He puffed at the cheroot, then watched the smoke curl from its tip into the darkness overhead. "They need you now more than the Guards do."

In his heart, Marcus knew that, too. Which was why he'd taken it upon himself to go through Elise's belongings when Claudia couldn't bring herself to do it, to pack up what he thought her daughter, Penelope, might want when she was older and to distribute the rest to the poor. That was how he'd discovered a letter among Elise's things from someone named John Porter, arranging a midnight meeting for which she'd left the house and never returned.

He'd not had a moment of peace since.

He rubbed at the knot of tension in his nape. His

friends didn't need to know any of that. They were already burdened enough as it was by settling into their own new lives now that they'd left the army.

"Besides, you're a duke now." Merritt flicked the ash from his cigar. "There must be some good way to put the title to use." He looked down at the party and clarified, "One that doesn't involve society balls."

"Or togas," Pearce muttered.

Marcus blew out a patient breath at their good-natured teasing. "The Roman theme was Claudia's idea."

"Liar," both men said at once. Then they looked at each other and grinned.

Merritt slapped him on the back. "Next thing you know, you'll be trying to convince us that the pink ribbons in you horse's tail were put there by Penelope."

Marcus kept his silence. There was no good reply to that.

He turned his attention back to the party below, his gaze passing over the crowded garden. He spied the delicate turn of a head in the crowd—

Danielle. There she was, standing by the fountain in the glow of one of the torches.

For a moment, he thought he was mistaken, that the woman who'd caught his attention couldn't possibly be her. Not with her auburn hair swept up high on her head in a pile of feathery curls, shimmering with copper highlights in the lamplight and revealing a long and graceful neck. Not in that dress of emerald satin with its capped sleeves of ivory lace over creamy shoulders.

Impossible. This woman, with her full curves and mature grace, simply couldn't be the same excitable girl he remembered, who'd seemed always to move through the world with a bouncing skip. Who had bothered him to distraction with all her questions about the military and soldiers.

She laughed at something her aunt said, and her face brightened into a familiar smile. Only then did he let himself believe that she wasn't merely an apparition.

Sweet Lucifer. Apparently, nothing in England was as he remembered.

He put his hands on both men's shoulders. "If you'll excuse me, there's someone in the garden I need to speak with. Enjoy yourselves tonight." Then, knowing both men nearly as well as he knew himself, he warned, "But not too much."

As he moved away, Merritt called out with a knowing grin. "What's *her* name?"

"Trouble," he muttered and strode down into the garden before she could slip back into the crowd and disappear.

Two

DANIELLE WILLIAMS SMILED DISTRACTEDLY AT THE story her great-aunt Harriett was telling the group of friends gathered around them in the garden. The one about how she'd accidentally pinched the bottom of—

"King George!" The crux of the story elicited a gasp of surprise, followed by laughter. Just as it always did. "I had no idea that the bottom I saw poking out from behind that tree was a royal one. Truly, doesn't one bottom look like all the rest?"

"I've never thought so," Dani mumbled against the rim of her champagne flute as she raised it to her lips.

Harriett slid her a chastising glance, although knowing Auntie, likely more for interrupting her story than for any kind of hint of impropriety.

"But oh, how high His Majesty jumped!" her aunt continued, undaunted. As always. "I was terrified—simply *terrified*, I tell you! I was only fourteen and convinced that I had just committed high treason."

Although Dani had heard this same story dozens of times, the way Harriett told it always amused her. Thank goodness. After all, she needed something to distract her, because this evening was the first time she'd been to Charlton Place since Marcus Braddock had returned from the continent. The irony wasn't lost on her. She was on edge with nervousness tonight when she'd once spent so much time here that she'd considered this place a second home.

"A pinch to a king's bottom!" Harriett exclaimed. "Wars have been declared over less offending actions, I assure you."

Dani had been prepared for the unease that fluttered in her belly tonight, yet the guilt that gnawed at her chest was as strong as ever…for not coming to see Claudia or spending time with Pippa, for not being able to tell Marcus what kindnesses Elise had done for others in the months before her death. But how could she face him without stirring up fresh grief for both of them?

No. Best to simply avoid him.

"Had it been a different kind of royal bottom—say, one of the royal dukes—I might not have panicked so. But it was a *king's* bottom!"

She had a plan. Once Harriett finished her story, Dani would suddenly develop a headache and need to leave. She would give her best wishes to Claudia before slipping discreetly out the door and in the morning pen a note of apology to the duke for not wishing him happy birthday in person. She'd assure him that she'd looked for him at the party but had been unable to find him. A perfectly believable excuse given how many people were crammed into Charlton Place tonight. A complete crush! So many other people wanted their chance to speak to him that she most likely couldn't get close to him even if she tried. Not that she'd *try* exactly, but—

"Good evening, Miss Williams."

The deep voice behind her twined down her spine.
Marcus Braddock. *Drat it all.*

So much for hiding. Her trembling fingers tightened
around the champagne flute as she inhaled deeply and
slowly faced him. She held out her gloved hand and lowered into a curtsy. "Your Grace."

Taking her hand and bowing over it, he gave her a
smile, one of those charming grins that she remembered
so vividly. Those smiles had always taken her breath
away, just as this one did now, even if it stopped short of
his eyes.

"It's good to have you and your aunt back at Charlton
Place, Miss Williams."

"Thank you." She couldn't help but stare. He'd always
been attractive and dashing, especially in his uniform,
and like every one of Elise's friends, she'd had a schoolgirl
infatuation with him. And also like every one of his little
sister's friends, he'd paid her absolutely no mind whatsoever except to tolerate her for Elise's sake.

Although he was just as handsome as she remembered, Marcus had certainly changed in other ways. The
passing years had brought him into his prime, and the
youthful boldness she remembered had been tempered
by all he'd experienced during his time away, giving him
a powerful presence that most men would never possess.

When he released her hand to greet the others, Dani
continued to stare at him, dumbfounded. She simply
couldn't reconcile the brash and impetuous brother of
her best friend with the compelling man now standing

beside her, who had become one of the most important men in England.

Harriett leaned toward her and whispered, "Lower your hand, my dear."

Heavens, her hand! It still hovered in midair where he'd released it. With embarrassment heating her cheeks, she dropped it to her side.

She turned away and gulped down the rest of her champagne, not daring to look at the general for fear he'd think her the same infatuated goose she'd been as a young girl. Or at Harriett, whose face surely shone with amusement at the prospect of Dani being smitten with England's newest hero.

No. She was simply stunned to see all the changes that time and battle had wrought in him. That was all.

But then, Marcus Braddock had always been the most intense man she'd ever known, with brown eyes so dark as to be almost black, thick hair to match that curled at his collar, and a jaw that could have been sculpted from marble, like those Greek gods in Lord Elgin's notorious statues that Parliament had just purchased. Broad-shouldered, tall and confident, commanding in every way...no wonder she'd not been surprised to learn of all his promotions gained from heroism on the battlefield or to read about his exploits in the papers. Only when she'd learned that the regent had granted him a dukedom alongside Wellington had she been surprised—not that he'd been offered the title but that he'd accepted it.

"You seem well, Duke." Harriett had the audacity to

look him up and down from behind the quizzing glass she wore on a chain around her neck. But her seven decades of age gave her the right to take liberties that few others would deign to claim, including so shamelessly scrutinizing the new duke when she should have done it surreptitiously. The way Dani was doing.

She gave him her own once-over while he was distracted with her aunt, deliberately taking him in from head to toe and finding him more impressive than ever. Despite her nervousness at seeing him again, a smile pulled at her lips. Only Marcus Braddock could appear imperial standing next to a papier-mâché statue of Julius Caesar.

Harriett finished her examination with an approving nod. "Life in London must be agreeing with you."

His mouth twisted with amusement. "I feel as if I've just been put through a military inspection, Viscountess."

Harriett let out a sound halfway between a humph and a chortle. "Better grow used to it, my boy! You were the grandson of a baron before, but now you're a peer. A duke, no less. Privacy has just become a luxury you cannot afford."

Although his expression didn't alter, Dani felt a subtle change in him. A hardening. As if he'd already discovered for himself the truth behind her great-aunt's warning.

"Lovely party." Harriett waved a gloved hand to indicate the festivities, the rings on her fingers shining in the torchlight. "So kind of you to throw it and invite all of London."

Dani blanched. Of all the things to say—

"Couldn't invite the best without inviting the rest," he countered as expertly as if the two were waging a tennis match.

Her eyes gleamed mischievously. "And which are which?"

"If you don't know—"

"You're part of the rest," the viscountess finished, raising her champagne glass in a mock toast.

In reply, he winked at her.

Harriett laughed, tickled by their verbal sparring match. "You happened by at exactly the right moment. I was just telling everyone about the first time I met His Majesty. Have I ever told you—"

"If you'll pardon me, Viscountess," he interrupted politely to avoid being caught up in the story. *Smart man.* "I'd like to ask Miss Williams for the next dance." He turned toward her. "Would you do me the honor?"

Dani's heart slammed against her ribs in dread. Being with him like this, surrounded by a crowd of friends and acquaintances where the conversation had to be polite and impersonal was one thing. But dancing was something completely different and far too close for comfort. There would be too many opportunities to be reminded of Elise's death, for both of them. *This* was exactly what she'd hoped to avoid.

"My apologies, Your Grace." Dani smiled tightly. "But I'm not dancing tonight."

His expression darkened slightly. Clearly, he wasn't

used to being refused. "Not even with an old friend returned from the wars?"

Especially not him. "Not at all, I'm afraid."

Something sparked in the dark depths of his eyes. A challenge? Had he realized that she'd been purposefully evading him? The butterflies in her belly molded one by one into a ball of lead as he smiled at her. "Surely you can make an exception."

Dear heavens, why wouldn't he let this go? "I haven't been feeling myself lately, and a dance might tire—"

"Danielle," Harriett chastised with a laughing smile. Beneath the surface, however, she was surely horrified that Dani was refusing not just an old family friend and the man of honor at tonight's party but the most eligible man in the entire British empire. "One dance will not overtax you."

Without giving her the chance to protest, he insisted, "If you grow fatigued, I promise to return you immediately to your aunt." Marcus turned the full charms of his smile on her and held out his hand. "Shall we?"

Now she knew what foxes felt like when they were cornered by hounds. With no more excuses for why she couldn't dance, the only way to avoid him now would be to flat-out cut him in front of his guests. *That* she would never do.

Marcus didn't deserve that. Truly, he'd done nothing wrong, except remind her of Elise.

She grudgingly nodded her consent and allowed him to place her hand on his arm to lead her away.

Once they were out of earshot of the others, she lightly squeezed his arm to capture his attention. "While it's kind of you to request a dance, it's perfectly fine with me if we don't take the floor. You shouldn't feel obligated."

"But I want to." He slid her a sideways glance that rippled a warning through her as he led her toward the house. "I was very happy to see that you'd attended tonight."

"I wouldn't have missed it." Although she'd dearly tried to do just that. Swiftly changing the topic away from herself, she declared, "This party is a grand way to celebrate your return as a hero. I'm certain that Claudia and Pippa are thrilled to have you home."

Regret surged through her as soon as the words left her lips, because her mention of them would surely only remind him of Elise's absence. She hadn't wanted to cause him more grief. After all, that was why she'd been avoiding him since his return. How could he not look at her without thinking of his sister's death? God knew Dani was reminded of exactly that every time she thought of him.

"And you—" she rushed to add before he could reply, pivoting the conversation in a different direction. "You must have missed England."

"I did." The way he said that sounded faintly aggrieved. "But I'm not certain England missed me."

"It did, a great deal." Part of her had missed him a great deal as well.

He chuckled at that, as if it were a private joke. "Very little, I'm sure."

Yet his amusement did nothing to calm her unease,

which wasn't helped at all by the hand he touched briefly to hers as it rested on his sleeve. The small gesture sent her heart somersaulting. But then, hadn't he always made her nervous?

Yet he fascinated her, too. Something about him stirred her curiosity... Of course, she'd found his life as a soldier intriguing and had loved to hear Elise talk of his adventures. His sister had been so proud of him that she couldn't stop bragging, and Dani had soaked up all the stories, especially those few she'd been fortunate enough to hear him tell himself during rare visits home before the fighting grew so fierce on the Peninsula that he'd not been able to leave Spain.

"But you're right. I did miss my family, and I'm very happy to be back with them." Another brief rest of his hand on hers, this time with a reassuring squeeze. "Although I suspect that they're ready to toss *me* back over the Channel."

She shook her head. "Not at all."

He lowered his mouth to her ear so he wouldn't be overheard by the other guests. "Then why else would Claudia torture me with a party like this?"

"She's not torturing you."

"Oh?" As if offering irrefutable proof, he muttered, "A plaster model of Vesuvius is set to erupt at midnight."

She laughed, her gloved hand going to her lips to stifle it. Amusement mixed with surprise. Being with him was quite enjoyable, when he didn't remind her of how much she missed Elise.

"And you, Miss Williams? Are *you* ready to toss me back?"

Her laughter died against her fingertips at the way he asked that. Not an innocent question. Not at all a tease. A hardness lurked behind it that she couldn't fathom.

"Of course not." She smiled uneasily as he led her through the French doors and into the house toward the ballroom that had been created by opening the connecting doors between the salon, dining, and drawing rooms. "Why would I want to do that?"

"Most likely for the same reason you've been avoiding me."

Guilt pierced her so sharply that she winced. *This* was what she'd feared during the past few months, why she hadn't come to Charlton Place—coming face-to-face with his grief over his sister and her guilt over avoiding him. She wanted no part of this conversation!

She tried to slip away, but his hand closed over hers again, this time pinning her fingers to his sleeve and refusing to let her go. Aware of every pair of eyes in the room watching them and not wanting to create a scene, she walked on beside him until he finally stopped on the far side of the ballroom near the musicians.

She pounced on this chance to flee. It was time for her headache to arrive. "If you please, General—" Remembering herself, she corrected, "That is, Your Grace—"

"Has your absence been because of Elise's death?"

She flinched beneath his bluntness. There would

be no avoiding this exchange. This was the reason he'd refused to let her decline the dance.

"No," she whispered, unable to speak any louder past the knot in her throat. "It's been because of you."

Three

DANI'S PULSE STUTTERED WHEN HIS EYES FLARED IN genuine surprise, then iced over. He demanded in a low voice, "What do you mean because of *me*?"

"I was the one who sent news of her death to you." She looked away across the dance floor as half of the couples moved off and more joined those who remained. "Why would you want to see me when I would only remind you of your loss?"

"You think me as weak as that?"

Never. Not him. "I think you…" How *did* she think of him, when he'd always paid her no more mind than a teacup? As his sister's friend and ten years younger, she'd expected no less, even as she'd admired him from afar. But now, seeing the man he'd become, she simply had no idea what to make of him. "I think you loved Elise a great deal. Even now, just speaking to me like this—it's making you grieve all over again."

His shoulders sagged almost imperceptibly. But she noticed. Given the hours she'd spent staring at him as a girl, of course she had.

"How could I bring that pain back into your home?" Or Claudia's? Or open herself again to fresh grieving? And sweet heavens, Pippa…did she deserve to be reminded that she'd lost her mother before she barely knew her, the same child who had already lost her father? "You've returned a hero, with a shining new future before you, and you've come back into your family's embrace. I didn't want to ruin that by reminding you of what you've lost. That is why I stayed away."

Tentatively, she placed her hand on his arm. She couldn't resist giving him this small gesture of reassurance. He deserved so much more from her, but this was all she could offer.

"I hope you understand." Her hand fell away to her side, yet her fingertips continued to tingle from the feel of the hard muscle beneath his jacket sleeve.

Not replying, he signaled to the master of ceremonies, who nodded and stepped onto the dais to speak to the lead musician. The violinist gestured toward the other musicians, setting them into a flurry of shuffling through their sheet music. Then they played the opening fanfare for the next dance—a waltz. Surprised murmurs went up through the crowd that the order of the dances had changed.

As Marcus gave her a low bow, Dani sank into an answering curtsy. But suspicion sparked in her belly for why he would order a waltz, of all dances, when he now knew why she didn't want to be close to him.

The music settled into sweeping strains, and he led her into the waltz, taking them expertly into their steps.

A pinch of uneasiness tightened in her chest as she glided along with him, her full satin skirts swooshing around his legs whenever they turned. Every pair of eyes in the crowd that watched them dance past only served to remind her that life was now so very different for both of them than it had been before the wars, and so very complicated.

Yet knowing that didn't stop her from enjoying the waltz. How could she not, when he led her so skillfully around the room? A natural-born athlete, he made every move seem effortless. Dancing with him proved just as wonderful as she'd always suspected it would be during all those evenings as a young miss when she'd watched him partner with other women beneath the glittering chandeliers at so many otherwise forgotten parties. Although nervous suspicion still lingered inside her, so did pleasure, helped along by the hard muscles in his legs that she tried unsuccessfully not to notice every time they accidentally brushed against hers in the tight turns they were forced to make on the crowded dance floor. She couldn't help but follow yieldingly in his arms, couldn't help but ignore the rest of the world spinning around them.

When his lips curled faintly into a smile, a jolt of raw attraction sparked inside her. It struck so unexpectedly that it shocked the daylights out of her.

"You seem surprised," he said, amusement coloring his voice. "You didn't think I could waltz?"

He'd misunderstood her stunned bewilderment. *Thank God*, because she couldn't have borne the humiliation if he realized how her body tingled in response to his.

"I thought you'd be rusty in your steps," she dodged.

"I didn't think you'd have had much opportunity to practice during the past few years."

"Not often, that's true. And my horse made for a damnably clumsy partner."

She laughed despite the fluttering butterflies in her
belly. "Four left hooves?"

"The rascal kept wanting to lead."

Another laugh bubbled from her as he twirled her into
a turn in the far corner of the room, then started a prome-
nade back across the floor. How had she not remembered
him being so witty? Brilliant, of course. Cunning even,
from the stories she'd read of his battle exploits. But such
a dry sense of humor was a welcome discovery, one that
was helping to cut through her unease.

The worst was over between them, apparently.
Hoping they could be friends, she teased, "Perhaps I
should be partnering with the cavalry at society balls."

But he didn't laugh at her joke, instead forcing a tight
smile as if distracted. Apparently, more lingered on his
mind than the reason she'd been avoiding Charlton Place.

Well, if they were going to find a way to be friends, then
she might as well be bold about it. "General, is something
wrong? You keep looking at me as if..." She shook her
head, puzzled. "As if you don't know what to make of me."

"Because I don't," he answered honestly, his brow
drawing down into a puzzled frown. His bluntness
was jarring, as was the sound of betrayal in his voice.
"Because I simply cannot fathom why you lied to me
about Elise's death."

Danielle stumbled.

Marcus caught her in his arms to keep her from falling. He held her against him to steady her, but in that fleeting beat, the sensation of her yielding body against his solid front passed through him like a warm breeze.

When he'd glimpsed her across the gardens, he'd thought she was beautiful. But up close, she was downright stunning.

The awkward young miss he remembered had completely disappeared. In her place was a woman in full, with ample curves, elegant lines, and an inherent grace visible in every move she made. She'd been replaced by a woman exuding confidence. That was the contradiction he now saw in her, one he found surprisingly alluring—that so much strength lay beneath that elegant exterior.

But he also saw a flash of stunned bewilderment cross her face. She hadn't expected him to accuse her of lying about Elise's death.

He led her back into the waltz. Anyone watching would have assumed she'd simply missed her steps if not for the way she stared up at him, as if he were a stranger.

Perhaps he was. He was beginning to wonder if he knew her at all. Had circumstances been different, he would have requested this waltz for the express purpose of getting to know her again. Perhaps even to become better acquainted than they'd been before. Spending time with a beautiful and intelligent woman would be a welcome luxury after so long away at war.

But Elise had been killed. Danielle had lied about it. And he desperately needed to learn why.

So he said as calmly as possible, tamping down the distrust she stirred in his gut, "You hid the truth from me about how she died."

"I told you everything I knew," she defended herself.

His eyes locked with hers as he expertly turned her through a half circle to move them away from the other couples. Although they kept their voices low, he couldn't risk being overheard. "What you wrote in your letter wasn't true. You said that she'd been found in the park, that she'd gone for a morning ride and been thrown from her horse."

"Yes." An emphatic nod. She was regaining her balance, both in the waltz and in the conversation. "She was found that morning in the park by one of the Horse Guards who had been out exercising his mount. The guards didn't know who she was. They came to me because they'd found my name on a note she had in her pocket. They asked me to identify—"

Choking on the words, she looked away, but not before he saw a stricken expression cross her face.

A pang of guilt pierced him for confronting her without warning like this, but he'd been trying to speak with her since he returned, only to be refused at every turn. But when he found that note among his sister's belongings, a deeper urgency to uncover the truth gripped him. Starting with discovering what Danielle knew.

She sucked in a steadying breath and continued, "They asked me to identify her body."

Despite admiration for her control, Marcus glanced away and twirled her into a tight turn, unable to bear the sight of her grief. Or to have her see his.

"They said that she must have fallen from her horse, that her mare was found nearby. That her neck was broken. What reason would they have had to lie to me? Or me to lie to you?" More than grief rose inside her now. Anger was beginning to simmer beneath her calm, collected surface. "As soon as I was able, I came here and told Claudia, informed the staff when Claudia was too overcome to do so herself, made arrangements for the funeral... And then I wrote to you."

Dear God, the hell those two women must have gone through here while he was hundreds of miles away, unable to help. His heart pounded brutally from the omnipresent grief that had shadowed him for the past two years, and from the guilt, which was made worse by this confrontation.

Yet it couldn't be helped. "That wasn't how she died."

"But the guards said—"

He whirled her through another turn. "She didn't die from being thrown from her horse."

Danielle frowned at him, bewildered. "How do you know that?"

"She didn't go out riding that morning. She'd left the night before to meet up with a man named John Porter and never came home."

Her voice softened as she repeated, her face paling, "How do you know that?"

"Because I found a letter from him among her things, confirming the date and time of their meeting." The information spilled out of him in a rush of frustration and grief. He didn't want to wound her, but now that he could finally challenge her with what he knew, he couldn't stop, for Elise's sake. "Then I tracked down the stable boy who had been working in my mews at the time of the accident. He said she often saddled her own horse and rode off alone. Apparently, she'd done that several times in the months leading up to her death. I think she did it that night, too."

He twirled her through a circle so unexpectedly that she glanced up at him, startled by the movement.

"Elise was too good of a horsewoman to be thrown from her mare. Certainly not on a morning trot through the park. Especially when she didn't go out on horseback at all that morning." His gaze fixed on hers with a hardness that told her he'd brook no dissembling. "So let's start over with the truth, shall we?"

"I did tell you the truth! I told you everything that the guards..." As her voice faded, the confusion on her beautiful face melted into anguish.

Her reaction pierced him. She certainly wasn't pretending the emotions behind that. Not even an actress at the Theatre Royal would have been good enough to fake such raw pain and sorrow.

Fresh guilt assaulted him. Good God, did she truly

not know? Had it never occurred to her that Elise's death hadn't happened at all the way she'd claimed?

He searched her face for answers. "You didn't know that she'd left Charlton Place at night, alone, to meet a man?"

"No. Or I would have stopped her."

Looking at her now, hearing the resolve in her voice, *that* he very much believed. "And John Porter?"

"I don't know who he is."

A bitter taste rose on his tongue. "Was he her lover?"

"No! Elise would never…"

Her cheeks flushed, and she glanced away in embarrassment. Danielle might have blossomed into a woman while he'd been away, but her reluctance to put to words that his sister had taken a lover assured him that she was still innocent. He had no idea why he should care, but he thanked God that some things hadn't changed.

"Why else would a widow meet up alone with a man at night?"

"*Not* for that." Irritation sparked in her eyes that he would assume that of his sister. Despite himself, a warmth blossomed in his chest at her defense of Elise's reputation. "Not her."

His fingers tightened around hers as he continued to waltz her around the room. "Are you certain she wasn't planning to elope?"

She gaped at him, thunderstruck. "What on earth makes you think that?"

"In his note, Porter wrote that everything was set for their vanishing that night."

She blanched and missed a step. If his arms weren't around her, she would have stumbled again. She rasped out hoarsely as she hurried back into step with him, "A vanishing?"

The way she repeated that, her haunted expression— *Good God*. Instantly, his blood froze. "You know more than you're telling."

She gave a fierce shake of her head. "I didn't know about any of this!"

"Did she die on the way to meet him or coming back?" His gaze narrowed, watching her closely as he dared to finally put voice to his fears. "Or did he murder her?"

She gasped, the strangled sound so pained that he flinched. "*Murder?*" The word came as barely any sound at all on her lips, and she began to tremble, so hard that she nearly shuddered in his arms. "Oh, God…Elise…"

"So I'll ask again." He twirled her through a tight circle, one meant to keep her off-balance. "Who is John Porter?"

"I don't know."

"What did he mean by their vanishing?"

She fiercely shook her head. "I don't—"

"And Scepter?"

At that, she halted right there in his arms, smack in the middle of the dance floor, bringing him to a stop with her. For one fleeting heartbeat, he saw fear grip her face, the same fear he'd seen on every man under his command the first time they'd charged into battle.

Then it was gone, and in its place came anger.

"How dare you?" Outrage filled her voice. "*This* is why you asked me to waltz? Not as an old friend of the family, not even to commiserate together in our grief—this dance was nothing but the battle strategy of a war-hardened general, to keep me from fleeing while you interrogated me!"

"My sister was murdered, and I'm damned well going to find out why." His own anger flared in response, yet he was aware of the crowded dance floor around them and kept his face carefully inscrutable. "John Porter warned Elise in his letter to stay away from them, as if he were afraid of them and what they were capable of doing." He searched her face for answers. "So tell me what you know. What the hell is Scepter? Why would he warn Elise to stay away from it? And where can I find the people behind it?"

"I don't know." The icy look she gave him was one of absolute obstinacy. "And for your sake, General," she said, her eyes practically glowing, "I wouldn't tell you even if I did."

He clenched his jaw. "I need to know what you're hiding about—"

"Stop!" she ordered hoarsely, pushing herself free of his arms. "*Please.* Just stop."

As the other couples continued to dance on around them, the attention of the room fell upon them, and everyone craned their necks to see what was wrong. But Marcus didn't care that whispers went up at the scene they were making or that Claudia now stood in the door-way, watching them curiously. Danielle Williams knew more than she was admitting. Far more. He wouldn't stop pressing until he had the entire truth and brought to justice the man responsible.

The waltz ended, and the last notes died with a flourish. When she stepped back, he had no choice except to let her go.

But this conversation was far from over.

Aware of the attention of the crowd still upon them and clearly wanting to lessen the spectacle they were making of themselves, she held out her hand and dropped into a curtsy as if nothing were wrong.

"Your sister was a good woman who dedicated her life to helping those in need," she said between deep inhalations as she gathered herself enough to put a smile onto her face for the crowd around them. "Keep that memory, and let the rest go. I beg you."

He took her hand and bowed over it, attempting to appear as if they were simply finishing the waltz. He murmured against her fingers, "I have no intention of letting this go."

Four

MARCUS HURRIED DOWNSTAIRS TOWARD THE ENTRY hall so he wouldn't be seen as he left the house. It was one of the reasons why he was up and dressed in his riding clothes so early despite not getting to bed until after three o'clock this morning. Even then, he hadn't slept, tossing and turning as he replayed in his head his conversation with Danielle and kicking himself for not handling it better.

She hadn't known about the murder. That was obvious. Yet she knew more than she was telling, he was certain. He wouldn't stop seeking her out until he had answers. Even if he had to waltz her halfway to Calcutta to get them.

Around him, Charlton Place was a hive of early morning activity. The servants were all busily cleaning up after the party, putting the furniture and rugs back in their proper places, and taking all the glasses and plates down to the kitchen. The Roman decorations were being removed one column at a time but quickly enough that the garden was beginning to return to normal. *Thank God.*

While the staff was spending their day doing this, it would be safer for him not to be anywhere near the house. A wise general knew when to retreat.

But he also wanted to clear his head. Because he needed to come up with a new strategy for dealing with Danielle.

"Marcus, you're sneaking away," Claudia chastised lightly as she entered the hall and caught him. "Again."

She was lovely in her morning dress of pale pink, her light brown hair carefully pulled into a stack of curls. As this season's Incomparable, she turned gentlemen's heads everywhere she went, but they were fools to chase after her. Only one man held her heart, and Marcus fully expected Adam Trousdale to offer for her by year's end. She'd put her own life on hold for the past two years to remain at Charlton Place and care for Penelope. But now that he had returned and assumed Pippa's care, she could move on, taking greater part in the events of the season, marrying soon, and establishing a household of her own.

At least one female in his family would live happily ever after. The blame he carried for not being able to give that to Elise clawed at him even now.

"I'm not sneaking away." He covered that well-meaning lie with a kiss to her cheek. "I'm going out for a ride."

She arched a disbelieving brow in that manner she had that reminded him instantly of his stepmother, so much so that his chest panged. Rachel Braddock had married his father when Marcus had been only nine. With a son to raise and dwindling finances to see to, his father had had no choice but to remarry. And quickly. But he'd chosen well, helped along in no small part by the family's good name and his grandfather's rank as baron. Marcus's new mother had been a dedicated, kindhearted, and intelligent woman who cared for him as if he were her own, and within three years, Marcus had two sisters whom he loved dearly.

Which was why he'd not stopped Claudia from throwing last night's party. Hosting it had made her happy, and he'd do anything to make his family happy. He slid a glance through the front door sidelights as Mount Vesuvius went gliding past, carried away by four footmen. He heaved out a sigh. Anything...even if it killed him.

Thankfully, she didn't challenge his very flimsy excuse for leaving so early. "We've been looking everywhere for you."

He tugged on his leather gloves. "We?"

As if on cue, his five-year-old niece, Penelope, skipped through the breakfast room door, dangling her favorite toy—a threadbare stuffed horse—by its hind leg. Pink ribbon laced through its tail. The same pink ribbon she'd knotted into his horse's tail last week. "Uncle Marcus!" She threw her arms around his legs in a big hug and tilted back her head to look up at him. Fresh out of bed, with her bare feet poking out from beneath the hem of her night rail and wrapper, she smiled at him as she always did right before she asked him for something he couldn't refuse her.

"Pippa." He scooped her up, and she snaked a skinny arm around his neck. "What are you doing down here? You should still be up in the nursery." Asleep. Just as he'd hoped so that he could make a clean escape for a few hours. But apparently, the entire household was awake, including the two Braddock women.

"I wanted to wish you a very happy birthday." With that explanation, she let go of him, completely trusting that he'd hold on tight to her and not let her fall.

But of course he would. *Always.* "That is very sweet of you."

She smiled, the one that would have gentlemen tripping all over themselves years from now when she debuted. She moved the horse back and forth over his waistcoat to let it gallop across his chest. "So does Brutus."

"And very sweet of him, too." So now the creature's name was Brutus. She changed it nearly every day, trying out new names the way society women tried out fashion styles. God help him when she grew older.

"Are you old?"

God help him *now.* He answered, deadpan, "Ancient."

She nodded somberly. "Auntie says you're old and that you need to get a wife soon or you'll be too old to—"

"Penelope," Claudia scolded, her face flushing. "I said no such thing."

Pippa cast her a dark look, spotting that for the lie it was. Then she brought her mouth close to his ear and countered in a whisper loud enough for Claudia to hear, "She did too say that!"

Marcus fought back a laugh at his sister's expense.

"Uncle Marcus." Pippa leaned far back to glance up at him. He knew that look—the one she used to twist him around her little finger. "Can I have a piece of cake from last night's party?"

"Cook's already made up a good breakfast for you. You wouldn't want to insult her by not eating it." Or make herself sick. He'd learned that lesson the hard way last month by letting her have too many sticky buns. How a stomach that tiny could cast up so much, he still had no idea. And with deadly aim on his boots, too.

"Not for breakfast. For playing soldier."

He frowned. During the past few months since his return, he'd become an expert on five-year-old logic, but this request bewildered the daylights out of him. "Why do you need cake to play at being a soldier, poppet?"

She stared at him as if he'd gone daft. "Because soldiers march with cakes on!"

Cakes? *That* was an interesting change to the uniform code.

Then it hit him. "Not cakes, darling—caissons." He grinned at her, ignoring the frown on Claudia's face that once more revealed her worry that Penelope would be raised by a bachelor soldier when she married and left Charlton Place. "Big boxes on carts. I'll show you the next time we visit the Horse Guards." Which, judging from Claudia's deepening frown, might never happen. "Now give me a kiss and scoot upstairs to get dressed."

She kissed his cheek.

"Thank you."

"And Brutus, too." She touched the horse's muzzle to his cheek and made the sound of a kiss.

His lips twitched. "Thank you, Brutus."

She neighed in reply.

He laughed and hugged her. If Claudia was worried about his niece being around soldiers and the cavalry, she'd suffer apoplexy to learn that he'd already bought Pippa her own pony, with delivery set for next week. He'd learned to ride when he was five. There was no reason Pippa couldn't as well, simply because she was a girl.

He set her down, and she ran upstairs to her nanny who waited on the first-floor landing, galloping the little horse through the air beside her as she ran. Mrs. Davenport took her hand and led her away toward the nursery on the top floor.

"You're so good with her, Marcus." Claudia gave a reassuring squeeze to his arm.

He turned his attention to tugging at his gloves. "She should have Anthony and Elise with her."

"She doesn't miss them," she said quietly.

"I know." But then, why would she? Her father had died in the wars when she was only an infant, without having ever laid eyes on his daughter. Then, when Elise died two years later, Penelope had barely been three.

Miss them? He bit back a pained and bitter laugh. She wouldn't even *remember* them.

"But knowing that doesn't make it any easier for you, does it?"

Hell no. And especially not when Pippa reminded him so much of Elise as a girl that sometimes he felt as if he were seeing a ghost.

"You *are* wonderful with her, Marcus. What you've done in getting to know her, even in just the short time you've been home, it's remarkable. And even though I give you a hard time about raising her to be a soldier rather than a society lady, you're going to continue to be a good influence on her."

"So will you."

"Less so." She bit her lip in a moment's hesitation, then confided, "Adam asked me to marry him, and I agreed."

His gaze jumped to hers. Not that he was surprised that Trousdale had asked, but the timing of it was sooner than expected. *Far* sooner. He'd counted on having another six months at least of calm in the house to give Pippa and him more time to adjust to one another before the frenzy of wedding preparations had to begin.

Her face fell. "You're not happy about it."

"Of course I'm happy for you." But damnably sad for himself that he would be losing her from the house right when he needed her help the most, both with Pippa and with the new dukedom. But he would never be selfish enough to prevent her from seeking her own happiness. "He's a good man with a solid future." He took her shoulders and placed a kiss on her forehead. "But I expected him to come to me first to declare his intentions."

"Adam's a modern man. He believes in asking a lady what *she* wants to do with her life rather than her male guardian." She sparkled with happiness. "But he's calling on you tomorrow to formally offer, so do try to act surprised, all right?"

With a light laugh, he hugged her. Still holding her tightly in his arms, his chin resting on the top of her head the way he'd done since they were children, he asked, "You love this man?"

"Very much."

"And he always treats you with respect and kindness?"

She leaned back to beam up at him. "Always."

"Then I wish you both a lifetime of happiness."

He released her and turned away, just in time to see two maids carrying the statue of Caesar down the front footpath. He grimaced at the sight. Judging from how far Claudia had gone with the party last night, her wedding portended to be a monstrous extravaganza.

He slid her a hopeful glance. "Any chance that I could talk you into eloping?"

"Not one." She waved a hand to indicate the party's aftermath lying all around them. "Last night was simply practice for the wedding breakfast."

Heaven help him.

She placed her hand on his shoulder, the simple gesture spinning affection through him. "You're a good brother, Marcus Braddock. You've always been my hero. Nothing will ever change that." She paused for effect, unsuccessfully stifling her grin at his expense. "Even if you are old as Moses."

He rolled his eyes. "Thank you."

She rose up on tiptoes to kiss his cheek. Then she was gone, gliding away toward the garden doors.

He stared after her. *Sweet Lucifer*...Claudia was

getting married, and he wasn't at all prepared for it. He was a soldier, for heaven's sake! What did he know about wedding ceremonies and breakfasts? Nothing in his life had trained him for this. If only he could rally some help around Claudia's engagement the way he used to rally troops. If only—

The solution popped into his head. He smiled. Oh, it was perfect!

Snatching up his hat from the hall table, he hurried back upstairs to Elise's room. He had a wedding to prepare for...and now the perfect excuse for staying close to Danielle.

Five

DANI READ THE NOTE THAT HAD BEEN DELIVERED TO her that morning and bit her lip.

"Bad news, miss?"

Forcing a smile, she glanced up at her maid's reflection in the dressing table mirror as the woman pinned up her hair. Unfortunately, she also caught her own reflection. And cringed.

Oh, she looked a fright! Dark circles surrounding puffy red eyes, pale skin, bloodless lips…but she wasn't surprised, given that she'd spent last night weeping into her pillow.

Her maid stilled as she placed a pin, frowning in concern. "Miss?"

Alice had been with her since Dani returned from school when she was eighteen and embarked on her first true season. But even though her maid was now one of her closest confidantes and one of the few people she trusted with her secrets, she wouldn't place the burden of Elise's death onto Alice's shoulders.

"It's nothing important," she dismissed, folding the letter and tucking it away into the pocket of her pelisse. "Just a note from Lady Hartsham."

Beatrice McTavish had been irksome of late, sending all kinds of notes. But from the excitable tone behind them, Dani assumed that Lord Hartsham had once more been attempting to control his wife's activities and so had been making the woman nervous. Again.

"Is it about Nightingale?" Alice whispered.

Dani darted a paranoid glance at the door to make certain no one had come in and overheard the name of her secret charity. Especially Harriett. The viscountess knew absolutely nothing about what Dani had been up to in the past four years since her father accepted a diplomatic position in the Court of St James's and her parents left for Italy. If her aunt ever found out—especially if she discovered that she was the reason for it all—she'd suffer apoplexy right where she stood.

Or more likely, knowing her aunt, she'd want to help. Which absolutely could *never* happen.

No. Danielle had to keep Nightingale a secret. Too many lives were at risk. Including her own. She owed that loyalty to Elise's memory and to all the women still in need.

Even now, a brewer's wife in Ealing was waiting for her help. Thank goodness she'd already planned to meet with Jenkins and Kimball tonight to make arrangements. The former smugglers, who knew her only as Nightingale, would gladly accept the generous payment she'd offer in return for their services in escorting a desperate woman out of London.

"I need you to deliver a note." Although they were alone, Dani lowered her voice. "To confirm tonight's meetings."

"Aye, miss." Alice nodded, knowing how to contact the men through the innkeeper's wife at the Golden Bell Tavern along the Strand by using false names and taking a circuitous route to return home. Neither the two men nor the innkeeper's wife knew Dani's true identity or those of the other women involved. That was exactly how she planned on keeping it.

Her shoulders sagged. The whole situation had become far too perilous. This wasn't at all what Nightingale was supposed to have been, but it had grown out of control. Now it was a burden that weighed upon her, one made nearly unbearable by what Marcus had revealed last night.

A vanishing. When Marcus had said that, she knew he'd told her the truth, that Elise's death had been exactly as he suspected. He wouldn't have known to use that word unless it was in the note, which wouldn't have existed at all unless Elise had established her own network behind Dani's back. To know that she had a part in her best friend's death had shattered her insides like glass, right there in Marcus's arms.

Elise had lied to her. The stubborn, reckless woman had gone and done exactly what Dani had warned her not to do. She'd put her life into unnecessary danger—

No. She'd gotten herself killed.

Sickening nausea roiled inside her. Last night, when Marcus revealed that to her, she'd wanted to flee, to cry and curse and scream! But she'd been trapped within his arms in the middle of the party, with nearly every pair of eyes in the room on them while he'd unwittingly taken Elise from her once again. And this time, so much more brutally.

So she'd fled behind her only possible defense—her temper. But that anger had come naturally once she realized why he'd asked her to dance, once she felt betrayed.

He'd wanted answers, but she couldn't give him any. Not when so many other lives were at risk. This secret she would take to her own grave. Just as Elise had. Too much had been sacrificed to betray those women now.

"Danielle!" Her aunt's shout rattled the windows on all four floors of the Bedford Square town house.

Dani rolled her eyes. Who needed a call bell around Harriett?

"Join me for breakfast!"

With no other choice, she yelled back, "Coming!"

"I don't think you are!"

Despite herself, Dani couldn't help but give a faint giggle when Alice burst into laughter. The release of that small laugh was a godsend given the weight that pressed in upon her. And thank God for it, because there had been a point last night when she wondered how she would be able to live with her guilt over Elise.

But now she knew she would find a way, that it would be the little things that would guide her through...like her aunt's antics and her maid's concern.

With a grateful squeeze to Alice's arm, Dani stood and made her way downstairs.

Harriett was a wonderful woman, kind and generous,

always loving, although her lack of propriety even in the most obvious circumstances entertained Dani to no end. It used to embarrass the daylights out of her. Those stories her aunt so dearly loved to tell at parties were enough to make a young lady faint from mortification. All apocryphal, all just odd enough to keep the attention of even the most bored lord, they usually involved one of Harriett's escapades from her younger and more exuberant days when she'd been one of society's most sought-after ladies. As an earl's beautiful daughter, she'd taken society by storm.

But then she married Viscount Bromley, and her life went horribly wrong.

When she was a girl, Dani had thought her great-aunt so very odd, relishing being the center of attention and flirting with the young dandies rather than sitting sedately with the matrons her own age. Harriett had come to stay when Dani was fourteen. At the time, she'd thought that her parents had taken her aunt in when the old viscount left for Ireland because Auntie was too irresponsible to stay by herself. Only later did she discover the truth. That Dani's mother had surprised Harriett with an unannounced visit to find that the viscount had beaten her to within an inch of her life. A beating that hadn't been the first.

Mama had spent the next sennight nursing Harriett back to health until she was well enough to travel. Once her aunt was safely ensconced with them in Bedford Square, her father paid a visit to the viscount. Dani would never learn what Papa said to him that day, but her great-uncle left England and never returned.

Since learning what happened, Dani had come to understand her aunt in a completely new way. She loved and supported Harriett however she could and greatly admired her strength and resilience.

If not her stories.

"Good morning, Auntie." She glided into the morning room to find Harriett at the little card table by the window with the breakfast dishes already in place. Her aunt offered her cheek for a kiss, and Dani obliged, then slid into her chair. "You should have started without me."

"Breakfast isn't nearly as interesting, my dear, when you're not here."

Dani didn't believe that for a moment. "No one else to fight with over the strawberries, you mean?"

Harriett winked. "Drummond doesn't brawl with the same spunk as you."

The butler stifled a smile as he stood by the door at the ready.

"That's because he gets paid to let you win." With a smile for Drummond, Dani popped one of the red berries into her mouth. "But I'll race you to the last one if you'd like."

She cackled out a laugh. "Agreed!" Yet she spooned several onto Dani's plate without any argument, then reached for the silver pot. "Chocolate?"

"Please." Dani held out her cup and did her best to hide her concern as she asked, "What was so important that I join you this morning?" Despite a dearth of berry fights, Harriett didn't normally mind eating alone. It gave her time to pore over the *Morning Post*, freshly ironed and left by her chair when Drummond carried up the breakfast tray. "Not enough news in the paper this morning to keep your interest?"

"News? Ha!" She topped off her own cup of chocolate. "I'm only interested in the gossip page. Such nonsense and twaddle, and about the best of society, too." Then she smiled gleefully, like the cat that had gotten into the cream. "I devour every word of it!"

With a laugh, Dani tore off a bit of toast and popped it into her mouth.

"And your meeting tonight?"

Dani froze in midchew. She asked carefully around the toast, "How do you know about that?"

"You told me. Remember? The lecture you plan on attending."

"Oh." Relief sank through her. Her secrets were still her own. "That."

Harriett stabbed a kipper with her fork and set it onto her plate. A deft stroke of her knife beheaded it. "I might attend with you."

"I don't think you'd enjoy it." Dani focused her attention on spreading marmalade across her toast. There was no lecture scheduled for tonight. That was simply the excuse she used whenever she needed to meet with her contacts for Nightingale.

When her aunt said nothing, waiting for her to

continue telling more about the nonexistent lecture, Dani shrugged as casually as possible. "It won't be at all exciting for you, Auntie."

"What is it about?"

She thought quickly—"Canals."

"Canals?" Harriett blinked as she absorbed that. "Venetian?"

"English."

"Oh dear."

"Yes."

Her aunt frowned, puzzled. "You think you'll find a lecture about the Bridgewater Canals interesting?"

"Well, I hope so." Dani couldn't look at Harriett during that lie and took a bite of her toast. She hated lying to her aunt, always had. After four years, she still wasn't used to it. "The Duke of Bridgewater has always struck me as an interesting man."

"I knew the duke."

"Did you?"

"I was once courted by the duke."

That didn't surprise her.

"Believe me when I assure you that Little Scroop, as we called him, was not at all interesting." Resting both elbows on the table, she held her cup between her hands as she pondered the man. "I daresay watching the water flow in one of his canals proved vastly more fascinating."

Dani put a strawberry to her lips to hide any traces of a smile.

"No wonder he died a bachelor."

At that, she popped the berry into her mouth to keep from laughing.

"If Marcus Braddock isn't careful, the same thing will happen to him."

She choked. She certainly hadn't expected that! Between coughs, she swallowed down the berry and let out a rasping, "*Pardon?*"

"Oh, I don't mean the boring part." Harriett waved a dismissing hand. "There's nothing at all boring about that man." She murmured dreamily, "I cannot imagine any woman wanting to watch water flowing in a canal when she could be watching him."

No. Dani couldn't either. She reached for her hot chocolate to clear her throat and kept her silence. How handsome Marcus Braddock looked was the last thing she'd comment upon.

"I'm surprised women aren't sneaking into his bed every night."

No. *That* was the last thing.

"He's eschewed society since he returned, you know. Lady Cunningham mentioned just yesterday that he's sent his regrets to every one of her dinners that she's invited him to."

Missing the Cunninghams' dinners was hardly a social hardship, and Dani didn't blame the general one bit for not wanting to attend. Lady Cunningham was notorious for her overly exotic meals and exceedingly dull conversation. "You speak of him as if he were a hermit."

"Just shy of one. Missing all the balls, dinners,

musicales, exhibits, outings…why, not even trying for a box at the opera or Vauxhall!" She waved her knife in the air. "Except for last night's party, no one has seen him."

"He's been away at war." Marcus Braddock was the last person she should be defending after his behavior toward her last night. Yet she understood his heartache and shared his grief. "He's returned to a different England, a different London." She inhaled a steadying breath. "And to the deaths of both his sister and brother-in-law. If he needs time to ease himself into society"—or into one of Lady Cunningham's dinners of roasted monkey—"no one should fault him."

Harriett scoffed as she slathered butter onto a cinnamon roll. "He doesn't have time for ease."

She frowned. "What do you mean?"

"He's getting up in years, my dear." She jabbed her knife at Dani to punctuate her point. "He doesn't have much longer to find a wife and produce an heir."

Dani smiled to herself. Given that the Earl of Margate had just fathered his youngest child at the ripe old age of sixty, Dani doubted that. Plus, Marcus Braddock was one of England's greatest heroes, eclipsed only by Wellington, and now a wealthy duke. A man like that would have no trouble finding a woman who wanted to marry him at any age and give him heirs.

Her smile faded into a frown. Or dozens of women.

Perhaps Harriett was right. Maybe women *were* sneaking into his bed every night. Was that why he was shunning society, because he didn't need to go to them when they were flocking to him?

She glared into her chocolate. It was no concern of hers either way…so why should she feel an odd prick at the thought of Marcus being intimate with a woman? He was a bachelor who was free to do whatever he wanted with whomever he wished. His private life was none of her business. Even if thoughts of it inexplicably grated.

"You're worrying over nothing." Dani placed her napkin on her plate. "Marcus Braddock is the most eligible gentleman in England. When he wants to find a wife and start a family, he will have no trouble doing so."

Harriett arched a knowing brow. "That's what they all said about Bridgewater, too."

Dani shook her head, saying nothing. She was done with discussing dukes of all kinds, boring, dashing, or otherwise.

"Tell me more about these lectures of yours, Danielle."

No, she really did *not* want to.

"Who all attends?" Harriett's eyes sparkled. "Anyone mad, bad, and delightful to know?"

"No one of note." Another dodge, another prick of guilt… She shrugged as if the answer were the most obvious thing in the world. "Canals, you know."

"Well, perhaps I'll accompany you next time, then. What's to be the subject of the next lecture?"

Her mind whirled to come up with a topic that her aunt would never suffer through—"The Pontcysyllte Aqueduct."

Harriett blinked, stilling for a moment. Then she slowly set down the roll and knife. "My dear, you really need to get out more." Daintily wiping off her fingertips, she muttered, "Unless you're seeking a husband in the canal business."

Dani smiled and reached for the pot to refill her aunt's cup of chocolate.

A knock sounded at the door, and Drummond cleared his throat. "My lady." He nodded at each of them in turn. "Miss. You have a visitor."

"A visitor? At this hour?" Harriett straightened in her chair, offended at the notion that someone would dare call so early. "The clock only just struck eleven!"

"Yes, ma'am. I told him that you didn't accept visitors until after one o'clock, yet he insisted."

"Well, send him away!" She gestured in the air with her cup. "Whoever it is can return at a decent hour."

"Marcus Braddock, my lady," he explained, a touch of awe lacing his voice. "The General His Grace the Duke of Hampton."

Six

Harriett's cup sank slowly to the table and clattered against its saucer. "Oh my."

Oh no. Dani's heart leapt into her throat. Until this morning, Marcus had the consideration to respect her wishes not to call at her home. But now she would have to receive him because Harriett would never send away a duke. Especially not *this* duke, given how he was currently the talk of the town. Drat him! The sly devil most likely knew it, too.

Her hand tightened around her cup. "I'm—I'm not feeling well. Suddenly. Must have been something I ate."

Harriett glanced at her empty plate. "But you've had nothing but a berry and a few bites of toast."

And was terrible at lying, apparently, except about canals. She placed her hand on Harriett's sleeve. "I do not wish to entertain him, Auntie. Not today."

"He's come at dawn, my dear. A military man arriving at dawn never portends good news." She set her napkin on the table and rose, oblivious to the true time on the mantel clock. "Whatever brought him here must be important. Come along."

Dani had no choice but to follow her aunt out of the morning room and into the drawing room at the front of the house, with its wide double bay windows and sky-blue wallpaper, its sapphire-blue brocade settees and matching Aubusson rug…and now with a very imposing general turned duke waiting by the white marble fireplace.

She paused, struck by the sight of him. He'd been handsome at the party, dressed in his evening finery and perfectly adorned, not a single strand of hair daring to stray out of place. But this… *Good heavens.* He wore tight buckskin breeches beneath a maroon redingote showing traces of dust. His black hair was mussed and his cheeks flushed from the morning air. His whole appearance had the effect of looking as if he'd been out riding and just happened to impulsively think of paying a call. With his stance solid and wide-legged, one hand clenched into a fist at the small of his back, Dani had never seen a more commanding man in her life. He was simply breathtaking.

And dangerous.

He faced them as Harriett swept toward him, reaching out both of her hands in a too-familiar greeting. "Duke!"

Marcus winced at her use of his title, although her aunt didn't notice as he sketched her a bow. "Viscountess, you're looking lovely this morning." Then his dark gaze moved to Dani as she entered the room far less enthusiastically than her aunt. "And you as well, Miss Williams."

"Thank you, Your Grace." She bobbed a curtsy. Unease rose inside her at his surprise visit, although she strongly suspected that he wanted to continue their conversation from last night, this time without fear of being interrupted by other guests or the very convenient end of the waltz. "It's a pleasure to see you this morning."

His eyes gleamed, recognizing that for the lie it was. "My apologies for both the hour and my disheveled appearance. I was out riding and decided to stop by. I hope you don't think me rude for calling on you so early."

"Is it early?" Harriett made an exaggerated show of looking at the long case clock in the corner. "I hadn't noticed."

Dani couldn't stop the roll of her eyes, but she also saw the answering amusement in Marcus's. Her aunt hadn't fooled him for a second.

"We're so happy that you stopped by." As she settled onto the settee, Harriett gestured with one hand for Marcus to join her and at the butler with the other. "Drummond, please fetch tea."

Remaining on his feet, Marcus stopped the butler with a shake of his head. "I'm afraid I don't have time. I only stopped by for a moment." He once more put his fist to the small of his back, as if finding strength in that commanding stance that must have been second nature to him. "I've come to ask for your help."

"Is something wrong?" Dani interjected, her lungs hitching with sudden concern as she sank onto the settee next to Harriett. *Please, God, no*...not his family, not again. "Is it Pippa or Claudia?"

"Nothing like that. But I admit that I find myself in a sticky situation." He gave a self-deprecating smile that won over Harriett immediately but did nothing to lessen Dani's unease. "Army training isn't at all helpful with matters of domesticity."

"Of course, we would be happy to help." Harriett beamed, thrilled to be of service. "Danielle and I are quite skilled with domestic matters."

Dani slid her a dubious glance. *Domestic?* The two of them didn't even know how to boil an egg.

"Claudia is being courted by Adam Trousdale," he explained. "He plans to offer for her, and I fully intend to grant my permission. Trousdale is a good man who will make her a fine husband."

Harriett gleefully clapped her hands. "Oh, how wonderful!"

Unease tightened Dani's belly. It truly was good news, and she was thrilled for Claudia... But what did it have to do with her and Harriett?

A concerned frown creased his brow. "With no female relatives to guide her through the betrothal and wedding, however, I fear she might become overwhelmed."

Harriett's hand went to her throat, alarmed for Claudia by just the thought of it.

Dani bit her cheek to keep from laughing. Her aunt's dismay was solely for the duke's benefit. Harriett was nothing if not theatrical.

"I know it's a great deal to ask, but I was hoping that you two would do her the kindness of providing that guidance." His smile widened. The man was certainly using all the charms at his disposal. "And take pity on an old soldier who knows nothing about wedding lace, breakfasts, and trousseaus."

Dani's gaze narrowed at how easily he tossed out that request for help. A wholly manufactured one, too, as Claudia was more than capable of surviving her betrothal and wedding just fine. And he certainly wasn't old or pitiable. What was the devil up to?

"Your help would be a perfect solution for Claudia."

Perfect, all right…most perfectly convenient *for him*. And a request he knew her aunt would never refuse. His battle strategy for wheedling more information out of her about Elise and Scepter was becoming clearer by the moment.

"We would be happy to assist her," Harriett answered quickly for both of them before Dani could refuse.

"Thank you." Then Marcus threw out casually, "Why don't you come to Charlton Place for dinner tomorrow evening? We can celebrate the betrothal and begin to discuss arrangements then."

That was a snare if ever Dani had heard one. And she had to put a stop to it. Now.

"Auntie, while it's very kind of you to offer our help," she gently contradicted, "surely Claudia doesn't need us. At least not until the engagement is formally announced." By which time Dani hoped to have thought of a way out of this mess that put her and her secrets in such close proximity to the general. A man who could never learn what she and his sister had been doing. "I would hate for His Grace to be burdened with hosting a dinner for us when our presence isn't yet necessary."

Harriett leveled a hard look on her and warned enigmatically beneath her breath, "Bridgewater."

Oh, for heaven's sake… Dani surrendered with a sag of her shoulders, seeing no good way of escape. Her aunt would never let her out of this.

Marcus swung a perplexed glance between the two women. As if realizing he'd never be able to fathom their secret conversation, he smiled. "I'm grateful for your help." Then he squared his shoulders, reminding Dani of a man preparing for battle. "Before I go, might I have a word alone with your niece, Viscountess?"

"Of course!"

"Auntie," Dani objected, panic pulsing through her. "I don't think that—"

Harriett patted her arm, misunderstanding Dani's objection. "Don't worry about the hour, my dear." She rose to her feet, forcing Dani to hers. "There's nothing scandalous about letting a man call before noon as long as his intentions are honorable."

Dani glanced at Marcus to find his dark eyes watching her. She wasn't at all certain of *that*.

"I'll be in the morning room when you're finished." Harriett held out her hand to Marcus. "We'll see you tomorrow, Duke."

He bowed over her hand but slid a sideways glance at Dani. "I'm very much looking forward to it, Viscountess."

Harriett glided from the room. Just as she was about to disappear into the hall, she looked back at Dani and mouthed, *Canals*.

Dani let out a long sigh. Somehow, she'd lost the battle before lines had even been drawn.

"Did I miss something?" Marcus asked, puzzled, as he stared after her aunt.

More than you realize. "Not at all." She forced a smile and folded her hands demurely in front of her. "What did you wish to speak to me about, Your Grace? Surely it could have waited until tomorrow." *Unless I figure out a way to beg off from dinner before then…*

He frowned. "You don't seem happy about Claudia's betrothal."

"Actually, I'm delighted for your sister. I'm very much looking forward to her wedding." But she didn't want to talk about Elise, and she was certain that was exactly what he was hoping for.

"Then please accept tomorrow's dinner invitation for what it is—my gratitude to you for helping Claudia. Nothing more."

"Nothing more?" Doubt colored her voice.

"Perhaps a bit more." His expression turned solemn. "It's also an apology for how I behaved last night. I'd like it to be a chance for us to start over."

She blinked. *That* was unexpected.

"I know that Elise's death was hard for you as well."

Not hard. Devastating.

"I shouldn't have confronted you like that." His expression melted with remorse. "It was badly done, and for that, I am sorry."

No, he shouldn't have, and for that, *she* had every right

to be furious. Yet she was unable to resist the solace that his apology brought.

"I understand why you did it. I truly do," she admitted discreetly. "But I don't have any more information than what you already know." *Please let this go...* "Nothing more can be gained by discussing it."

A tight smile pulled at his lips. "The invitation to dinner isn't a bribe."

Guilt consumed her. "I didn't mean to imply—"

"But this is." He reached into his jacket and withdrew a little box the size of a pocket book, wrapped in white paper and tied with a pink ribbon. He held it out to her and added dryly, "Although the soldier in me prefers to think of it as reparations."

She ached for him. He'd gone through so much in the past few years, with the coming months most likely to be nearly as difficult. He had Pippa to raise now, Claudia to deliver safely into marriage, a dukedom to oversee...*alone.* He wasn't in the army now and couldn't fight his way through life any longer. She had a tingling suspicion that Harriett was his first attempt at calling in civilian reinforcements to win a battle and that she was his first attempt at diplomacy.

Knowing all that, how could she refuse to accept this gift?

Mumbling her thanks, she carefully took it from him, then pulled loose the ribbon and let the paper fall away—

She blinked in surprise and traced her fingers over it. "A music box?"

"An apology."

The polished mahogany box shone in the morning sunlight as she turned it over in her hands. She carefully unfastened the tiny clasp and opened the lid to reveal the circular brass plate and winding mechanism that made it play.

"I cannot accept this," she whispered. Yet how dearly she wished she could! But they weren't courting and never would, and this was far too expensive a gift from an acquaintance.

Not looking at her, he said quietly, "It was one of Elise's." He pulled a brass key from his waistcoat pocket and inserted it into the tiny keyhole. "She would want you to have it."

If it had been any other gift, she would have accused him of attempting to use it to manipulate her, just as he'd used the waltz. But not this. Not even a battle-hardened general would use her love of his sister against her like that.

This much of his apology, at least, was heartfelt.

His unexpected kindness warmed through her. "It's beautiful." And the most thoughtful gift she'd ever been given. She swallowed down the knot of emotion in her throat. "Thank you."

A single tear slipped down her cheek, surprising her. So many tears had been shed that she didn't think any were left, yet she couldn't stop it, her heart torn between grief at Elise's death and indescribable joy that he'd given this to her. This piece of the woman who would always be the most special friend she'd ever have.

She wiped the tear away with her fingertips before he could see it, then gave the key a single turn. Just enough to play the first few notes…a lullaby. The same lullaby that Elise had sung to Pippa when she was a baby, cradled in her arms and drifting to sleep.

Dani held the music box tightly to her chest as if she could magically embrace Elise through it. Without a thought except that she desperately needed to show her gratitude, she rose onto tiptoes to kiss his cheek. Only a brief and chaste touch, to show what she couldn't put into words.

But he startled and turned his head. Her mouth unexpectedly caught the corner of his. He inhaled sharply against her lips at the accidental contact. Suddenly, that touch to the cheek had become so much more, and despite herself, a yearning thrill sparked inside her.

He tensed beneath her hand that rested on his shoulder for balance as she lowered herself. But the hard muscle under her fingers felt so solid and strong that for one desperate moment, she didn't want to step away. She wanted to step into his embrace and absorb his strength.

His hands went to her arms to steady her—no, to steady both of them as they stared into each other's eyes, both momentarily stunned.

Her cheeks flushed as she stammered out in embarrassment, "I didn't mean to…kiss you…like that."

"Damnable shame, then," he murmured deadpan, which made her flush turn absolutely burning.

"My apologies. I was overcome." What she'd just done

was wholly inappropriate. Yet she couldn't stop herself from rising onto her toes again, this time to bring her mouth to his ear and whisper with little more than a hint of a voice, "Thank you...so very much."

She stepped away to place the box onto the mantelpiece, turning her back so he couldn't see the emotions on her face.

Good heavens. She'd *kissed* him. Oh, she'd truly gone and proved herself a goose this time! Put herself into foolishness up to her neck.

Oddly, though, she couldn't find it within her to regret it.

By the time she'd gathered herself and turned to face him, she'd managed to put a smile into place, and his own shocked expression had been squelched. As if nothing at all had happened, as if she hadn't just had her mouth on his. But tension flared between them, and she remained by the fireplace, where she could easily grab the poker and hit herself over the head with it should she be so idiotic as to attempt to kiss him again.

"I hope that means that you've accepted my apology," he drawled.

She nodded, although suspicion nagged at her that his mission to wring answers from her was far from done.

"Shall we start over, then, as if we'd never waltzed?" He sat casually on the arm of the settee. Although she knew that he was now attempting to be nothing more than her best friend's older brother, he looked so perfectly like a rake in that position that her pulse spiked.

"Perhaps you'll be willing to give me a second chance at tomorrow's dinner."

"Perhaps." Her fingers plucked at her skirt, that old nervous habit she'd had since she was a girl. Fitting, because she'd been nervous around him since she'd been in braids and never more than at this very moment. "Although I might find that you're just as poorly behaved at dinners as at parties."

His sensuous lips curled into an amused smile, which did nothing to take her mind away from wondering how it would feel to kiss him again. A *real* kiss this time, too, not an accidental one. One that the raffish soldier in him would enjoy. "Ah, but at dinner, I'll be surrounded by chaperones who'll be there to keep me in line. Including your aunt."

"You don't know Auntie very well." She arched a brow. "She'd be thrilled to be part of something shocking. More fodder for her stories."

"Then we must be on our best behavior. I'll promise to behave if you do."

Hmm...wishful thinking on his part or a direct lie? Yet she answered, "Agreed."

His smile didn't lessen, and she sensed a hardness in him that gave her pause. As if he wanted her to promise to a lot more than simply that. But she couldn't. No matter how much she wanted to ease his grief and her guilt.

He stood. With a polite nod, he made his way to the door. "Until tomorrow, Miss Williams."

Then he was gone.

Dani's knees gave out, and she sank slowly onto the settee. Gripping the armrest, she gulped down several mouthfuls of air to calm her pounding heart and stop her shaking.

Although it had been an accident, she had no business kissing him like that, no matter how kind he was to give her the music box, no matter how chivalrous to apologize...no matter how dashingly intriguing he'd looked in his riding clothes, his dark hair mussed and curling against his collar like that, his muscular thighs so well defined underneath his breeches—

She groaned. Oh, she was an absolute goose!

And if she wasn't careful, her goose would be good and cooked before this was all over.

Seven

WHAT THE DEVIL WAS SHE UP TO?

From a dark corner in the back of the crowded Golden Bell Tavern, dressed inconspicuously in the plain work clothes of a warehouse porter, Marcus watched Danielle as she sat at a little table positioned in front of the grimy windows. She'd been there for almost half an hour, and he'd been right here since shortly after she'd entered, following her inside and keeping watch. And doing his damnedest to figure out why she was here.

This wasn't the haunt of any gently bred miss. Not the daughter of a baron. And certainly *not* alone.

Neither was she dressed in clothes befitting a lady. No, she wore the plain, coarse clothes of a laboring woman, one who might have spent her days working in a market stall just down the street. A dress of gray worsted wool covered her from ankle to wrist to neck, along with sturdy shoes and a cap that hid her hair. She'd tried her best to appear ordinary, yet her natural grace couldn't be hidden. Neither could her fine features or the delicate softness of her hands.

No one would ever mistake her for a laborer. So the question was…why did she want them to?

Since their waltz, he'd been left with more questions than answers, so he'd set about watching her. When she'd left her town house tonight under the cover of darkness and wound her way through the streets of London, he'd followed. But he hadn't expected her to lead him to the Golden Bell.

The bells of St Bride's Church struck midnight and echoed faintly through the black night over the Strand, just barely heard above the noise of drunken revelry. A man entered the tavern as if on cue and hesitated just inside the doorway. Then, spotting Danielle, he made his way through the crowd to sit at her table.

Marcus lifted the tankard of ale to his mouth, watching them over the rim as the two engaged in private conversation. They leaned close together to be heard above the noise.

So…another midnight meeting with a man. Just like the one planned in Elise's letter. And based on what he'd seen tonight, this wasn't Danielle's first.

He had to give her credit for her artfulness. When she'd left the house, she'd worn a velvet cape edged in ermine over a blue muslin gown. She'd also been in the company of her maid, who was acting as chaperone in her aunt's absence. All perfectly proper for a society outing.

Except that she didn't go to one.

Instead, she'd set out a goose chase. He'd followed her on horseback, easily keeping out of sight in the shadows as the baron's town coach rolled its way toward Westminster. When it reached the Queen's House and stopped on an empty side street, Danielle emerged, the cape and dress gone. In their place was the worsted wool costume she now wore. He'd watched as she hired a hackney and was off again, this time winding through the streets toward Covent Garden. Another change of carriages there, and a second hired hackney brought her to this tavern. Watching from the shadows down the street, he hadn't heard what she said to the driver when she paid him, but the carriage stayed right there on the cobblestones, waiting for her to return. Marcus stabled his horse and followed her inside.

His gaze narrowed. What was she doing, laying down a chase like that through the dark city to meet a man? Not the kind of man a baron's daughter should be spending time with, either. Coarse and rough, he was dressed like any other riverfront worker, in dirty tan clothes and a tweed cap. He could have been any age from twenty to forty, weathered by too many cold London winters and the harsh life that came from clawing out a living in a city that could be brutal. Even more so now that the wars were over and too many men were seeking the same too few jobs, now that food prices had shot up to the heavens.

What the hell *was she up to?*

He had no idea, but as he watched Danielle surreptitiously hand a bag of coins beneath the table to the man, he became determined to find out.

"'Nother ale?" A barmaid pointed at his tankard.

"Please." Marcus slid a coin across the table toward her, then asked, "Can you help me with something else?"

Misreading his question as an opening for a solicitation, she propped a round hip against the table and leaned toward him, her large bosom nearly falling out of her tightly laced bodice as she reached to trail her hand down his arm. "What you have i' mind?"

"Information." He watched her eye the first coin, then set down a second and pushed it toward her. "There's a woman in a gray dress at a table in front of the windows." He withdrew a third coin and set it on the table in front of him with the others, but he kept this one pinned to the table beneath his finger. "The man who's with her. Do you know him?"

She stiffened coldly when she realized that he didn't want to take her upstairs. Yet she very much wanted the coins and glanced over her shoulder. Her face hardened when she saw Danielle, as if she was her competition tonight. With an unimpressed sniff, she looked past her to the man sitting across from her.

"He comes in 'ere e'ry now an' again fer supper an' ale." She reached down to scoop up the first two coins. She gave him a bright smile as she slipped the coins down inside her bodice, still wrongly thinking that she could persuade him to tup her. "His name's Jenkins. Works down a' the river."

"What else do you know about him?"

"Nothin'."

"Are you sure?" He pushed the coin toward her but didn't remove his finger. "Has he ever spent time with you or the other barmaids?"

She laughed. "Not 'im! Stingy bloke that one. An' ne'er seen him crack a smile." She jerked a thumb toward

Danielle. "That one's wastin' her time if'n she thinks she'll get any blunt out o' him." Then she shook her head and leaned lower to give him a better view of her breasts. "That one don't know what she's doin', dressed like an old church matron. But I do." She smiled seductively, revealing a wide gap between her front teeth. "I'll make it good fer you. Give you a satisfyin' ride."

Marcus hadn't been intimate with a woman since he'd returned from the continent. He had to be careful, given his new position and fortune, and becoming involved with the wrong woman was a mistake he didn't want to make. But he wasn't so desperate for female intimacies that he had to stoop to paying for them.

"Just the ale." He removed his finger from the coin and sat back. "Thank you for the information."

She reached for the coin with an irritated scowl.

Without warning, he brought his hand down over hers and pinned it to the table. Her mouth fell open in surprise.

"One more thing." His voice was low and controlled, despite the hard clench of his gut. "Do you remember another woman meeting with that man here at midnight? About two years ago. A young woman about three and twenty, with light brown hair, piercing sky-blue eyes, pale skin."

She'd remember seeing his sister, even after two years. No one who saw Elise could forget her. She'd made an impression on every room she'd entered.

"Not 'im!" She cackled out a laugh. "Ne'er seen 'im wi'

any other woman but that one. He just comes in fer a bit of stew an' ale, sits by 'imself, eats by 'imself, then leaves."

Frustration growled inside him. "Are you absolutely certain that you've never seen him with another woman?"

"Swear it on me mum's grave."

He released her hand. She snatched up the coin and spun on her heel to walk away. If he had any luck at all, she'd not bother him again.

His gaze drifted back to Danielle. He had enough trouble with females tonight as it was.

The man stood and left. From across the tavern, the barmaid shot Marcus an *I told you so* look so hard that it could have cut glass.

Danielle remained behind, no doubt to wait long enough before leaving that no one who might be outside would assume she and that man had met together in the tavern. There was no need for Marcus to keep watching her. She'd retrace her steps all the way home, he would have bet his fortune on it.

But the man she'd met with was a different story. One capable of providing answers.

When Jenkins slipped outside onto the street, so did Marcus.

Marcus followed after him, moving quickly but silently. No longer bothering to stay to the shadows, he closed the distance between them until he was only a few feet behind. When the man turned down an alley cutting toward the Thames, Marcus lunged.

He grabbed Jenkins by his shoulder and tossed

him back against the wall, then pinned him there with his forearm against the man's neck. His other hand wrapped around his own wrist for additional leverage, turning his forearm into a bar across Jenkins's throat. He could easily crush his windpipe with a single forward step.

"Relax," Marcus calmly ordered, his voice nonthreatening. "I don't want your money."

Jenkins said nothing. Marcus had easily surprised him. Like most men, he'd been too focused on what lay before him to worry about what was sneaking up from behind. Marcus had seen more soldiers than he wanted to count who had fallen victim to the same short-sightedness on the battlefield.

"I want answers. About the woman you met with tonight."

Jenkins's gaze narrowed as he accused harshly, "Yer after one of 'em, then."

He frowned. "One of what?"

"The women."

Women? First Elise, then Danielle…how many society ladies were arranging clandestine midnight meetings?

"Got none with me, so yer old lady or yer tart ain't here. Ain't no vanishings set for t'night neither."

Vanishing. The word that had been in Elise's note. The same word that had raised such panic in Danielle last night. "What do you mean?"

"'Xactly what I said! No one's disappearin' t'night, including whate'er bit you're looking fer. If she ain't at home, then she done run on her own. None o' my business."

"And the woman you met with in the Golden Bell? What did she want with you?"

"Nightingale hired me."

He pressed harder against the man's throat—a reminder not to lie. "To do what?" And who the hell was Nightingale? Was Danielle using a false identity? *None* of this made any sense, and none of it was giving him any answers about Elise.

"I help wi' the vanishings an' transfers." His brow pulled into a deep furrow. "You ain't a husband or pimp, then? You ain't tryin' to locate one o' the missin' women?"

"What women?"

The man smiled, his eyes gleaming as he realized that Marcus wasn't who he thought. Although who Jenkins thought he was, he had no idea. "Ask Nightingale yerself." He jerked his head in the direction of the tavern. "'Cause she ain't at all what she seems."

He was beginning to learn that himself. "And Scepter?"

Jenkins blanched, his face paling visibly even in the darkness. "What do ye want wi' them bastards?"

Marcus kept his face inscrutable against his rising frustration. "Who are they?"

He laughed, an evil and rasping sound that echoed off the damp stone walls. "If'n ye figure that out, guv'nor, we both'll be rich in reward money!"

Then the man clenched his jaw and refused to say anything more.

Knowing he would get no more useful information tonight, Marcus released his hold on Jenkins's neck and stepped back.

The man scurried down the alley, half turning to make certain Marcus didn't change his mind and come after him. In a matter of seconds, he'd disappeared into the foggy darkness.

He'd gotten no more answers. It was time to deal with Danielle.

He returned to the tavern just in time to see her slight figure emerge into the street. But instead of walking toward the waiting hackney to retrace her circuitous path home, she turned in the opposite direction.

Marcus followed behind, staying a dozen strides back and careful not to be seen. But no matter if he lost her. He knew where she'd left her father's carriage and could intercept her there.

When she reached a narrow passageway leading off the main street, she paused to glance in both directions. Marcus flattened himself inside a doorway in the shadows, out of sight. Then he watched as she foolishly headed into the dark passageway alone.

With a curse, he shoved himself out of the doorway and hurried after her.

He darted into the alley and saw Danielle standing only a few feet away, her back against the brick wall. In front of her, a large man towered over her, blocking her escape. The man was tensed and ready to attack, and a knife gleamed in the hand dangling at his side.

"Get away from her!" Marcus shouted and rushed forward.

The man raised his knife to strike at Danielle, but Marcus dropped his shoulder and plowed into the stranger's gut. His body blocked the downward arc of the knife, and he grabbed at the winded man's arm, twisting it forcefully back at an unnatural angle to his elbow. A painful curse tore from the attacker's lips, and his fingers opened with a convulsing shudder. The knife dropped with a clatter onto the ground.

Marcus kicked it away at the same time as he pulled back his arm and landed a hard fist into the man's jaw. The attacker staggered backward from the strength of the blow. Marcus drew back his arm to deliver another punch.

The man dove for the knife, snatching it up as he rolled across the ground. He came up facing Marcus on the balls of his feet, crouching low and prepared to fight.

Marcus glanced around the alley. No weapons, nowhere to dash for safety, Danielle to protect—retreat was his only option. He grabbed her hand and ran. He pulled her down the alley toward the avenue, hoping the attacker was too cowardly to follow them into the moonlit street.

He hurried her to the waiting hackney. The driver stared in wide-eyed surprise as they ran toward him. Marcus threw open the door and shoved her inside the compartment.

He swung up after her and called out to the driver as he slammed shut the door, "The Queen's House!" He pounded his fist against the ceiling. "Go, now!"

The carriage jerked to a start and pulled out into the street.

He grabbed Danielle's arm and pulled her across the compartment toward him, putting her off-balance and halfway onto his lap. "Why are you meeting with men in taverns and alleyways?" He lowered his head until his mouth was only a hairsbreadth from hers and growled, "And what the hell happened to my sister?"

Eight

DANI YANKED HER ARM AWAY AND SAT BACK ON THE bench opposite from him, her breathing labored. Even in the darkness, she could see anger blazing in his eyes and was certain that it matched the intensity of the fear in her own.

"Why were you at that tavern tonight?" he demanded.

"I was meeting with the men I'd hired, to give them instructions," she breathed out, too upset to find her voice.

"For what exactly?"

She refused to answer that. He was asking her to endanger all of Nightingale. Something she would *not* do.

"That man was going to kill you." He leaned toward her, the hardness in him visible even in the dark shadows. "I've spent years studying how a man moves his body when he's readying to attack, how he holds a weapon that he's about to plunge into your gut. I can read the tension in the way he holds himself and know when he's going to strike. Not if. *When.* And I saw all of that in your man just now. He wasn't holding that knife ready in case someone else came upon you. He was raising it to strike. At you."

Her stomach lurched. She'd been working with Kimball for years, trusted him to carry out his duties and not give her up, just as Jenkins wouldn't—

But he'd turned on her. If Marcus hadn't been there, Kimball would have killed her.

She pressed her hand against her belly. Oh God, she was going to be sick!

"Why would someone want to attack you, Danielle?"

Praying she didn't cast up her accounts, she shook her head. She couldn't tell him that. It would mean divulging everything about Nightingale.

"You might as well answer me. I have no intention of letting you out of this carriage until I know what you're involved in, because I have a feeling that it also involved Elise. So I'll keep us circling Westminster until the horses drop dead if I have to."

"Siege warfare, General?" She seethed breathlessly at his audacity.

"Whatever it takes, including telling your aunt. You're keeping secrets from everyone, but there won't be any more secrets if I tell her what you've been up to. No more midnight meetings in dark alleyways." He leaned forward, elbows on knees, to punctuate his point. "No more trips to the Golden Bell to arrange vanishings."

Her heart lodged in her throat. "How do you know about that?"

In the shadows cast by the glow of the lamps, he arched a silent brow, indicating that he planned to keep secrets of his own. The rest of his face was too dark to see his full expression, but she knew he would be wearing that soldier's mask of his, the inscrutable countenance that so carefully hid his true thoughts.

"If that man was willing to come after you tonight, then he'll be willing to do it again," he continued, ignoring her question. "Perhaps in your own home."

"No," she whispered, forcing herself to breathe normally. "Kimball doesn't know who I am or how to find me." In that much, at least, she felt secure.

"Tell me why he wanted to harm you." He waited patiently for her to answer as the horses trotted on toward Westminster. When several long moments had ticked by with no answer, he pressed, "Or would you prefer to tell your aunt?"

The night was closing in around her like a snare, yet she refused to answer.

"When I was on the Continent, I lost a lot of men," he said as casually as if he were simply telling another one of his stories of camp life that he'd shared with her so many years ago, when she'd been nothing more than an infatuated girl. But so much had changed since then. "I would have done anything then to help them. So let me help you now."

She longed to let him do just that, so much so that she ached at the temptation. How wonderful it would be to unburden herself, to let him carry even just a small part of the weight resting on her shoulders.

And yet…

"You can't," she rasped out. "Too much is at risk."

"It seems to me that too much was already risked and lost," he said quietly with a brother's grief. "Let me help you. I'll make certain that man never comes after you again."

Let me help you... The same plea Elise had given when she'd asked to join Nightingale. He had no idea how brutally the memory of those words pierced her, or how much she wished he could do just that.

"What kind of trouble are you in, Danielle? How can I save you?"

Save her? She strangled back an ironic laugh that swelled up from the overwhelming emotions roiling inside her. "You misunderstand. I don't need to be saved." The burden, the endless lies, the unbearable secrets... She sucked in a deep lungful of air, gathering her courage to confide in him—"I *am* a savior."

His only reaction was a stiffening of his spine. He stared at her in the darkness, saying nothing, as if he knew that a single word might change her mind and silence her once more.

"I run a charity—a network," she began, turning toward the window. She couldn't bear to look at him. She'd never told anyone else what she was about to reveal except the women who worked with her. She prayed that there would be absolution once this agonizing confession was over.

"Nightingale."

She nodded, not surprised that he knew. "We help women who are being abused. Wives, daughters, sisters—women made to work as prostitutes, girls forced into slave labor in mills and factories, those who are beaten by husbands and brothers... We help them start new lives."

"We?"

"Other women who are part of the network."

Surprise crossed his face. "Society women?"

"Not all of them. A few."

"Who?"

"I won't tell you." She'd take that secret to her grave, because some of those women were battered themselves but unable to escape. God help them if their husbands ever discovered what they'd been doing. "But when a woman asks for our help, we work together to rescue her."

"A vanishing," he murmured.

"Sometimes, yes, if there's no other option. We help them to vanish into new lives, never to be seen again."

He leaned forward intently. "How?"

"It's not complicated, not really." Telling him was diffi-cult, but the words came more easily the more she shared, the burden slowly lifting. "When a woman decides that she can no longer tolerate her situation, she contacts Nightingale to ask for our help." *Tolerate?* She nearly laughed. Most women only contacted Nightingale when they realized that their lives were in danger. "She's heard about us because one of us is aware of her situation and has made contact with her. We don't approach the women directly, but through other people, like barmaids, prosti-tutes, housemaids—"

"The men you've been meeting with," he interjected.

"No. Jenkins and Kimball work with us only once the women have left their homes, if they need to flee London." She idly traced a trembling fingertip over the edge of the bench seat beneath her. "Once a woman asks for help, we work together to help her. We usually relocate the women into homes with relatives who will protect them. But sometimes, we have to make the women disappear completely and create new lives for them, usually in America."

She could practically feel the puzzled frown he gave her through the shadows. "How many of you are there?"

"Less than a dozen." That was as detailed an answer as she ever planned on giving. "There are also contacts we work with outside the network, such as innkeepers and shopkeepers, who don't know our real names or identities. People like Kimball and Jenkins, the two men tonight. They're former smugglers who know how to get in and out of London and the ports unseen, who are only involved for the money." Which brought its own layer of distrust. But she'd always thought money could buy a certain level of anonymity and protection, until tonight. "Every meeting is carefully arranged so that the contacts outside the network never learn the women's true names or where they lived. It's how we keep both the women and ourselves safe."

"Is that what happened tonight, do you think? That one of the men discovered what you were doing and hired that man to kill you because he wanted revenge for you taking away his wife or sister?"

"Unlikely. Harming me wouldn't tell them what happened to the women who had fled from them."

"And Elise?" His icy voice sent a chill tingling through her. "She was part of your network, wasn't she?"

"Yes."

"Why?" Frustration and confusion pulsed from him. "For God's sake, why would *she* be involved in something like this? Her husband was a good man. He never laid a hand on her."

"Your sister was the most selfless person I've ever known. She would never turn her back on anyone in trouble, whether it had a direct effect on her own life or not. Those women needed her help. That was all she had to know to devote herself to them."

"And it killed her."

She shook her head and stared down at her hands, now folded uselessly in her lap. "She wasn't working for Nightingale that night." Dani knew that much with certainty at least. "I personally arrange all the vanishings. I know when they're going to happen and how, if an additional transfer is necessary—I make all the final decisions. There was nothing scheduled that night."

When his expression darkened, she knew he understood what she meant. "Elise arranged it on her own." He leaned forward, his gaze piercing as he sought answers she couldn't give. "That's why you didn't recognize John Porter's name, because he wasn't one of the men who worked for you. She'd hired him on her own and didn't tell you."

"Yes." But that answer did little to ease down her rising guilt. "I believe so."

He reached for her hand. When she tried to pull away, his fingers tightened around hers. Instead of letting go, he moved across the compartment to sit beside her and covered both of her hands with his.

"I need answers, Danielle." He squeezed her fingers. "I need to know that my family is safe, and the only way I can do that is to uncover the truth about my sister."

"I can't give you any more answers." She turned toward the window and the dark city beyond. "I don't even know them myself."

"You have to try." He cupped her cheek in his palm and gently turned her face to look at him. "Please."

Nodding faintly, she began in a voice that was little more than a whisper, "I told Elise about Nightingale because I needed her help with the money. We couldn't use a bank because women aren't allowed to open an account without a man to sign for them, and we couldn't use our household accounts without husbands or relatives seeing. Except for Elise. Her husband was dead, and you were away at war. No one was at Charlton Place to question why large sums of money were being moved through the accounts."

"That was all she did, help with the money?"

"With Nightingale, yes. We all had our own responsibilities. I arranged the vanishings, other women made certain the women had everything they needed for their new lives, and Elise served as the bank. It worked well, for a while. But you know how your sister was. She wanted to *do* things. Secreting out money wasn't nearly enough for her."

"No, it wouldn't have been." He tenderly stroked her cheek. "What happened?"

She tightened her fingers around his hand as he continued to hold hers, and she tried to explain in a way he would understand. "There are certain women whose situations are so dangerous that helping them puts their lives at risk, and ours. If we attempt to help them and something goes wrong, they might be hurt even worse. Or killed. Sometimes we simply can't help them," she admitted in a guilt-rasped whisper. "But Elise wanted to rescue everyone, and as soon as possible. We argued about it. When I refused to change how Nightingale operated, she wanted to start her own network so she could arrange her own vanishings. I told her that it was too dangerous, that she would be putting her life at risk—" She choked. Swallowing hard, she finished, "She promised me that she wouldn't."

"But she did anyway, didn't she?"

She nodded, lowering her face so he wouldn't see her grief. "I believe so."

"And she hired John Porter to help her, a former smuggler like the men who work for you?"

"I suppose, but..." When she hesitated, he stroked his thumb over her bottom lip in entreaty for her to continue. "But he might be connected to a brothel."

He paused, his thumb stilling as it looped up to lightly trace the outline of her lips. "Why do you think that?"

"The women who are in the most dangerous situations are usually connected to brothels. They're forced to sell their bodies and are beaten by the managers if they don't. But it's all about profit for the owners. If they discovered that someone was helping their women escape and hurting their profits…"

"They'd put a stop to it," he finished grimly.

When she nodded, he leaned forward and brought his lips to her forehead in a gesture of understanding and gratitude for trusting in him.

"Marcus, I'm sorry…" She buried her face against his shoulder as she clung to him, not caring how weak she must have seemed. Not caring about anything except how much she needed to absorb his strength to keep from breaking down completely. "It was my fault that she died." In her grief, she could barely speak the words. "I asked for her help—she died because of me."

"It isn't your fault," he murmured into her hair, his arms tightening around her.

Oh, how much she wanted to believe that! But simply saying it didn't make it true.

She squeezed her eyes shut. She'd told him all she was willing to share, and still it wasn't enough to bring solace. There was nothing left that she could do or say to give him the peace he sought, or bring any to herself.

"Danielle," he whispered, his voice an agonized rasp. Then his lips touched hers.

She inhaled sharply at the unexpected contact. It took a moment for her to realize what was happening, that Marcus Braddock was kissing her.

No, not a kiss. Nothing as simple as that. It was so much more.

The comfort he gave her soothed the raw edges of her

grief and provided an absolution of the guilt she carried and most likely always would. She drank him in, wanting desperately to end the pain. As she let go of his lapels and brushed her hands over his waistcoat to feel the power and life pulsing within him, she wanted nothing more than to find a way to be engulfed by his strength and steely hardness. To find a way to capture the solace she knew he was capable of giving—

"Marcus." His name was a plea against his lips.

In response, he deepened the kiss. She knew as his mouth moved more insistently against hers that he was seeking his own comfort in her, and the sweet touch of lips to lips transformed from a soothing caress into shared consolation. And then into need.

He shifted her in his arms, bringing her onto his lap as his mouth captured hers, now more demanding in claiming this taste of her. His hand slipped to her nape and tugged her down to him, until her breasts flattened against his hard chest.

She lay against him so scandalously, yet she couldn't bring herself to stop him. Hadn't she wanted this since she was sixteen, to be in Marcus's arms? Hadn't she always been jealous of the other women she'd watched him dance with, take for drives through the park, smile at flirtatiously, and whisper God only knew what kind of sinful things into their ears that made them laugh so wickedly? Now that she was the woman in his arms, his kisses were just as wonderful as she'd imagined. *Heavenly.*

When the tip of his tongue coaxed at the seam of her

lips, she couldn't deny herself this pleasure and opened her mouth in invitation.

His tongue slipped between her lips to claim all of her kiss. He made slow but deep and exploring sweeps into her mouth, then encouraged her to kiss him back by giving a velvet-soft stroke over her tongue.

More nervous than she wanted to admit at this new way of kissing, she repeated the little movement. But her unschooled tongue twined around his in a motion far more wanton than she'd intended.

A low groan rumbled from the back of his throat. He began to thrust his tongue between her lips in a sinfully seductive motion that stole the air from her lungs. *Sweet heavens.* An intoxicating warmth bloomed low in her belly, and she melted against him, completely losing her battle to resist.

Slow and deliberate, each thrust of his tongue now came as a decadently smooth and unhurried slide between her lips. A restless ache settled between her legs, intensified by his other hand that moved reassuringly in slow strokes over her back, in caresses that were some-how both so innocent yet surprisingly erotic that she shivered.

When he slid his mouth away from hers, to trail kisses along her jaw, she whispered his name. What emerged instead was a low moan, one that made him smile against the fragile skin below her ear.

She was lost in the spicy, masculine taste of his kisses, the sensitive caresses of his hands over her body, wishing he would dare to touch her in a way no other man had ever attempted before…because she would let him. This man, at this moment, when every touch between them was a healing benediction.

"Danielle." Her whispered name reached her through the arousal engulfing her.

A slow caress of his thumb over her bottom lip made her eyes flutter open. She stared at him, seeing such an expression of desire that she lost whatever breath she'd managed to regain.

"We're in Westminster."

She blinked, her kiss-fogged brain momentarily confused. But a quick glance out the window at the Queen's House confirmed his simple statement.

Alarming clarity washed over her, replacing the confusion with humiliation. Oh, what a fool she was! To be so weak as to capitulate to him, both with her kisses and her secrets.

Cheeks burning, she slid off his lap and onto the other bench. When he didn't move to open the door, the urge to flee overwhelmed her. She grabbed for the handle herself—

"Wait." His hand clasped her wrist. Even at that innocuous touch, her pulse pounded wildly like a drum. "We need to talk."

She refused to look at him. "There's nothing more to talk about. I've told you all that I can." *Please don't mean the kiss! Please don't mean you want to talk about that…*

"Are you in danger?"

The concern with which he said that pierced her. "No," she answered honestly, "I don't think so." No one knew her real name or where she lived. They wouldn't be able to trace her any further than the Golden Bell. "And Kimball had nothing to do with Elise, I'm certain of it."

"You will tell me if anyone threatens you." Not a question, an order. "If you need my help."

His concern might have been genuine, but all the worry in the world wasn't enough to make her be so foolish as to let down her guard again. Next time, she wasn't certain her heart could survive it.

She flung open the door and hurried to the ground so quickly that she surprised the horses. Leaving Marcus to pay the driver, she rushed along the avenue toward the little side street where she'd left her carriage. She didn't glance behind to see if he was following and tried to convince herself that she didn't care either way.

Apparently, now she was even lying to herself.

Nine

GRITTING HIS TEETH, MARCUS SLAMMED HIS FIST into the large leather bag filled with sawdust and grain that dangled on a chain from the overhead beam. Then again. And again.

The frustration inside him from kissing Danielle was still too hot, too raw, and he needed to purge it completely before he could return home to Charlton Place tonight. Despite the sweat that rolled down his face and bare back, he wasn't anywhere near reaching that point.

Around him, the old armory building was dark and silent. Its ten-foot-thick, windowless stone walls and iron doors kept out the noise and confusion of London and provided a place of sanctuary. The only light came from the lamps he'd lit and placed around this part of the central octagonal-shaped room that he'd turned into a training area. The only sounds were the rattling of the chain with each punch or kick to the bag. Exactly how he preferred it.

That was why he'd kept this property as it was instead of turning it into a warehouse, even though its location just north of the City made it financially valuable. He needed somewhere he could go to get away from Charlton Place and from society, in a way he couldn't by going to the club or taking a long ride. And that was why he came here tonight after returning to the Strand to fetch his horse once he'd made certain that Danielle was safely back home. Only here could he let out his frustrations and pent-up energies like this.

Only here could he be himself.

But if anyone at court or in the Lords ever saw what he'd done with the building—how he'd hung bags from the rafters to practice fisticuffs, how he'd constructed men from sawdust and thick leather coverings that he could attack with swords and axes, how he'd put together a collection of various weights and clubs meant to enhance his agility and build sheer strength—they'd think him mad. But he couldn't survive without this place to escape to.

Especially tonight.

Kissing Danielle like that… What the *hell* had he been thinking?

He punched the bag with all the force he could muster. The jolt of contact reverberated up his arm and shuddered painfully through his shoulder.

He'd been caught up in his grief for his sister, in the shock of watching Danielle being threatened in that alley, in the betrayal he felt that she'd been keeping such dangerous secrets—

Lies. He'd kissed her because he'd wanted to. No other reason.

Clenching his jaw, he kicked at the bag, driving his bare heel deep into it. So hard that it went sailing in a wide arc away from him and jounced noisily on its chain.

He was a damned fool to kiss her.

When the bag swung back toward him, he pivoted in a circle and kicked at it again with the same foot from behind, sending it arcing high into the air.

And an even bigger fool to let her run away.

The large metal door to the outer courtyard clattered loudly as it opened and closed, followed a few seconds later by the creak of rusty hinges on the inner door to the building itself. He didn't need guards to keep anyone from sneaking inside. The old building announced visitors' arrivals on its own.

"We were summoned here by General Braddock," Merritt called out as he and Pearce walked into the central room from the narrow entry hall. "Looks like we found Gentleman Jackson instead."

Marcus grimaced as he grabbed the bag to stop it from swinging.

"No," Pearce corrected as his gaze roamed around the room and took in all the training paraphernalia and weaponry. "I've been to Jackson's saloon. It isn't half as good as this." Then his attention landed on Marcus, and he arched a brow. "What is this place?"

My sanctuary. "A former armory." He reached for a towel lying over a rack of metal weights and wiped off the sweat clinging to his bare chest. He was soaked with perspiration, including his loose-fitting trousers that hung low around his hips and were the only piece of clothing he wore, but the frustrations inside him had barely eased. "I purchased it last winter to turn into a warehouse."

"But you turned it into something else." Merritt

muttered with a faint trace of awe as he scrutinized the weapons on the wall, "A fortress."

Marcus unwound the long strips of cloth he'd wrapped around his hands as mufflers to protect his knuckles. "A place to escape to." During the past few months since his return, this place had become a safe haven for him. That he'd turned it into a small arsenal meant nothing. "Some place where I can work my muscles and maintain my fighting edge." Perhaps *almost* nothing. Since he'd returned, he'd also felt hunted, and keeping his edge by training here put him at ease. "And Claudia thinks claymores clash with the wallpaper at Charlton Place."

"And the rifles over the door with the Aubusson rugs," Merritt agreed as he pulled a war rapier down from the wall and examined it.

"Do you often feel the need to escape, General?" Pearce's somber gaze narrowed on him.

Marcus answered with brutal honesty, "Don't you?"

Before Pearce could reply that purchasing an armory was a damnably unusual way to escape, Merritt called out to Marcus and tossed the rapier to him. He easily caught it and smiled grimly when Merritt took down a second sword.

Merritt Rivers was one of the best swordsmen His Majesty's army had ever produced. Normally, Marcus avoided sparring with him, to save his pride a certain beating. But tonight, he felt just masochistic enough to engage.

As Merritt shrugged out of his jacket and tossed it

aside, Pearce leaned against the wall and folded his arms over his chest, settling in to watch. "What made you come here tonight?"

"Undoubtedly a woman." Merritt pulled off his cravat and tossed it over his jacket, then rolled up his shirtsleeves. "Probably the one he was so enamored of at the party." He grinned as he came forward, brandishing the sword in quick, slashing arcs through the air to gain the feel of the blade. "Turned you down, did she?"

"She is the Honorable Danielle Williams, daughter of Baron Mondale, and I am not enamored of her." No, he just inexplicably turned into a nodcock whenever he was around her. "And I don't proposition innocent misses."

"No," Pearce agreed dryly. "As a duke, you marry them."

He leveled a hard look at the earl, saying nothing. There was no good reply to that.

When Merritt took his position across from him on the open stretch of floor, Marcus ignored Pearce's baiting and raised his sword in salute. Merritt did the same.

"*En garde*," Pearce called out, acting as de facto referee. The two men turned their shoulders toward each other, their swords pointed at the floor. "*Prêt?*" Both men readied their stances, bending their front legs and shifting their weight onto their rear feet. Their swords raised. "*Allez!*"

Merritt lunged, immediately gaining the offensive. Marcus parried the thrust and deflected Merritt's sword. There was no blunt tip on either rapier, but each man had trusted the other with his life on the battlefield, just as they trusted now in each other's skilled control to keep from injuring the other. Although Marcus would be lucky if he managed to touch Merritt at all, who now advanced and retreated with expert footwork that made getting close to him nearly impossible.

The metallic ring of blade striking blade echoed off the stone walls and filled the large space that stretched three floors above their heads. When Merritt fended off a thrust with a circle parry, the defensive move separated the two men by several steps, giving Marcus a moment to catch back his wind.

"So why ask us here tonight, General?" Merritt's voice was barely winded, his reflexes still as quick and deadly as they'd been when he'd been commissioned.

"Because I need your help."

Pearce called out, "With what problem?"

A problem, all right. Marcus smiled tightly as the two men engaged once more. "Miss Williams."

Merritt thrust again, this time with a circling flick of his wrist as his blade ran down the length of Marcus's. He easily twisted the sword from Marcus's hand. It landed on the stone floor at his feet with a clatter. Merritt grinned, retreating to let Marcus pick up his rapier. Had this been a real duel, Marcus would be dead. "You're losing your touch, General."

Doubtful. Merritt was simply that good. Always had been. Still, he acknowledged, "My skills can dull a bit. We're not reconnoitering the French."

"No. A society lady." Merritt saluted Marcus with his sword. "In my experience, far more dangerous than the French. I've seen how they use those parasols. As deadly as bayonets."

Pearce made a wry face. "No quarter either. When they capture a man, it's for life."

"Best not let them capture you then." Despite his grin, there was a low warning in Merritt's voice.

But capturing Danielle Williams to wife wasn't at all why he'd asked Merritt and Pearce to join him here tonight.

Certainly she was attractive, and the woman she'd become held little in common with the girl he remembered. Like a butterfly from a cocoon, Danielle had transformed into a graceful, lithe, and curvaceous lady, one who possessed a regal air and self-confidence that were simply alluring. When they'd danced, she'd moved in his arms as if she belonged there, matching him step for step and faltering only when he'd challenged her about Elise. And good Lord, how sweet she'd tasted when he'd kissed her...a decadent mix of honey and wine.

How she'd managed to turn twenty-five and remain unwed he had no idea. Neither was he the man to end that. His concern for Danielle went only as far as gaining justice for his sister's death.

"I'm not one to get himself leg-shackled by the enemy," Marcus countered as they once more took up their bout.

Merritt's eyes gleamed knowingly as he deflected a slashing strike. "Even by one in petticoats?"

He gritted his teeth and shoved Merritt's blade away with sheer strength, pushing his friend backward several feet. "*Especially* one in petticoats."

"Then why do you need our help?" Pearce called out, still leaning against the wall and safely out of the way.

Marcus sidestepped Merritt's slash of the rapier. "Because she has information I need."

"About what?"

"Elise's murder."

Stunned, Merritt halted, his sword hand falling to his side as he stared in disbelief.

Marcus flicked the tip of his sword across Merritt's chest in a well-controlled slice that cut through his waistcoat and left a gaping tear in the silk brocade.

Panting hard to catch his breath, not all of it lost from physical exertion, he tossed away his rapier. It banged against the stone floor in an echoing clatter, the only sound in the armory as his two closest friends continued to stare at him, unable in their shock to find their voices.

Not wanting to see their startled expressions, Marcus snatched up the towel. He rubbed it over his face to wipe away the rivulets of sweat stinging his eyes, taking this moment's pause to collect himself. Then he flipped the towel over his shoulder and crossed the room to a little cabinet pushed up against the wall. He kept his attention on the cabinet, still unable to bring himself to look at them.

"Elise was killed the night before her body was found, I'm certain of it. She didn't break her neck falling from her horse. Someone murdered her." His hand trembled as he reached into the cabinet and withdrew three glasses and a bottle of brandy. They would all need a strong drink after this. "When I was packing away her things last month, I came across a note."

As he poured brandy into each glass, he told them what he'd found, what the letter had said, how the details that Danielle had shared about Elise's death simply didn't fit together. He fixed his gaze to the golden liquid in each glass as he unburdened himself. Gratefully, both men kept their silence.

When he finished with his story, including what he felt was safe to share about Nightingale, he turned around and held out the glasses.

Somberly, both men came forward to claim them, then took contemplative swallows, not knowing what to say. Their silence was fine with Marcus, because he didn't know what he needed to hear. Except...

"How can we help, General?"

He warmed with gratitude at Pearce's quiet question, spoken with no doubt of offering assistance. After all, they considered themselves to be brothers, the bond between them forged by blood and hellfire on muddy battlefields stretching from southern Spain to Belgium.

"I need to find the man she was supposed to have met with that night." He took a large swallow of brandy and welcomed the burn down his throat. "John Porter. Miss Williams believes he may be connected to a brothel. And I need to learn more about Scepter."

"Is that wise?" Pearce finished his brandy. "From what you've said, they sound dangerous."

So am I. "If this group had any connection to Elise's death, I need to discover what it was." And wouldn't stop until he did. "Can I count on your help in finding Porter?"

The two men exchanged dubious glances at the paltry bit of information they had to work with.

"We'll ask around, but…" Pearce shook his head at the improbability of finding one specific man in all of London based solely on his connection to a brothel.

"I know." Marcus's mouth tightened at the task he was giving them. "But I appreciate whatever help you can offer." More than he could say.

"We should call on Clayton," Merritt suggested, frowning thoughtfully into his glass. "He has the resources of the Home Office at his fingertips."

Clayton Elliott had served under Marcus as a major in the last year of the fight against Napoleon. Of all his closest friends from the army, only Clayton seemed to be thriving now that the wars were over. But then, he hadn't strayed too far from the ranks, simply moving from the governing auspices of the War Office to the Home Office, taking a position as an undersecretary.

Pearce nodded and took the rapier from Merritt. "Good idea. He can reach out to his contacts while the two of us work through London in person." He paused. "Unless you don't want anyone else to know, General."

Eventually, all of England would know when he found the person responsible for Elise's death and had him hanged. But now, it was better to be cautious, especially after how Danielle was nearly attacked tonight. She'd sworn that Kimball's betrayal had nothing to do with Elise, but a niggling doubt pricked at his gut.

"Tell Clayton but no one else." He dropped the towel to the floor. "Until we know what we're dealing with, we can't take any chances."

Not with Danielle's safety hanging in the balance.

"We'll start first thing in the morning," Merritt assured him, resting a hand on his shoulder. "We won't let you down."

His throat tightened. This was what he missed about the wars, what he would trade his new title and every penny of his fortune to possess forever—this bond of brotherhood.

"If we're all done here, then I'd like to head home." Pearce hung the rapier and its mate into place on the wall. "It's been a long night, with the promise of an even longer day tomorrow, and I have a warm bed waiting for me."

"With a warm widow in it, I'm sure," Merritt added knowingly.

Pearce grinned as he moved toward the door. "Who am I to complain if a beautiful woman wants to comfort a poor soldier recently back from fighting Old Boney?"

"A poor soldier who recently inherited an earldom," Merritt corrected, which only widened Pearce's grin.

"That damned title might as well be good for something besides giving me a headache." He opened the door and amended over his shoulder as he stepped out into the night, "Who am I to complain if a beautiful woman wants to comfort a wealthy earl recently back from fighting in the Lords?"

Then he was gone, the doors closing behind him with a rusty squeal and a banging clatter.

Merritt reached for his jacket and slipped it on. "Pearce complains about that title incessantly." He tugged his sleeves into place. "But between you and me, I think it might just save him."

Marcus's chest clenched. He knew his men had suffered difficulties in readjusting to life in England, but he hadn't realized that Pearce was struggling as much as Merritt implied.

"If he can't be a field officer anymore, then the next best thing is overseeing his estate and caring for the village and parish there. It gives him purpose, and we all need that these days." Merritt hung his cravat around his neck, not bothering to tie it, and mumbled half to himself, "Some of us more than others."

Marcus frowned. Had he been wrong about Merritt? The man had returned to the law to take up at the bar right where he'd left off six years ago when he joined the Coldstream Guards, and by all accounts, he was successfully proving himself. He had family to support him, a career, a future—

No, Merritt simply needed reassurance. "Don't worry. You'll take silk soon." Marcus carried his glass back to the cabinet to refill it. "And your father will finally be able to brag that his son is a King's Counsel."

"I've got the law. Pearce has his estate. Clayton has the entire Home Office." His face softened with concern. "What's going to save you, General?"

"I don't need to be saved." Those words triggered a memory of Danielle, wearing an expression of such bleak misery that it had sliced through him. *You misunderstand. I don't need to be saved...* More than she realized. "I need to find John Porter."

Merritt held his gaze for a long moment, not satisfied with that answer. But he knew not to press and instead turned his attention to finishing his last swallow of brandy.

"But I do need another favor." Marcus picked up the long strips of cloth that he'd used for mufflers. "Can you hire a couple of men from the old guard to watch over Miss Williams and keep her from harm?" He winced inwardly at the thought of the tongue lashing he'd receive from her if she ever found out that he'd placed guards. "For God's sake, whatever you do, don't let her know."

"Of course." Merritt grinned at his expense. "You should marry this one, General. Sounds like she's got spine enough to keep you in your place."

"And how is that a benefit in a wife?" He wrapped his hands again for another set-to with the bag once Merritt left, carefully layering the strips of cloth over his knuckles and tying them off in small knots against his palms.

"It isn't. Just damn amusing for the rest of us!"

With a slap to Marcus's back, Merritt strode out the door.

Not bothering to muffle a curse of frustration, Marcus plowed a fist into the bag as hard as he could.

Ten

"BUT THAT CHICKEN WOULD NOT LEAVE THE GENERAL alone!" Harriett exclaimed to the entire dinner table at Charlton Place as she told a story about the first time she met George Washington. "I think he was in love with the general."

Dani bit her bottom lip to keep back a laugh. Thankfully, at least, no stray bottoms were involved with this tale.

"When Washington went inside the house, it threw an absolute fit that it couldn't follow. Flapping its wings, pecking its beak at everyone, crowing and carrying on as if a weasel had gotten into the henhouse. So Washington ordered that the chicken be let inside, and it followed him everywhere!"

Laughter went up from around the table, including from Adam Trousdale, Claudia's fiancé, who had never met the Williams women before and had no idea what to expect. That he hadn't run fleeing as fast as he could when the viscountess began telling her stories had certainly earned him favorable points. When he became the brother-in-law to a duke, he would have to interact often with society women at all levels of rank.

"Washington was convinced the chicken was a British spy."

And all levels of madness.

"They named it Major Andre."

Even Dani couldn't keep a laugh from escaping at that. It was the first genuine moment of amusement she'd felt in an evening of nearly unbearable tension between her and Marcus, so intense that surely the others also felt it. The man kept staring at her from the head of the table as if he couldn't decide whether to throttle her or kiss her.

"Auntie," she chastised mildly, leaning in close to Harriett, seated beside her.

"You said I couldn't tell the story about pinching King George's bottom," the viscountess countered in a low voice meant only for Dani but which everyone overhead. "You never said anything about Washington and the chicken."

"Because I didn't know about this one," she muttered, "or I would have."

"Before you're done," the viscountess accused, "you'll have an entire book filled with stories that I'm not allowed to tell."

"Exactly."

Marcus laughed.

Dani looked up and froze when she found him watching her. But when she saw the sparkling in his eyes, she smiled at him, happy to find an ally in her embarrassment.

But then his gaze fell to her mouth, and the memory of last night's kisses returned unbidden and with enough intensity to make her tingle. The tension hummed between them like electricity.

"What happened to the chicken?" Mr. Trousdale asked as he raised his wineglass to his lips, not knowing the viscountess's stories well enough to avoid stepping into that trap.

She matter-of-factly dabbed her napkin to her lips. "We had it for dinner."

He choked on his wine. "You're making that up!"

Her aunt feigned insult. "Would I lie about the fate of Major Andre?"

"To finish a good story?" Claudia piped up from across the table. "Yes, you would."

As the three of them argued good-naturedly about chicken dinners and American rebels, Dani took another glance at Marcus, this one curious as she tried once more to fathom why he insisted that they still have this dinner, even after all of last night's revelations.

But this time when he smiled at her, she didn't look away. Her pulse surged at that subtle connection between them. Wariness lingered inside her because she still expected him to corner her and interrogate her more about Elise and Nightingale, but now there was...curiosity. About her.

She'd rather have had his ire. Anger she knew how to deal with, while his pointed interest in her as a woman completely undid her.

Needing air—and distance from his dark stare—she placed her napkin on the table. "And on that, Claudia, perhaps you should take us all through to the drawing room so we can change the conversation to the reason we're here tonight." She flashed Claudia a happy smile. "Your upcoming wedding."

"Hear, hear!" Harriett seconded.

While Marcus assisted Harriett from her chair and Mr. Trousdale helped Claudia from hers, Dani took the opportunity to slip quickly from the room. She needed a few moments to herself, to attempt to relax before subjecting herself to the rest of the evening under Marcus's dark stare. She also desperately needed to collect her thoughts so that she could keep her wits about her and prevent him from catching her alone, when he would undoubtedly press her for more information about Nightingale. Information she refused to give.

And why not sneak upstairs to look in on Pippa in the nursery while she was here? Oh, how she missed that precious little girl!

"Danielle!" Claudia ran down the hallway after her. When she reached Dani, she linked their arms. "I need to talk to you. *Alone.*"

Worry tightened her belly. "What's wrong?"

Claudia placed a finger to her lips and glanced up and down the hall to make certain no one saw, then reached for the nearest door. "In here." She led Dani into Marcus's study, which was lit by a single lamp and the mellow glow of a banked fire. She closed the door to ensure their privacy and sent wariness spiraling through Dani when she leaned back against the door, as if she were afraid Dani might go running out. Did she know about last night with her brother?

Or worse…had Marcus told Claudia the truth about Elise's death?

"You know how much you mean to me," Claudia announced in a nervous rush. "You're like a sister to me."

"I feel the same."

"And I'm so pleased!" Claudia surprised the daylights out of Dani by throwing her arms around her and hugging her tightly.

"Oh?" Dani stiffened.

Claudia nodded as she took both of Dani's hands in hers and squeezed them. "Having you and the viscountess help me with my wedding like this is such a relief. You have no idea how worried I was that Marcus would try to interfere with it. If he had his way, we'd be married in some dank parish church without any wedding breakfast or party whatsoever."

"I doubt that."

Claudia silently arched a brow in challenge.

"I don't believe the church would be dank," Dani corrected with a knowing smile, collaborating in Claudia's characterization of her brother.

"No dank churches, no dour vicars…and an absolutely grand party!" She bounced with happiness. "You will help me plan every detail, won't you?"

"Well, the viscountess would be better at planning a party than I would be. But I will help you secure the church and vicar." Or more than likely, once her aunt was given free rein, St Paul's Cathedral and the archbishop of Canterbury.

"Thank you!" Another tight hug. When she pulled back this time, a seriousness that made Dani uneasy darkened her face. "There's one more thing."

"Oh?"

"Marcus is going to walk me down the aisle, of course, and Pippa's going to be my flower girl." Claudia hesitated before adding, "And if Elise were here, she would have been my matron of honor."

Grief panged hollowly in Dani's chest.

She squeezed Dani's hands again and said in hesitant stops and starts, "So I want to ask you...if you would...as my honorary sister...be my maid of honor."

Her throat stung with emotion. "I would be delighted."

Another hug, this one lingering, most likely so that both women had the time to control the tears threatening at their lashes.

"I'm worried about Marcus," Claudia whispered, taking the conversation in a new direction without warning. "Truly worried."

Surprise darted through Dani. Slowly, she pulled out of the hug and cupped Claudia's face between her hands. "He's been through a lot. But now that he's home, everything will be fine. You'll see."

"It won't be," she whispered, her face long. "He's so distant these days. He seems lonely, even when he's in the same room with us. It's as if—as if he draws back into himself, as if his mind goes some place far away. Surely you saw it for yourself tonight during dinner."

Dani had. But unlike the others, she knew exactly

where he'd gone in his mind. Into the private hell she'd helped cast him into.

"He hasn't yet adjusted to being home." She mustered a reassuring smile. "Just give him time."

"No, it's not that." Claudia turned away and aimlessly crossed to the large desk to run her fingers over the smooth desktop. A worried frown pulled at her brow. "He seems…lost. As if his life has no meaning."

"He has his family," Dani reminded her.

"It isn't enough. Don't misunderstand me. He's wonderful with Pippa and is the best brother I could have ever hoped for, and he's taking all this wedding and marriage news in stride as best he can. But he needs other things to fill his life beyond Charlton Place—*important* things. And not even a new dukedom or a seat in Parliament seems to make up for what he's missing." Inhaling a tremulous breath, she turned toward Dani, a pleading expression darkening her face. "Will you help him?"

That question knocked the air from her lungs. "*Me?*" she squeaked out. "What do I know about retired soldiers?"

"Nothing." Claudia shrugged. "Which makes you perfect for it. He doesn't need someone who treats him like a general or a war hero—he gets enough of that already and is thoroughly sick of it. And he definitely doesn't need to be treated like a duke. The society sycophants are already falling all over themselves to become ingratiated with him." Her mouth twisted wryly. "He has me and Pippa, so he doesn't need anyone who will treat him like a brother either."

Well, *that* would be an easy one to avoid. Dani's thoughts of Marcus certainly weren't brotherly.

"He needs someone to hold his feet to the fire, who will stand up to him and read him the riot act if he deserves it. Someone who will push him to find that new purpose." In exasperation, Claudia dropped her hands to her sides and stared pleadingly at Dani, as if willing her to understand. "He needs to be rescued from himself, and you're the perfect one to do it."

Dani shook her head. "What you're asking…" It was one very big favor, and more of an uphill battle than Claudia realized, given what had happened last night. Dani couldn't bear to spend more time with Marcus, which she would have to do to fulfill Claudia's wishes. No, if she were to continue her work, then she needed to stay as far away from him as possible. Meaningful life be damned.

"I know. And I wouldn't ask it of you if I had anyone else to turn to." Her eyes darkened with worry. "But you know how my brother is."

Dani once thought she did. Now, though, she wasn't at all certain.

"At the very least please help me to distract him until after the wedding."

She bit her lip. Oh, this wasn't at all a good idea… "I'll help however I can," she vaguely offered, her resolve vanishing beneath Claudia's pleading expression. "But I make no promises."

"Thank you! You have no idea how relieved this makes me. With you looking after him, Marcus is now one less problem I have to worry about."

Hmm. *That* was yet to be seen.

Claudia kissed both of Dani's cheeks, then bounced over to the door. "I'm going to dash upstairs to peek in on Pippa. I promised her that I'd stop up after dinner. I'll be back in a moment, and then we can discuss flowers for the wedding. I want hundreds of white roses!"

Then she was gone, slipping into the hall and closing the door after herself.

Dani rolled her eyes heavenward. Dear Lord, what had she gotten herself into now?

Pressing her hand to her forehead, she began to pace the large room, now needing to burn off her uneasiness even more than before. Help Marcus Braddock to find purpose in his civilian life? What a laugh! Even if the man were willing to accept help, which he would certainly *not* be willing to do, she was the absolutely most wrong person in the world for the job.

If he ever found out what she'd just agreed to—heaven help her. But her acquiescence had put Claudia at ease. Given how nervous and emotional she would become as her wedding day drew nearer, this was the least Dani could do for her.

And if there was any bright spot to this fiasco—and she wasn't at all certain there was, given how Claudia would now expect her to spend more time with Marcus while Dani would do everything she could to avoid him—at least no one would suspect anything more between them than distant friendship. To the world, they would be nothing more than two people forced together by Claudia's wedding. Certainly not two people who were hiding secrets of life and death, who had so shamelessly enjoyed being in each other's arms.

The door opened behind her with a soft click, and her shoulders sagged. Claudia was back, most likely having forgotten some other promise she'd intended to wrangle out of Dani.

But she didn't have the strength for more right then. Heaving out a long exhale of exasperation, she faced the door. "Claudia, I don't—"

She froze. Not Claudia.

Marcus.

He stood in the doorway, surprised to find her here. Alone. But of course he was. After all, Dani had been as thick as thieves with Claudia and Harriett tonight, not moving from either lady's side for fear of exactly this happening—finding herself alone with Marcus. She'd wanted to avoid at all costs a continuation of their last conversation in the carriage.

Apparently, fate was out to get her.

He stepped into the room and closed the door. But when he stalked slowly toward her, his dark gaze daring to trail over her and heating her skin everywhere he looked, it wasn't panic that spiraled through her but something else just as intense, just as unsettling.

"If you're looking for Claudia," she interjected

before he could speak, "she's gone up to check on Pippa."

"I wasn't."

When he stopped in front of her, she lifted her chin, readying for battle. "If you were looking for *me*, then you should know that I—"

"I wasn't," he repeated with a lift of his brow.

Well, *that* stung. Yet it wasn't enough to tamp down her suspicions. "Then why are you here?"

In answer, he stepped around her to the liquor cabinet and held up a bottle. "The best port in the house. If Trousdale and I are to be subjected to talk of weddings and trousseaus for the remainder of the evening, then we'll need to be properly fortified for it."

"Oh." She frowned with chagrin, feeling like a goose for thinking he'd sought her out. Most likely, he hadn't given last night's kisses a second thought, when they'd been practically all she'd been able to think about. "So if we're here, and Claudia is upstairs with Pippa, then poor Mr. Trousdale—"

"Is alone in the drawing room with the viscountess," he finished as he removed two glasses from the cabinet.

Poor Mr. Trousdale indeed. "By all means, you should return and rescue him."

"I think Trousdale can fend for himself against an old woman for a few minutes."

"Then you don't know Auntie very well. At any moment, she's likely to launch into her story about Napoleon."

"Let me guess." He poured the dark port into both glasses. "Boney had a pet pig who helped him invade Russia."

"A greyhound named Pierre, actually."

He froze for a beat, then replaced the bottle. "You are making that up."

"I wish I were," she sighed.

He sent her a pleading look over his shoulder. "Don't make me go back there."

"Well, you cannot stay in here with me." *Alone.*

"Why not? I think we have a lot of things to discuss, don't you?"

"And I think I've said all that needs to be said about those things."

"Not even close." Walking back to her, he held out one of the glasses.

She glanced down at the port, recognizing it for what it was. Not a drink but a challenge. And not to see if she would dare to take it or decry that proper ladies didn't drink port but if she were bold enough to remain here with him.

But she'd never backed down from a challenge in her life and accepted it. "Thank you."

With a knowing smile tugging at the corners of his mouth, he crossed behind his desk and gestured toward the pair of wingback chairs across from him in invitation for her to sit.

Dani hesitated. She knew she shouldn't. In fact, she should have already left to rejoin the others in the drawing room. Sitting would only invite him to delve further into her secrets and to chastise her once again for the dangers of Nightingale. Yet she couldn't help herself. This was her opportunity to put an end to all his prying...and other things he had no business doing with her.

"This is a first." She sat gracefully, then raised the glass to take a small sip of the sweet liquid. "I've never been invited to join the gentlemen after dinner for port."

"What a shame." With an amused smile, he leaned back in his chair, kicking out his long legs in a position of complete ease and relaxation. Yet behind the desk, he somehow looked even more masculine and powerful. And drat her heart, that the foolish thing leapt into her throat and beat a wild tattoo at the sight. "Those other men don't know what they're missing."

Her fingers tightened around the glass in irritation. "You really mustn't—"

"Beautiful company, biting wit, interesting conversation," he mused, studying her over his glass. "Or at least, I hope there will be interesting conversation, especially as you've been avoiding speaking to me all evening."

"I have not been avoiding you. We had a perfectly pleasant conversation over dinner."

"Surrounded by family," he corrected, "when we couldn't say what needs to be said."

"There's nothing to be—"

"Such as what happened in the carriage." His voice turned shiveringly intense. "We kissed last night."

They'd done a lot more than simply kiss, and the

memory of it tightened all the tiny muscles in her lower belly. She took another sip of port to calm her fluttering nerves. "I'm sure you've kissed quite a few ladies since your return."

"Just one, actually." His dark eyes gleamed. "You."

"Well, we all make mistakes."

His sensuous lips twisted in amusement, and he murmured a bit too huskily for comfort, "Didn't feel like a mistake to me." He kept his gaze locked on hers as he raised the glass to take a sip. "We kissed last night, and I strongly suspect that we both want to do it again." His head tilted slightly as he studied her. "If I came around this desk and took you into my arms, would you stop me?"

With that question, it wasn't her belly that he made ache.

She had to put a stop to this. *Now.* "I don't wish to discuss this."

"All right, then. So tell me more about Elise and what she was doing in the days before she died." He hadn't changed position, hadn't moved a single muscle, but she sensed a hardening in him. The intensity turned deadly. "Tell me how I can find John Porter and the men responsible for her death."

"I don't wish to discuss that either," she whispered from behind the rim of the glass, raised to her lips to give her something—*anything*—behind which she could hide. Yes, she was keeping secrets from him. So had Elise. But she wasn't prepared to be treated like an enemy under interrogation.

"Then it's back to why you keep kissing me whenever we're alone together."

Indignation sparked through her. "I do not—"

"You kissed me first over the music box."

"And *you* kissed me in the carriage!"

A rakish grin spread across his face as he drawled, "Yes, I certainly did."

A hot blush seeped into her cheeks, and she had to look away before he glimpsed it. Drat the devil! No wonder so many French soldiers wanted to kill him if he battled like this. "This conversation is improper and wholly unseemly for a duke."

"Dear God, I hope so."

Her gaze darted back to him in surprise. He'd meant that as a sarcastic reply, but the sincerity beneath it struck her like a slap. "You don't want to be a duke?"

His smile tightened. "We're not talking about me."

"We are now." She sat forward, balancing the glass of port on her knee, and critically assessed him across the desk. "If you don't want to be a duke, why did you accept the title?"

"I had no choice."

"Of course you did. Prinny could have given you a lesser title or a knighthood and an estate to go with it. You still would have been well rewarded and—"

"I had no choice," he repeated.

She stared at him, unable to fathom the inscrutable expression that fell over him like a veil. Why on earth would he put himself through all these changes, all the pressure of running a dukedom and sitting in Parliament, if he didn't—

"You damn fool," she whispered as the answer pulsed icily through her. Claudia's earlier pleas regarding her brother now made terrible sense…why he seemed so lost, why he lacked purpose. He hadn't accepted the title for his own gains, had never wanted it or the obligations that came with it, had hated every moment of it—"You did it for Claudia and Pippa."

"To give them the protection and wealth of a dukedom? Of course I did." He sat forward himself, placing his glass onto the desktop. "What wouldn't you do, Danielle, to protect the ones you love?"

He meant Elise, and a burning formed behind her eyes. Apparently, she hadn't done enough. "I would do all that I could," she breathed, the sound little more than the brush of a feather. "*All* that I could."

He rose from his chair and circled the desk to stand in front of her, to be closer and catch every whispered word from her lips. "Me, too." He leaned back against the desk in a casual pose, but she knew every muscle in his body was tensed and alert. "What else do you know about the days leading up to Elise's death? What else are you keeping from me?"

"Nothing." She leaned back in the chair and out of his reach. "I've told you all I know about your sister."

"And the men and women who might have been working with her? You've said almost nothing about them."

"Because I don't know."

"I've got men tracking down John Porter." He pulled at his cravat as if it choked him. Although it might very well have been the turn of conversation that pained him. It was certainly distressing her. "But there were women involved, I'm sure of it. If Elise had created her own network, one modeled after Nightingale, then she would have made use of her friends for some of the same tasks that you do. Perhaps even the very same women."

"I will never give up their names," she resolved firmly. She would go to her grave before she shared their identities. "If you value your sister's memory, do not ask me again."

"All right then." He pushed himself away from the desk and stopped directly in front of her. "It's back to the kisses."

Not this again! "I will *not*—"

"Did you enjoy them?" He placed his hands on the arms of the chair and leaned in over her, bringing his gaze level with hers.

She kept her lips closed. Any answer to that would only provoke the rascal to keep discussing it. Or worse, attempt to kiss her again right here.

"Surely you did," he answered for her, a knowing smile pulling faintly at the corners of his mouth. Then he leaned in to brush his lips against her temple.

Dani closed her eyes against the sweet torture. Even now, she trembled at his nearness, unable to hide the effect he had on her.

"I certainly did," he murmured.

"Stop staying things like that." But her order emerged as an unconvincing, throaty rasp.

"Then tell me your last secrets, Danielle." His warm lips caressed down the side of her face to her jaw. "Share the names of the women with me."

"I won't tell you that."

He placed his mouth against her neck, to lightly nibble at the tender flesh just below her ear and send a shivering heat sparking out to the tips of her fingers and toes. She put her hand against his chest, but she couldn't find the willpower to push him away.

"John Porter?" he pressed in a low murmur.

"I know nothing about him." She knew what he was doing, teasing her with kisses that weren't true kisses, hoping she would crave the inevitable reward of his mouth on hers that he would give if only she named the women. But she wouldn't, no matter how much her traitorous body longed to be back in his arms, and she stifled a whimper. "Neither do any of the women in Nightingale."

"And Scepter?"

Her heart stopped. In that moment's brutal stillness, she felt her blood turn cold.

"Porter cautioned Elise about it in his note," he murmured against her ear, not realizing that every word stirred icy fear inside her.

She swallowed. Hard. "John Porter gave good advice. You should heed it, too."

He shifted away from her, just far enough to look down into her face. "What is Scepter? Is it a person or a club—a network like Nightingale?"

"I don't know exactly. An organization of men from

London's underworld with ties to all kinds of crimes. Smuggling, fencing stolen goods, running brothels, extortion—" She shook her head. The rumors of what Scepter had been doing, the ruthlessness of the men behind it—God help her, *why* was he asking about them? "No one knows how large it is, how far-reaching."

"How do I find them?"

His appearance hadn't changed; his expression was still sober and hard. But she felt the change in him, a yearning so subtle that she nearly missed it—*Revenge*.

"Stay away from them," she rasped.

"If they're responsible for Elise's death—"

"Then they'll kill you, too."

He stiffened at her warning, his body tensing beneath her hand as it rested on his waistcoat.

Under her fingertips, his heart beat strong and steady, and she couldn't resist the urge to curl her fingers into the hard muscle of his chest. He was warm and alive, and she fully intended to keep him that way, no matter how many secrets she had to hide from him.

"Leave them alone, Marcus. They're not the kind of men you want to bother."

"I'm not afraid of them, Danielle."

Of course he wouldn't be. Not this man, who had charged into battles against the enemy in some of the bloodiest fighting the world had ever seen, repeatedly putting his life at risk.

Yet she warned, "You should be."

His eyes flickered darkly, but she couldn't tell if he

would pay heed to her cautions or dismiss them outright. Marcus Braddock was just infuriating enough to do either.

"Just one more question," he pressed.

Her shoulders sagged with exasperation. She pushed at him to shift him away, but he didn't budge. "Marcus, please—"

"Have they threatened you?"

Her throat tightened at the concern in his voice. "No." But then, why would they come after her? She admitted, so softly that her voice wasn't even a whisper, "I've been cowardly enough to avoid them."

"You're not a coward." He cupped her face between his hands. "You're the bravest woman I know."

Brave. She wasn't that at all. But for this moment at least, with the heat and strength of him there for the taking, she could let herself believe that she was.

"You need to stop your work with Nightingale." The firm warning was tempered by caresses of his fingers across her cheek and a brush of his thumb over her bottom lip. "Before you get hurt."

"Never," she countered breathlessly.

She closed her eyes, knowing he was going to kiss her. None of those half kisses either. This time, he would be just as hungry as he'd been last night, just as—

A scream tore through the house.

Fear seized her as she looked up into his startled face. "Claudia!"

Eleven

MARCUS RACED UP THE STAIRS TOWARD THE UPPER floors, taking them three steps at a time. The screams continued, chilling his bones with terror. Not Claudia—*please, God, don't let her be hurt!* How would he survive losing another sister?

"Claudia!" he bellowed as he reached the second floor landing. His lungs burned as he sprinted down the hall toward the bedrooms in the east wing. The door to Elise's room was open, the light from the hallway lamps spilling inside—

He halted, freezing in midstep as two forms emerged from the shadows…Claudia and an intruder who stood behind her, holding a knife to her throat.

"Marcus!" she cried, but the man held her by her hair and yanked hard to silence her. Tears spilled down her pale face.

"Let her go," Marcus ordered. He widened his stance and balled his hands into fists, preparing to attack.

"Let me pass," the man shot back as he dragged Claudia with him as he circled the edge of the room, making his way toward the door and escape.

"Don't hurt me, please," she whispered. "Please…"

With no other choice, Marcus stepped to the side. Helplessness seared the inside of his chest. Christ! He couldn't do anything to help, not as long as the man held the knife to her. If he attempted so much as a small move in the man's direction, he would slice her throat. All he could do was watch and wait for the exact moment to pounce.

And then he would kill the bastard with his bare hands for daring to harm his family.

Step by slow step, the man circled the room, keeping Claudia in front of him like a shield. She was so terrified that she shook violently, most likely still on her feet only because the man held her up by her hair, his fingers twisted painfully into her curls. They reached the doorway. With his eyes never leaving Marcus, he backed deliberately toward the hall.

"Marcus!" He heard Danielle rush down the hall, not seeing the intruder until it was too late.

Startled, the man spun around to face her, leaving his side vulnerable to Marcus and lowering the knife in surprise.

Now. Marcus drew back his leg and kicked. His boot slammed into the man's knee, which buckled beneath him with a loud groan of pain.

The intruder shoved Claudia to the floor and staggered back into the hall. He brandished the knife at Marcus to force him to stay back, then at Danielle as she pressed herself against the hallway wall less than ten feet away. She snatched a lit candle from the wall sconce and threw it at him, forcing him to duck.

Marcus pivoted on his foot and twisted around to

kick with the other, landing another strike, this time hard into the man's chest.

A flash of motion at the top of the stairs caught his attention. *Pippa.*

In that moment's distraction, the intruder thrust the knife. The sharp blade sliced through Marcus's jacket and sleeve, cutting into the hard muscle beneath. Flinching at the searing pain, he jerked back, his punch missing the man's jaw and flying through empty air.

The man swung the knife again, and Marcus dropped his shoulder as he dove forward. He hit the floor and rolled, popping back onto his feet and snatching up a silver candlestick from one of the tables lining the hall. Brandishing it like a sword from his uninjured arm, he positioned himself between the intruder and the stairs, keeping Danielle and Pippa behind him.

White-hot fury burned inside his gut. Never. That bastard would *never* lay another hand on the women he loved.

"What on earth...?" The viscountess's panicked cry surprised him. He glanced over his shoulder to see the older woman kneeling behind Pippa to take the child protectively into her arms and a flash of motion as Trousdale barreled down the hallway at the intruder.

The man turned and sprinted for the rear stairs to flee the house, too fast for Trousdale to catch him.

The candlestick fell from Marcus's hand and banged onto the floor as he fell back against the wall, bruised, bleeding, and exhausted.

"Uncle Marcus!" Pippa cried and shoved away from the viscountess and past Danielle to launch herself up into his arms and cling to him.

Marcus winced at the blinding pain, but he would never drop her. *Never.*

"Your arm," Danielle rasped out as she hurried to him and placed her hand worriedly on his shoulder.

"I'll be fine," he ground out. He'd suffered much worse on the continent.

But the dubious expression on her face told him that she didn't believe him. She turned her attention to his niece.

"Pippa, come here. It's all right," Danielle cooed as she gently pulled the little girl from his arms. She turned to hand her off to Mrs. Davenport as the woman finally arrived, huffing and puffing from running down from the nursery. "Please take her back upstairs—"

"Noooooo!" Pippa wailed, her arms tightening around Danielle's neck, and refused to go to her nanny.

Danielle cast a silent plea at her aunt for help.

The viscountess came forward immediately to take Marcus's good arm and help him away from the wall. "That wound needs to be dressed, Duke."

Ignoring her concern for him, Marcus glanced at Claudia, who sat on the floor in Trousdale's arms, crying in both fear and relief.

"I'd checked on Pippa," she explained, her chin resting on Trousdale's shoulder as he held her in his arms. "On the way back, I stopped in Elise's room to see if I could find her wedding veil." A jerking sob tore from her. "I wanted to show Danielle and the viscountess… Then I saw that man…going through her things…"

Trousdale rubbed her back to calm her, but his caresses did nothing to ease her shaking.

"I tried—I tried to get away, and I screamed…but he was too fast…that knife…"

Her words died away as she buried her face in Trousdale's waistcoat and cried.

Marcus's eyes stung as he tore his gaze away from Claudia. The icy truth slammed through him, as palpably as the burning pain of his cut arm. His family would never be safe until he found the men responsible for killing Elise.

And when he did…God help them.

_____

"Claudia found him in here, going through the boxes." Marcus led Clayton Elliott inside Elise's room. For once, he didn't feel the pang of grief that always struck him whenever he stepped into her room. But tonight, he blamed that on worry and anger.

Nodding, Clayton went to the window and checked the sill and shutters, his brow frowning in concentration as he ran his hand along the sash, feeling for any unusual marks.

One of the best officers who had served under Wellington, Clayton had been a major in the Grenadier

Guards and one of the many men who had gone through the fires of Waterloo. Unlike the others, though, he'd managed to avoid losing his way in civilian life by continuing his service to crown and country during the peace. Now fully ensconced in the Home Office as an undersecretary, he held responsibility for overseeing surveillance of half of England. Which half, though, he refused to say.

Clayton moved to the second window and began his inspection again.

He'd arrived here at Charlton Place only moments ago, after Marcus had sent a footman to find him and tell him they'd had an intruder. The man had tracked him down at his club, and Clayton came immediately, still in his evening clothes and smelling faintly of brandy and cigars. A better man to help with this Marcus could never have found.

"He was searching Elise's belongings," Marcus said quietly. Every inch of his home felt like it had been invaded and ransacked, although nothing seemed out of place.

Except for him. The surgeon had just finished with his medical treatments when Clayton arrived. *Thank God*, because the viscountess had insisted on being at his side while the man had sewn up the wound. He didn't know which was worse—the pain of the needle sticking repeatedly into his flesh or her attempt to distract him with a story about swimming in the Thames with Benjamin Franklin.

But the wound was now clean and sewed up tight, even if the shirt he still wore was soiled with his blood, not yet having found the time to change into fresh clothes. He'd been too busy securing the house and giving orders for all the servants to check every room, cabinet, nook, and cranny to make certain no other intruders lurked anywhere in the shadows.

"He didn't come in through these windows. There's no sign of forced entry here." Clayton straightened away from the casement, then turned and cast an assessing look around the room. "Most likely, he saw that you were having a dinner party and took advantage of the distraction to break his way inside through another window or door without being seen. This was probably the first room he came to where he thought he might find valuables worth taking."

A niggling doubt at the back of his mind told Marcus it wasn't as ordinary as Clayton made it sound.

Clayton stepped out into the hall to glance up and down its length. "With everyone in the dining room and kitchens, no one would have noticed if he'd slipped up here and searched the rooms. No one was up here to catch him."

"Except for Pippa and Mrs. Davenport, sleeping just above in the nursery," Marcus ground out, his jaw clenched. "And Claudia, who simply walked upstairs."

"None of them were hurt, General," Clayton reminded him.

Only by the grace of God. "To break into a house like this, when even more people than usual are here... This wasn't a typical burglary. That's why I sent for you."

Marcus lowered his voice even though they were alone in the hallway and solemnly revealed what he could. "Elise became involved with some dangerous people, right before her death."

"Who?"

"Have you heard of an organization called Scepter?"

Clayton gave a slight nod. "Criminal activity in the rookeries and stews, smuggling and fencing, prostitution…" He paused, his eyes narrowing. "Your sister was involved with them?"

"I think she stumbled across them by mistake."

Disbelief flashed across Clayton's face. "How would a society lady even come into contact with men like that?"

"It's not as impossible as you would think," Marcus muttered, thinking of Danielle and Nightingale. He sucked in a ragged lungful of air. "I can't tell you how, but Elise strayed into their world. I believe she crossed them, and they killed her for it."

His friend muttered a low curse, momentarily stunned. Then Clayton nodded his sympathy, knowing not to voice any more arguments or worthless condolences. He stepped back into the room and swept his gaze around it once more, this time taking in the boxes and trunks.

"It's very unlikely that the man who broke into your house tonight is involved with Scepter or had anything to do with your sister's death." He opened one of the trunks and looked inside. "Why take that risk? And now, two years after her death? For what?"

Marcus rubbed the knot at the back of his neck. "Damned if I know."

There was nothing left in the trunks and boxes except clothes and other whatnots that hadn't yet been donated to the poor. Nothing at all that seemed important.

But then, *he* hadn't known himself that anything important had been among her things until he stumbled across the letter. God only knew what else was hidden here that the men who had killed her would want to keep from coming to light.

"Whoever killed your sister," Clayton said, closing the trunk, "she's not a threat to them anymore."

But Marcus was. He'd watch those men swing, no matter what it took.

"As a favor to an old brother in arms, can you call on your Home Office contacts to learn more about Scepter, what it's been doing and who the men are behind it?" Marcus placed his hand on Clayton's shoulder, the bandaged and blood-stained arm stretching out between them as a reminder of the gravity of the situation. "I'd be more at ease if I knew my family won't be threatened by them again."

Especially once he had their names and put them into their graves.

"I can't do anything officially," Clayton offered, "but I will ask around, see what I can discover on my own. I can't promise that I'll learn anything. You know how it is with criminal groups like this. If they don't interfere with legitimate business interests or those of the crown, they're mostly allowed to carry on unchecked. The Home Office simply doesn't have enough men to go after all of them."

Marcus's hand dropped away. "Nor does Parliament or the king care if the poor are killing and cheating themselves."

"As long as it doesn't spread outside the rookeries," Clayton confirmed with a sardonic lift of his brow. "Then they might actually have to do something about the fact that the poor are starving and dying instead of simply ignoring them."

These days, many of those same poor and starving were soldiers who had returned from the wars to find vacant jobs nonexistent and their commissions worthless, with no way to support themselves or their families. The aristocracy did their best to ignore their existence, and the middle class blamed the poor themselves, calling them lazy and ignorant. The truth was that those same men would have gladly taken any job that put food on the table and a roof over their heads, but those jobs simply didn't exist. And what did Parliament do? Passed import laws that protected their own profits by raising the cost of corn and food while taking away resources for the poor. They'd even gone so far as to make being poor a crime by passing vagrancy laws and allowing the death penalty if a man poached a single hen in order to keep his wife and children from starving.

They'd fought to stop the tyranny of Bonaparte, yet a worse tyranny had befallen their own countrymen, and at the hands of the men who were supposed to be protecting them. Marcus knew better than to believe that military men turned politicians, like Wellington, would make any difference to the ones who needed help most.

"In the meantime, I'll post men around the property for the next few days," Clayton offered as Marcus walked him from the room and down the hall toward the stairs. "I'll tell the Home Secretary that someone broke into the house but spare the other details. Because it's you, he'll take it seriously enough to post a guard." Clayton shot him a darkly amused look as the two men descended the stairs. "Can't have England's newest hero harmed after he's returned safely to English soil. We'd be worse than the French."

Marcus grimaced. "He wouldn't give a damn if I were still only a general."

"That's where you're wrong." They reached the ground floor, and Clayton accepted his gloves, hat, and coat from the footman. Slipping into his overcoat, he tapped his gloves to Marcus's chest to make his point. "If Marcus Braddock were still only a general, he'd have men watching you around the clock." His grin hid the seriousness of his words as he lowered his voice. "Your men loved you, General—still do. Don't think their loyalty to you and their willingness to do whatever you asked of them went unnoticed in Westminster. The French had a king once, too, before they killed him and made a general their emperor."

He slapped Marcus on his good arm as he turned to leave and doffed his hat to the women inside the drawing room as he passed by, the room's double doors open to the hall.

As Marcus followed to see him out the front door, he glanced inside the drawing room. The others were all still there. They took comfort in one another's presence even now, with Trousdale's arm far too familiarly looped around Claudia as they sat on the settee in the corner. Danielle and the viscountess were together on the sofa. Pippa nestled in Danielle's arms, not yet willing to release Danielle as she continued to talk in hushed tones to the little girl and rub her back in an attempt to ease her into sleep.

As Clayton waited for the footman to open the door, he appealed to Marcus beneath his breath, "Promise me that if I bring you information about Scepter that you won't do anything reckless."

"I won't let them hurt the people I love." That was the only promise he'd give.

Danielle looked up and somberly met his gaze over Pippa's head. At her worried glance, something twisted deep inside him.

Since his return, she'd come to mean a great deal to him. As much as his own family. Yet she was unnecessarily putting herself at risk with Nightingale, the same way Elise had, and the stubborn woman refused to stop.

One way or another, though, he was going to put an end to Nightingale and save her from herself. He knew at that moment that he would protect her the same way he would Claudia and Pippa.

With his life.

Twelve

THE MAN WAS FOLLOWING HER.

Again.

Dani didn't have to glance behind her as she strolled down Bond Street to know he was there. She felt it in the tingle at her nape. It was the same electric jolt she'd gotten two days ago when she'd looked out her bedroom window and noticed the same man lingering in the square across from her house, keeping watch. On her.

That's what he'd done ever since—kept watch and kept his distance, always following after her whenever she went out but never approaching her, never coming to the door, never making his presence known beyond his mistake of letting her see him the morning after dinner with Marcus at Charlton Place. Now she saw him whenever she went out, always there just at the periphery of her vision, always lingering far enough behind that no one else would have noticed him.

But she had. *Of course* she had. Working with Nightingale over the years had trained her to notice such things.

The man wasn't dangerous. At least she assumed so, trusting that he would have attacked her by now if he were. Which meant that he was watching her house and following her for a different reason. Because Marcus had asked him to.

But she'd had enough of secrets and surveillance to last a lifetime, and this afternoon, she planned on teaching that man a thing or two about following innocent women. Along with the man who'd hired him.

Smiling slyly to herself, she darted into the dressmaker's shop.

Inside, the seamstresses and assistants barely glanced her way, having grown used to having her here. Oh, she spent a great deal of time here, too, because this was where she had all of her own dresses made as well as those for the women whom Nightingale vanished. Many of them had nothing but the clothes they'd been wearing when they disappeared from their old existences. They needed new clothes to match their new identities, all of which the network provided.

With a little help. In gratitude, she waved a gloved hand at Mrs. Harris, the shop owner and one of the first women Nightingale had rescued, as she walked through to the rear of the shop.

She passed through the front showroom, with its beautiful dresses on display, brocade chairs, and bone china tea services for the ladies who patronized the shop, and disappeared behind the door that separated off the work rooms in the rear. Back here, the small army of assistants made the fine gowns and accessories that had earned Mrs. Harris her reputation as one of the best mantua-makers in London. The rooms on the floors above served as warehouses for the material, beads, lace, and other fripperies used to make the gowns, as well as dormitories for the girls who worked long hours in the workshop. They'd also served many times as hideaways for women Nightingale had moved about London when other places weren't safe.

Dani had enough trouble finding the money to reimburse Mrs. Harris for the dresses. She would never be able to repay her kindness for hiding the women.

"Thank you, Mrs. Martin," Dani whispered, using the woman's real name to herself as she snatched up a day dress from a pile of folded dresses waiting to be delivered to clients. She held it up to judge its fit. "This will do nicely." She plucked up a pair of pale pink stockings that matched the dress. "And so will these."

Then she stepped into a little fitting room at the rear of the building and flung closed the curtain.

Oh, if Marcus could only see her now! This little quick-change act would prove that she was more than capable of hiding her identity and taking care of herself. His efforts to convince her to shut down Nightingale were completely unwarranted. And would certainly come to nothing in the end, as she had every intention of continuing to rescue women just like Mrs. Harris.

He might have been a determined general, but she was a stubborn society lady. His unstoppable force had just met her immovable mountain.

With a mischievous smile, she quickly began to undress. She'd show the man who was following her, and undoubtedly still lingering on the street and waiting for her to emerge from the front of the shop, that keeping watch on her wasn't as easy as it seemed. She'd leave through the rear alley door, wearing a different dress and a bonnet that hid her hair and face. She'd be long gone before he realized that he'd been fooled.

"That'll set him on a merry chase," she mused as she reached behind her to unfasten the short row of pearl buttons at the back of her bodice.

She peeled herself out of her dress with a few contortions of her arms and twistings of her spine that left her cursing herself for leaving Alice at home this afternoon. A ripping of fabric—she winced. But it couldn't be helped. Then off came the petticoat and her white stockings, until all she wore were her short stays and the thin shift beneath.

She held up the dress again and frowned at the bodice. With aggravation, she undid the front lacing of her corset and then began to tie it again, this time much more tightly, in order to restrict her breasts enough to fit into the smaller dress. Unfortunately, all that seemed to do was push them up higher. But it would have to do. Somehow.

Deciding to find a spencer that she could button up to her neck and hide whatever flesh spilled over the neckline, she propped her foot onto a stool in the rear of the fitting room and quickly rolled up the stocking to her knee.

Behind her, she heard the curtain's grommets scrape against the rod as it was slowly pulled aside. She called over her shoulder without looking, "An emergency, Mrs. Harris. You can add the expense to my personal account."

She smiled as she secured the first stocking, dropped her foot to the floor, and bent down to pick up the second stocking. "I do have to say, though, that these stockings are absolutely beautiful."

"I agree."

Startled, she wheeled around at the sound of the deep voice.

She stared, surprised speechless, as Marcus held the curtain open with one hand and leaned his opposite shoulder against the doorpost in a pose so rakish that her pounding heart sank all the way down between her thighs. It continued to beat relentlessly there, stirring up all kinds of wanton yearnings.

His gaze slipped slowly over her, and he murmured, "Absolutely beautiful."

"What are you doing here?" The question emerged as a hoarse whisper.

"Hoping to see you." He arched a brow and helped himself to another lingering look at her curves. "I simply didn't expect to see so much of you."

"Stop that!" She grabbed the curtain from his hand and used it to cover as much of herself as possible. She glanced past him, which wasn't easy, given how his tall, broad body filled the fitting room doorway. The workshop behind him was oddly empty, the assistants having all disappeared. "How did you get back here?"

"I'm a duke." He crooked an arrogant grin. "People let me go anywhere I wish."

"How convenient," she drawled archly.

"Decidedly so." Then the devil had the audacity to reach out for a stray curl that had come loose from its pins while she'd been dressing and rubbed it between his fingers and thumb. "I think I've finally found something that makes possessing the title a pleasure."

"Stop that," she repeated, but she couldn't keep the husky purr from her voice. Nor did she find the resolve to slap his hand away, not even when he dared to trail a fingertip along her jaw. "What do you want, Marcus?"

"I'd say to learn all your secrets." He took a single step to close the distance between them, then peered over the curtain to take a new view of her backside. "But I don't think you have many of those left."

"And fewer every day, apparently." Although it wasn't embarrassment at being seen half-dressed by him that pricked at her, particularly since the way that he stared at her made her tingle in all kinds of delicious ways. It was disappointment that he didn't think her competent enough to take care of herself. "Especially when you set a guard to watch me."

No surprise flashed over his face at being caught. Instead, he simply smiled that she'd figured it out and touched her cheek again. But this time, the caress didn't spark a tingle inside her so much as a pleasant warmth. A sensation that was just as disconcerting.

He murmured, "I protect the people I care about."

She wasn't foolish enough to believe that he meant anything more by that than friendship. Still, her silly heart danced a little jig, although her sober head knew better. "To watch over my house, you mean? To follow me everywhere I go?" In indignation, she tapped her finger on his waistcoat, only to catch her breath at the steely hardness of the muscles in his chest. "Will he waltz with me at Lady Northrop's ball next week, too? Fetch me ices when I go strolling through the park? Save me a chair at the art exhibition?"

"Society events?" He gave an appalled shudder. "I'd never ask a man to sacrifice himself like that."

Her patience snapped. Dropping the curtain, she grabbed his shoulders, wheeled him around, and gave a hard push to send him staggering out of the fitting room. "Out!" With a glaring scowl, she flipped the curtain back into place, then shoved a hand out to wag a finger at him. "Don't even *think* about opening that curtain, sir."

He replied with a low chuckle. Drat that devil!

With a titillating tingle at knowing that he stood only a few feet away as she finished dressing, she loosened her stays with a grateful sigh of relief and release. But she also couldn't help thinking of the predatory gleam in his eyes when he saw her breasts, thrust up beneath the tight corset. And of how much she'd enjoyed it.

"How did you know to follow me in here?" She tugged on the petticoat. Perhaps if she kept him talking, he would keep his distance long enough for her to change back into her own clothes.

"I spotted you walking on the street. When I saw you duck inside the shop, I knew what you'd planned."

She paused, the dress halfway over her head. "You knew?"

"You forget that I've already had a glimpse of your quick-change talent."

Her lips twisted with vexation. "Your man would never have figured out where I went."

"I know." From the tone of his voice, he wasn't at all pleased to admit that. "You'd have outsmarted him."

Pride warmed her at that unintended compliment as she slipped on the dress and shimmied her hips as she pulled the skirt down into place. But there was far more to him being here than he let on.

"I have a feeling that your man has orders to do more than guard me," she drawled, once more irritated at his lack of trust as she pulled on her stockings. "Following me everywhere I go like this, he'd surely report back the names of any ladies I might meet with so you could figure out which ones are involved with Nightingale."

"No. I'd never ask him to do that. I'd never breach your trust like that. His only responsibility is to keep you safe."

This time, it wasn't pride that fluttered inside her but something stronger. Perhaps he did care, and enough that she could begin to trust in him.

"I won't deny, though, that I'm pleased with how it worked out," he commented. "Now that you know you're being watched, you'll be less likely to work for Nightingale." His voice faded slightly. She pictured him moving around the workshop, curiously looking at the various women's items, his interest snagged by a pretty silk shawl, or running his hand over a silk nightgown meant for a lady's wedding night. "Which means you won't be putting yourself into danger."

"Ah, so there's your ulterior motive," she quipped, irritated that he was once more attempting to put an end to Nightingale. As she quickly pinned up her hair as best she could in the small mirror hanging from a nail, she couldn't help but feel that she was suiting up in armor for a battle.

"If that's what it takes to keep you safe, so be it."

She bit back the retort that it wasn't his job to keep her safe, because a part of her liked the idea of being protected by a strong man far more than a modern woman like herself should admit. "Yet you feel no hesitation to risk yourself."

"That is what a man does."

But in his solemn answer, she heard the truth. *That is what a soldier does.*

Slowly, she opened the curtain and stepped out of the fitting room, one hand carefully clutching her loose bodice to her bosom. He stared at her from across the small workshop with the same predacious stare as before.

"Undressed…dressed…" he mused in a low drawl. "Beautiful either way."

She ignored the heat that flushed her cheeks. "And you shouldn't waste your time attempting to flatter me into giving away my confidences." She turned her back to him. "Button me, will you?"

"I am your humble servant, madam."

She couldn't hide a smile at that. This man was no one's servant.

He came up behind her, and she felt the heat of his hands lingering on her back as he slowly fastened the half dozen little pearl buttons.

"I didn't spout empty flattery, you know." His fingers brushed against the bare skin just above her undergarments. "You truly are beautiful, Danielle."

Her belly fluttered. She had no idea what to say to that. With his hands on her, his body so close that she could feel the heat of him lingering against her back, she needed to change the topic. Quickly. "How is Claudia?"

"Better. She's still a bit shaken, but Trousdale's been a strength to her."

"And Penelope?"

"She's decided to set traps around the house in case anyone attempts to break in again." She heard the consternation in his voice, but also patience and love. "She's organized the servants into rigging wires across the halls, noisemakers on the stairs, bells on the doors... So far, she hasn't caught any intruders, but she's trapped two footmen, one coal deliveryman, and the neighbor's dog."

Her chest sank with pity. "Poor Pippa."

"*Poor* Pippa?" He leaned over her shoulder to give her a dubious look before returning his attention to the last button. "That little poppet's on her way to world domination."

She smiled. "You'd best refrain from teaching her battle strategy then."

She expected a low chuckle from him, the kind that would twine down her spine and create that same sensation of arousal low in her belly that he seemed to stir inside her every time they were together.

But this time…silence.

She looked over her shoulder to find him frowning as his fingers played with the last button even though he'd already fastened it. He was a man with the weight of the world on his broad shoulders, or at least a deep worry for his family. She understood that and ached for him. After all, she loved Claudia and Pippa as dearly as if they were her own.

"I won't give up the names of the women currently working with Nightingale," she stated with quiet resolve as she turned toward him. "No matter how often you ask. Their lives are just as important to their families as Claudia and Pippa are to you."

"Of course."

"But…" She bit her lip.

"But?"

"There is a woman, someone who helped with Nightingale only tangentially and who has nothing to do with us now," she explained, hesitating with each bit of information she offered. "But Elise might have been working with her to identify women who needed to be rescued."

"Who?"

She squeezed her eyes shut, feeling like a traitor. Trust had always been important to her, and now she was betraying the network. But he deserved answers, even if this small bit of information was all she was willing to provide. "Lady Hartsham."

"The Countess of Hartsham?" He clarified in disbelief, "Beatrice McTavish?"

She didn't blame him for sounding incredulous. Beatrice was nothing if not a mouse afraid of her own shadow. "She's not the most daring of women, I'll admit."

He arched a brow at that whopper of an understatement.

"She'd been involved with Nightingale when we first started—nothing important, but she knew people. Her father had owned one of the largest breweries in England, so she still had connections at inns and taverns where we could move the women if necessary."

"At the beginning, but not now," he surmised from her words. "Why not? I thought her husband and your father were good friends."

"They are." The Earl of Hartsham was an old family friend, one of the gentlemen her father trusted to keep watch over her while her parents were in Italy. "But Beatrice had nervous fits that the network might be discovered. She'd prattled on in worried rants about what would happen if Lord Hartsham ever learned what she'd been doing, how furious he'd be with her." Dani certainly couldn't fault the woman's concern, although she had to admit that her excitability had been distracting. And grating. "So I eased Beatrice out of Nightingale completely."

"You stopped working with her just in time for Elise to take her on."

"I think so. It would make sense if she did. Elise wanted to help women in the brothels. Perhaps Lady Hartsham's connections extended that far."

"But you never asked that of her?"

"Absolutely not." It would have been too dangerous to take on brothel owners, as well as far too easy for Nightingale to be tracked down through the personal connections that Beatrice had. But Elise... She bit her bottom lip. "Yet your sister might have."

"If she did, then Lady Hartsham might know who else Elise was working with during those last days and how to find John Porter. She might know who wanted Elise dead."

"But if she wasn't," Dani warned, placing her hand on his arm, "we might very well be putting her into danger by approaching her."

"Then we need to be very careful when we do."

Excitement began to tease at her toes. "How?"

"I'll have Lord Hartsham invite me to be his guest of honor at Vauxhall."

He'd have Hartsham... She blinked. "Why would he do that?"

"Haven't you heard?" He leaned against the wall with a confident grin, crossing his arms over his chest. "I'm England's greatest hero next to Wellington. And a damned duke. If I suggest to Hartsham that he host me in his private box at Vauxhall, he won't pass up the favors he'll be certain to believe he'll gain from it. He'll also use it as a grand opportunity to invite others who want to ingratiate themselves by having the chance to speak with me. Peers and patronage…as thick as thieves."

He would despise every moment of it. What he was suggesting epitomized everything he hated about society and its sycophants. "You don't have to do that."

His eyes softened on her face as his smile faded. He pushed himself away from the wall and crossed to her, then stroked his thumb across her bottom lip and elicited a heated shiver from her. "Yes, I do." Then he tapped her on the nose and earned himself a scowl. "And you're coming with me."

"Pardon?" she squeaked out, not at all prepared for that.

"I can't approach her myself."

Well, that was true.

"And if Lady Hartsham was worried that the earl would find out about Nightingale, then having me there to distract him while you speak with her should help calm her fears."

"I suppose…" But apprehension pricked at the backs of her knees, not the least of which was because she would be there as his personal guest. The situation would all be nothing but a ruse, of course, yet it would also be far too close to how they would act if he were actually courting her. And far too enjoyable. She couldn't help herself. The idea of being courted by Marcus Braddock sent butter-flies twirling in her belly, and she didn't want to risk her heart by having to accept his attentions when they were nothing but pretense. "Or I can just pay her an afternoon call."

"Vauxhall's better. I'll be there with you to make certain nothing goes wrong." The resolve behind that statement told her that he'd brook no argument about this. It was Vauxhall, with him, or nothing. "Surely you'll be able to find a moment to maneuver her aside for a private conversation. No one will think twice if the two of you have to speak into each other's ears to be heard over the noise of the music and fireworks."

"You devious man," she murmured, finding new appreciation for his battlefield cunning. "But I cannot attend with you. Aunt Harriett is away visiting friends, and my maid Alice won't do at all for a proper chaperone." The little thing would give away everything on her face. She was trustworthy and dependable, but she knew too much about Nightingale to carry off the relaxed, uncaring—even bored—expression of a lady's companion necessary in the midst of sharks. "Unfortunately, Claudia won't work either. As Elise's sister, her presence would make Lady Hartsham too nervous to confide in me."

"Perfect. Lady Hartsham can serve as your chaperone, then."

She gaped at him. The man had lost his mind! "How on earth is that perfect?"

"Because you'll have an excuse to remain close to her side all evening, from the moment their carriage arrives at your town house to collect you until it returns you home. No one will notice you two exchanging words when you'll be expected to do so all evening." His dark eyes shone. "By the time we leave, we'll finally have answers."

We... She warmed with the thought that he now considered them partners. That he no longer thought of her as the enemy. And yet—

"Aren't you afraid I'll be placing myself in danger?" she challenged. "The same way you wrongly think I do with Nightingale?"

"You *do* place yourself in danger for that network." When she began to argue, he cut her off. "But at Vauxhall, you'll be surrounded by people and less than ten feet from my side. I don't plan on letting you out of my sight all evening."

His plan was madness and would most likely not turn up any new information at all about what trouble Elise had gotten herself into during her last days. But she couldn't resist the chance to help find justice for her best friend.

She eased out a long exhale of acquiescence. "You have it all figured out, don't you?"

"When the enemy changes position on the field, a good general has to adapt his battle plan or be defeated."

"Indeed." She was beginning to think she needed to study battle strategy if she ever hoped to understand this man. "Is that what I am, then? Part of your battle plan?"

"I think you're worth fighting for."

He tossed that comment off almost teasingly, yet

the jolt that pierced her at its implications was decidedly serious. God help her. For one tempting beat, she wished his hands were on her again, but this time *not* to button her up. This time to peel away her dress and all the layers beneath, to reveal her bare flesh to his hands and mouth—

"Yes," she whispered, her foolish heart blurting out her answer before her logical head could stop her. "I'll help you at Vauxhall."

He took her hand and raised it to his lips to place a kiss to her palm. "Thank you."

"Don't thank me yet." She slipped her hand away before he could feel the spike in her pulse. "I haven't yet delivered terms of repayment."

With a laugh, he watched her walk away toward the front room of the shop. For propriety's sake, he lingered behind before following after her, but she felt his wolfish gaze on her back the entire way.

Thankfully, no clients had come into the shop while they'd been talking, but Dani suspected that Mrs. Harris would have known to make enough noise to alert them if anyone had so that Marcus could slip unseen out the rear door. After all, even though Mrs. Harris owed a large debt to Dani, she also had her own reputation to protect, and allowing former soldiers to scandalously approach unmarried misses in the rear of her shop while they were changing would severely damage her business. Even if they were dukes.

Dani pasted a smile on her face to hide the way he'd

made her tremble. "You should have warned me," she whispered to the dressmaker, checking her appearance one last time in the little mirror sitting on the front counter.

Good heavens, her cheeks were bright pink! One look at her, and anyone would have assumed that the two of them had done far more in that fitting room than simply strategize.

"His Grace's sister is a client," Mrs. Harris replied.

Dani arched a chastising brow. "You'll need a better excuse than that."

Her eyes gleamed mischievously. "Then how about because you, of all women, deserve the attentions of a handsome hero?"

Her mouth fell open in surprise. Before Dani could find her voice to answer, Marcus sauntered from the rear of the shop, looking like any other gentleman strolling along Bond Street that afternoon, tending to errands and paying off accounts.

Oh, who was she attempting to fool? *Nothing* about him was ordinary, and the shopgirls noticed it, too, all of them pausing in their work to watch him as he walked past. Other men might have been more dashing and handsome. Others might have somehow been more powerful and commanding. But put all that together into one man...*breathtaking.*

He stepped up to her side.

"How lovely of His Grace to meet with me this afternoon in your shop, Mrs. Harris, exactly as we'd planned,"

Dani announced, loudly and quickly, declaring the excuse for why he was in the shop in case anyone dared to spread rumors about the two of them being alone together. "Why, at dinner just the other evening, he offered to pay for the all dresses that you've been making as a charity for poor women in need."

"He did, did he?" he muttered, realizing the trap he'd stepped into.

"Oh yes! *All* of them." She tapped the counter. "Do you happen to have your account book handy, Mrs. Harris?"

"Right here." The woman snatched the book out from beneath the counter, along with the pencil she used to mark the shaped strips of paper she kept for each client that noted their measurements. She flipped open the book and ran her finger down the column of figures. "Here we are—the total for the past quarter's tick." She turned the book around and tapped the tally so that Marcus could see it. "Shall I send someone to your home to collect payment, Your Grace?"

He gave a tight smile as the snare closed around him. He couldn't deny it without scandalizing both women. "No need." He reached into the inside breast pocket of his jacket. "I'm always happy to help a charity whenever I can." He muttered low enough that only Dani could hear, "Or whenever I'm coerced."

She swallowed down a laugh at his expense.

He withdrew several banknotes and placed them one by one onto the counter. "That should bring the account to current."

Dani's lips curled into a smile in private victory. "Thank you, Your—"

"And consider this an advance on next quarter's bill."

She stared, stunned speechless, as he added several more bills to the pile.

"Thank you, Your Grace," Mrs. Harris purred with a beaming smile. "You are a very generous man."

With an amused expression that Dani simply couldn't fathom, he took the pencil and scrawled a note to Mrs. Harris in the margin of the account ledger. "And this, too, please, as a personal favor."

The woman read the note. Her eyes flared wide for a moment before her face melted into a knowing smile. "Certainly, sir."

"Good day, then." With a tip of his hat to both women and a tug at his gloves, he excused himself and left the shop.

Dani remained by the counter, taking a moment to gather her wits and calm her pounding heart as Mrs. Harris left her alone to go into the rear of the shop. Thank goodness the woman knew not to ask any questions about Marcus or the true reason he'd followed her into the shop, recognizing the ploy about paying the account as nothing more than a convenient excuse.

How was it possible that he could tie her belly into aching knots with only a smile? That he was such a good man that he'd not really minded about being tricked into paying Nightingale's bill? Or that he had her longing to be not only in his arms but also in his life, and in more ways than helping gain justice for his sister?

But he did just that. And if he kept it up, she'd be lost. Because she knew that with a man like Marcus, surrender would never be unconditional.

"Thank you, Mrs. Harris," she called out as she placed her hat on her head and stepped toward the door. "You are greatly appreciated."

"Wait!" Mrs. Harris hurried out of the shop and onto the street after her, carrying a small white box in her hands, tied with a red ribbon. "His Grace requested this for you."

Surprised, Dani thanked her and took the package. What on earth? As Mrs. Harris returned to her shop, Dani glanced around at the busy street, but there was no sign of Marcus in the crowd, not one clue of explanation.

She untied the ribbon and lifted the lid to look inside—

The silk stockings she'd tried on in the fitting room.

"Oh, that man," she murmured, then smiled to herself as she traced her fingers lightly over them.

Thirteen

MARCUS ACCEPTED A GLASS OF ARRACK PUNCH FROM the Vauxhall attendant. As he took a slow swallow of the sweet liquid, careful not to let the evening's libations dull his wits in this sea of sharks, he glanced at Danielle, who stood on the other side of the crowded supper box.

Around them, the pleasure gardens were a flurry of noise and activity as the suppers being held in the long rows of multistoried galleries lining the main alley finished and a small army of attendants began to serve trays of punch to guests who were already half-foxed from bottles of wine and champagne. Two different bands played at opposite ends of the alley, their music meeting in the middle in a loud cacophony, seemingly right at the Earl of Hartsham's box. Acrobats tumbled past while tightrope walkers sauntered back and forth overhead. Members of the *ton* walked slowly past in their evening finery so their presence would be noted. Other people who didn't want to be noticed strolled past with their identities hidden behind masks and fancy dress, headed toward the close paths at the rear of the gardens, where the lanterns had already been extinguished by amorous couples who wanted to take advantage of the dark. And each other.

Inside the box, a different kind of spectacle was taking place.

The earl had invited over a dozen men and their wives
to cram into the box for supper, all men with influence at
the Exchange or in Westminster—men whom Hartsham
was clearly hoping to win favors from by introducing
them to Marcus. They'd fawned over him all evening in
attempts to ingratiate themselves.

He tolerated all of it with a smile and feigned interest in their conversations, but his attention had barely
strayed all evening from Danielle.

Dear God, she was beautiful. Even in the diffused
light of the dim lanterns, she simply glowed. Every
smile shone, and her eyes gleamed like diamonds as she
talked and laughed with the others. She wore her hair
down tonight, draped teasingly over her right shoulder
in a thick riot of chestnut curls that accentuated the sap-
phire blue of her gown. Everything about her appearance
announced boldly that she wasn't some unmarried miss
out for her first season but a woman with confidence, ele-
gance, brilliance…a woman capable of matching a man
like him in every way.

Except she refused to stop putting herself in danger.

She looked up and found him watching her. A faint
smile for him teased at her lips, and the softness of it
wrapped around him like a velvet ribbon.

He raised his glass to her in a toast. She hesitated only
a moment before returning the gesture, then smiled a bit
shyly into her glass as she brought it to her lips and took
a sip, her cheeks pinking alluringly.

He frowned. She was frustration of the first order.

Her devotion to Nightingale bothered him to no end, how she was willing to put her own reputation and life in jeopardy in order to help other women. He should have admired her for her courage. Instead, she worried the daylights out of him.

Of course, it didn't help his frustration that he'd thought of little else during the past few days except for how she'd looked in the dress shop. Standing there so delectably in only her undergarments, rolling that silk stocking slowly up her leg... He'd nearly laughed when she'd asked him to button her up, when he had to fight for restraint not to tear off her clothes and bare her to his eyes.

Was the little minx wearing the stockings? He would have given his right arm to be able to kneel at her feet and ease up her skirt, to reach beneath and run his hand up the curve of her calf to feel for himself if—

"Duke!"

Marcus hid his distaste for the man as William McTavish, Earl of Hartsham, sidled up to him. Palming two glasses of port in his large hand, he slapped Marcus good-naturedly on the back. "I cannot begin to tell you how pleased I am that you agreed to join us for dinner. Very pleased!"

Oh, Marcus was certain of that, even though he'd invited himself. As far as he could tell, the earl had made good use of currying favor with the other men at Marcus's expense. He drawled with a tight smile, keeping the sarcasm from his voice, "How good of you to host me."

"I'd been hoping to throw a spread like this since I heard that you'd returned to England." Hartsham audaciously removed the glass of punch from Marcus's hand and discarded it onto a passing attendant's tray, then replaced it with one of the glasses of port in his hand. With a grin, he tapped his own glass against Marcus's in a small toast and raised it to his lips. "Here's to the future."

At least *that* toast Marcus could drink to, and he took a swallow. The fine port trickled smoothly down his throat. Apparently, Hartsham had spared no expense tonight.

"And how has life been for you since you've returned?" Hartsham gestured boisterously around the box at the other guests. Clearly, the evening's drink was having an effect on the earl. "Society seems to be welcoming you with open arms."

An embrace Marcus wasn't keen to accept. "It will help for the fights in Parliament."

"Fights not nearly as exciting as the wars, I'm sure."

"War isn't exciting." Anyone who claimed so was either a damned lunatic or had never been in the heat of battle. War was destructive, horrifying, sickening…sheer hell.

Yet that terrible life was predicated upon a sense of purpose deeper than he'd ever known. One he missed every day.

"How have you been adjusting to London life, then?"

Unease pricked at the base of his spine, as it always did whenever he thought of all that he'd left behind when he resigned his commission. "It's been an adjustment, I'll admit." He twisted his lips in a half smile at the private irony as he drawled, "But London's an exciting place to be these days."

"So it is! And what do you think of England now that you've returned?" Hartsham studied Marcus over the rim of his glass. "Can Parliament win the peace now that the army has won the wars?"

"It can, under the right circumstances." Marcus fully believed that. But from what he'd seen of the depth of the poverty and crime in London, the struggle before them would prove to be as great as the one against Napoleon.

"Perhaps Parliament, but what about the crown?" Hartsham's voice lowered despite the piercing glint in his eyes. "Do you have any confidence in the monarchy now, given the old king's madness and Prinny's arrogant behavior of late? His disdain for English dignity and restraint? His determination to bankrupt us by spending our treasury on himself? Surely it galls you to see that buffoon parading around like a peacock in a field marshal's uniform as if everything that uniform symbolized were nothing more than fancy dress."

Marcus took a silent sip of port. He'd served at the pleasure of the crown and now held a dukedom because of it. Yet how many times had he and his most trusted friends grumbled about the very things Hartsham had just mentioned while pinned down in the Spanish countryside as artillery fired around them and the real colonels of the Light Dragoons charged bravely into battle?

But he wasn't daft enough to utter his agreement aloud, especially in this sea of sharks. *Especially* given current tensions among the regent's ministers and the increasing power of the Home Office to arrest Englishmen on charges of sedition.

"It's up to men like us to make certain the country moves in the right direction," Marcus drawled noncommittally.

"Agreed." Hartsham's eyes gleamed. "Perhaps we'll be allies, then."

"*If* you're willing to put your reputation on the line to commit to change." Marcus certainly was. Danielle's devotion to helping others had rubbed off on him, apparently. For the first time since he'd returned to London, he felt a sense of purpose, however faint, sparking inside him. One not related to finding answers about Elise. "I'm willing to fight to make a difference. Are you?"

"Very much so," Hartsham assured him, but the way the earl said that slithered coldly down Marcus's spine.

Once more, his attention drifted across the box to Danielle. She smiled at something one of the ladies said, yet her head was turned just enough that she could look at him with a sideways glance. She knew he was watching, and that realization warmed through him.

"Ah, the lovely Miss Williams," Hartsham half purred, following Marcus's attention across the box. "She's certainly a special one."

"Indeed." She'd become more special to him than he would ever have imagined.

"Are you courting her?"

The directness of that question surprised him, and he hesitated to answer.

"Oh, come now!" Hartsham tapped his glass to Marcus's shoulder as the earl turned to stare blatantly at Danielle. "No need to pretend humility. For heaven's sake, look at her—a baron's beautiful daughter. Gentlemen must be lined up a dozen deep at her door and fighting amongst themselves to call on her." When the man raked a slow gaze over her, Marcus had to force down his rising hackles and not pummel him for daring to look at her so lecherously. "What man wouldn't be willing to brag if he'd snagged the attentions of a woman like her?"

He raised the glass to his mouth to hide his scowl at the idea of men calling on her. And being received.

"I understand your reluctance to admit to it. If you do, you'll be breaking the hearts of marriage-minded mamas across the empire." Hartsham grinned as if the two men were university chums rather than practically strangers. "His Majesty's Most Eligible going to the gallows of marriage!"

"Those women have nothing to fear," he assured Hartsham. But even as he said that, Danielle turned her head to look fully at him, then frowned slightly, as if she knew the two men were talking about her. "Miss Williams's tastes are too refined to find any lasting interest in an old soldier like me."

The truth of that stung more than he wanted to admit. Discovering the truth about Elise's death had brought them together. Once they had their answers, would they return to being nothing more than distant acquaintances? In just a short time, she'd filled an empty space in his life, and he wasn't at all certain he wanted to let her go.

"I can help you find female companionship if the London ladies aren't what you're looking for," Hartsham tossed out casually, gesturing a greeting over the heads of the crowd to two gentlemen who had arrived late to supper. "To quench any needs that might arise."

Marcus's lips twisted. Nothing ever changed. He might be hundreds of miles away from those suppers that he and other officers had shared at various Allied headquarters across the continent, but the after-dinner conversation among men proved to be just as crude here at Vauxhall. "You're mistaken." He smiled icily. "I have no need of a mistress."

"Oh no, not a mistress. Nothing at all that tame!" Hartsham laughed and moved away, weaving his way through the crowd to personally greet the new arrivals.

Marcus frowned after the earl. If this was how his conversations would go with fellow peers, God help him.

Another troupe of acrobats tumbled past, snaring the attention of the guests inside the box. The crowd shifted, with the ladies maneuvering for better views at the railing and the men for new glasses of punch.

Excusing herself from the conversation, Danielle smiled brightly at no one in particular as she slowly circled the box toward him as if having no specific destination in mind except to pluck up a sugared orange slice from the tray of sweets on the sideboard. She nibbled at it casually, then smiled at him as she feigned surprise at unwittingly finding herself standing next to him.

Oh, she was good at navigating the perils of society's unwritten rules of propriety. Another stark reminder of the differences between them.

When she stopped beside him and turned so that they stood shoulder to shoulder at the side of the box, his skin tingled at her nearness.

"Wonderful evening, isn't it, Your Grace?" She kept her voice low, yet they still couldn't speak openly. Not here, surrounded by people who were eager to overhear every word they shared.

"Very much so, Miss Williams. I trust that you enjoyed dinner." As the daughter of a baron, order of precedence put them on opposite ends of the supper table, with several countesses and viscountesses between them. They hadn't had the chance to speak privately all evening. "And all the entertainments that Vauxhall offers."

She smiled apologetically as one of the ladies lingered so close to catch their conversation that she accidentally bumped into Danielle's side. "Actually, I haven't had a chance to venture out into the gardens yet tonight."

"That's a shame," he commented, falling into a private language the eavesdroppers wouldn't be able to understand. "You'll certainly want to take a stroll along the alley before the fireworks start."

"Yes," she agreed, a breathless undertone in her voice indicating that she understood perfectly what he meant—he wanted a moment to speak with her outside the box. Alone. "I think I will."

In an innocuous gesture, as if simply jostled by the crowd, she briefly rested her hand on his arm. But he felt her fingers give a quick squeeze into the muscle beneath his jacket sleeve. That small touch shot up his arm and straight into his chest.

Before any of the women pressing in around them could elbow their way into tagging along with Danielle when she left the box, she sidled up to Mrs. Slater, the wife of a wealthy mill owner and the woman who had sat next to her at dinner. According to Hartsham, Slater had been called away on business in Dover, yet he'd sent his wife and his apologies. Danielle leaned in to speak into the woman's ear, ostensibly to be heard over the noise of the band marching past the box, but Marcus knew it was to keep from being overheard by the other nosey women lingering nearby. Then she gestured faintly toward the door.

Mrs. Slater nodded with a glance of her own in the direction of the door...until her eyes slid sideways to take a fleeting glance at Marcus. She froze for only a beat, then smiled.

Then the two women linked arms and entered into rapid conversation as they ambled toward the door, so rapid that no one else would be able to interrupt and invite themselves along on their stroll. They paused only to select masks from a pile on the table before slipping out the door.

As he watched the two women leave, Marcus took another sip of port to cover the knowing smile pulling at his lips. He had a new appreciation for the sharpness of Danielle's mind. Of course she'd sought out Mrs. Slater, a woman whose position at the edge of the *ton* made her less devoted to propriety. Danielle would have a proper chaperone for strolling through the gardens, yet one who knew to wander off at an opportune time so that the two of them would have the chance for a private conversation.

Marcus finished the port a few minutes later. When he stepped into the cool night air, he found the mask she'd left behind for him on the rear railing.

Grinning to himself, he snatched it up and sauntered down the alley after the women.

Fourteen

Mrs. Slater tightened her hold on Dani's arm and slowed both of them almost to a stop as she pointed with excitement at a juggler who tossed flaming batons high into the air. "Look at that!"

"Amazing." Dani smiled. It was the fifth time in as many yards that the older woman had stopped them since they'd left the box. But Dani knew that it wasn't the performers that had captured her attention but a desire to go slowly to give Marcus time to catch up with them. Apparently, this wasn't her first time acting as chaperone.

They lingered until the juggler caught each baton and one by one extinguished them in his mouth, then took a bow to astounded applause and the tossing of coins into a sack at his feet. Then they strolled along the wide alley fronted by three-story galleries toward the giant Chinese pavilion.

"Aren't masks wonderful things?" Mrs. Slater held up the half mask she'd taken from the box, letting its ribbons dangle along her skirts as she contemplated it. "If I had my way, every society event would be held behind masks."

"Because then no one would know who you are," Dani agreed with a long sigh. How many times during the past few years had she simply wanted to be anonymous and left alone to live her life as she chose? Nightingale gave her that anonymity, but it also came with a price.

"Because then no one would be able to see how bored you are," the older woman corrected. "Heavens, how tedious these things are! This is the first good time I've had all evening."

"But you came to tonight's supper, even without your husband. Surely you could have used his absence as an excuse to beg off."

"Because Mr. Slater asked me to." She patted Dani's arm as she took a surreptitious glance over her shoulder. "Future business ventures always come first."

When Dani's gaze followed after, she saw nothing but a crush of bodies and entertainers in the dim light of the lanterns strung overhead.

"He knew how important this supper was to Hartsham and thought I would enjoy the evening." Mrs. Slater smiled nostalgically. "He's always been so attentive to me and my interests."

Dani's throat tightened. Would Marcus ever care for her like that?

"I didn't have the heart to tell him that I'd rather have spent the evening at home. Besides, I knew that my being here would be important for his business, to show his support for the men in the room."

Did she mean Marcus? "How so?"

"They've all gotten involved in some kind of business venture together. Lord Hartsham and the others have hinted that it could be quite substantial if my husband gives them the financial backing they're hoping for. And his loyalty." She sent a sideways glance at Dani. "I'd assumed that was why they were hosting His Grace this evening, to bring him into the venture as well, since he has powerful connections in the military and Westminster."

That wasn't the reason for tonight's supper at all, but Dani didn't dare reveal that. Although what she'd learned of Mrs. Slater by conversing with her tonight over dinner made her consider the possibility of bringing her into Nightingale, the woman couldn't yet be trusted. "I wouldn't know."

"Wouldn't you?" Her sly expression deepened, followed by another glance behind them. "I thought that surely he would have told you."

"His Grace and I don't have that sort of relationship." Although what sort they did have, Dani had no idea. The kind that involved aching kisses, bared bodies, caresses that sent her out of her mind and had her longing for all kinds of things she had no business wanting…but not a single discussion about politics or business.

"Hmm." That sound of disbelief answered her, and Mrs. Slater stopped them once more. This time to release her arm. "Oh, I do love a mask," she remarked offhandedly as she raised hers to her face and tied it behind her head. "Makes for all kinds of wonderful opportunities for secret meetings, don't you think?"

A conspiratorial smile blossomed on her face, and Dani secured her own mask in place. "I agree."

With their identities now safely hidden behind the

masks, the two women wandered onward again, this time toward the refreshment booths surrounding the pavilion.

"Oh, look!" Mrs. Slater pointed to one of the booths where brightly uniformed attendants served ices. "I wonder if they have peach ice. I haven't had that since I was a little girl on my first visit to London."

"Well, perhaps you should go see if they do." She rested her hand meaningfully on the woman's arm. "I'll wait here."

"Or over there, out of the way of the crowd," Mrs. Slater amended, gesturing at the close walks snaking off behind the pavilion. "It's a very long line for the ices. I might be waiting a good while."

"Indeed."

"Perhaps twenty minutes or so."

Dani smiled from behind the half mask that covered only her eyes.

"We might even become separated."

"Most likely."

"If so, then there's no need for you to linger here. We'll meet back at the box. But I'd like to investigate the rear steps, to find out if the fireworks will be visible from there. So you might find me there rather than inside the box."

"Of course." Dani knew exactly what Mrs. Slater meant. Oh, Mrs. Slater would be a fine addition to Nightingale!

If her mask hadn't been hiding her face, Dani was certain she would have seen a knowing lift of the woman's brow as she turned to walk toward the refreshment booths.

Dani hesitated a moment, her gaze searching the milling crowd around her but not finding Marcus. Where was he?

Trusting that he would come to her, she started forward toward the shadowed paths behind the pavilion. She chose one and started slowly down it.

She moved carefully through the shadows, her pulse pounding with every step. The path narrowed as it receded into the depths of the garden and grew darker. The sounds from the main alley became muffled by the wilderness until she could no longer hear the music and cheers from the crowd. Her chest tightened with unease, but she walked on, even more slowly now. She passed several groves of trees, moss-covered stone walls meant to resemble tumbled-down Greek temples, a thick hedge that lined part of the path—all capable of hiding secret assignations.

She passed a few couples who were meandering along the path, poking their heads behind walls and trees to judge how private and dark the spaces were beyond. Around her, the lanterns had been extinguished, and from the darkness rose female giggles and masculine groans.

A masked woman raced by, her skirts hitched up to her knees. She slowed only to look behind her, then burst into laughter and ran on, jumping off the path and darting behind a row of bushes. Behind her, a man dressed as a harlequin chased after. Heedless of anything but catching the woman, he knocked Dani aside in his hurry to follow after her into the undergrowth.

A squeal cut through the darkness just behind her, and Dani jumped, startled. Apparently, the man had caught the woman.

Oh, this was madness! She'd never find Marcus searching for him like this, not when the trees around her were so dark that they seemed to press in upon her, yet all of the woods felt strangely alive. For the first time since she started Nightingale, she felt afraid in the darkness.

She turned around and headed back toward the main area of the garden with its lanterns and torches, its crowds and music. With each step she took, her heartbeat eased and her lungs—

A hand shot out of the darkness and grabbed her arm. Too startled to scream, she was pulled off the path.

A man's arms encircled her waist, swinging her off her feet and into the shadows. But she didn't punch or kick against him despite her gasp of surprise. Because she knew those strong arms and shoulders, that firm jaw, the gleam of his dark eyes even from behind the mask—

"Marcus."

He maneuvered her behind the wall of a folly, into a secluded and dark corner of the fake ruins. Then he lowered his head to capture her mouth in a kiss that left her weak and tingling to the tips of her fingers and toes. Her arms wrapped around his neck, and she arched into him, eagerly giving herself up to be kissed and caressed.

A deep groan sounded from the back of his throat when she opened her lips and allowed him inside to plunder her mouth. An aching yearning started at her toes and fanned up through her, and she simply couldn't kiss him deeply enough to keep it at bay or quash the throbbing he stirred between her thighs.

When he finally tore his mouth away from hers, he murmured against her cheek, "I've been wanting to do that all night."

"Have you?" Her voice was just as raw with desire as his as she admitted, "I thought I was the only one."

With a laughing growl, he kissed her again, this time languidly and leisurely, as if he could take his time to savor her now that he'd satisfied that initial longing.

A peal of laughter from the path broke the stillness of the night. Startled, Dani jumped away from him. But she didn't go far from his arms and sagged against the stones behind her, staring up at him through the shadows. Her hand rose to touch her fingers to her lips, finding them warm and wet and aching to be kissed again. God help her, the taste of him was sheer addiction.

Safely shielded from the world by his strong body and cocooned privately in the shadows, she dared to reach a hand to touch his cheek. So warm and strong…

As if knowing what she was thinking, he turned his head to kiss her palm. She trembled with longing.

"I didn't know if you were going to follow, if you understood what I wanted you to do," she whispered, but even that seemed to echo loudly against the muffled night surrounding them. "Then, when I looked for you in the crowd, I couldn't spot you. I thought…"

He covered her hand with his and gave her fingers a squeeze. "What?"

"That you'd changed your mind." She slowly pulled her hand from his to step into his embrace, her arms once more encircling his neck. "That you weren't following."

"I knew where you were at every step," he assured her, his warm breath tickling her ear. "I wouldn't have let you out of my sight."

His answer sparked a liquid warmth inside her. She pulled back, but only far enough to tease her fingers into the silky hair at his nape. "Because you've been watching me all evening." She'd happily noticed that, how his gaze never left her for long, even during the supper when their attentions had been required by the people on either side of them at the table. "A less confident lady might be rather nervous to realize that."

His eyes flickered brightly behind the mask. "And a confident woman like yourself?"

"Flattered." The truth behind that would have heated her cheeks in a happy blush…until reality turned her cold. "Until she realizes it was only to keep watch on her."

"No respectable gentleman would do less when that woman is in his care for the evening."

"Is that what I am—in your care?"

"Would you mind if you were?"

"No, I don't believe I would." That sincere admission

turned into a subtle flirtation, one that tickled deliciously at the backs of her knees. "But given that it took me to rescue you from those cloying gentlemen in the box, it seems to me that tonight, you're in *my* care."

"Am I?" His sensuous lips curled in amusement.

"Would you mind if you were?" she repeated his words and delighted when he gave a low chuckle in response.

"Definitely not."

A thrill surged through her at that half growl, and her arms tightened around his shoulders, not to keep him close but to keep herself from falling away.

"But that wasn't the only reason I watched you," he admitted.

"And what other reason would there be?"

He shifted into her, bringing her soft front against his hard chest. "Simply to watch you."

Her fingers stilled in his hair. It would be so easy to believe his flattery, to let herself go deeper into this new—and refreshingly direct—flirtation that she'd never dared attempt with a man before. That had all the little muscles in her belly tightening with a mix of uncertainty and utter enjoyment.

But a reminder of why they were there in the gardens tonight crept out from the back of her mind, and it wasn't because he wanted a secret assignation with her in the shadows.

"I haven't had the chance to speak to Lady Hartsham alone yet." She slipped out of his arms to put space between them and find her equilibrium. "There have been too many people around. But I promise that I will before the evening is over."

He didn't reach for her, but his eyes stayed keenly bright as they studied her from behind the mask. "You don't have to, you know."

"But I do. That's what this evening is for, why we're here."

He shook his head. "If you think this is too dangerous—"

"It isn't." Yet she couldn't stop a faint trembling from traveling up her legs to her knees. She wanted to believe it was because of the danger, but that would be a lie. It was only because of Marcus.

"If you've changed your mind," he said pointedly, lightly grasping her upper arms, "I'll understand, and the evening will become nothing more than an outing to Vauxhall. I don't want you placing yourself in unnecessary danger."

"We're in the middle of a pleasure garden." She gestured a hand at the property around them. "The only danger here is of drinking too much arrack punch and suffering a fierce headache in the morning."

What she could see of his expression from behind the mask remained somber, the tightening of his jaw not eased by her teasing assurances.

But his overprotectiveness made her nervous, especially when she'd been so excited earlier to know that they were working together as a team. She couldn't bear the thought of being left behind now.

So she quickly changed subjects. "By the way, when

you paid for all those dresses the other afternoon, I know that I cornered you into it. You really don't have to. I'll make certain you're reimbursed."

"Consider it my contribution to Nightingale." Yet he didn't seem happy about being a benefactor.

"Thank you."

"And the other?"

She couldn't see his expression behind the mask, but she knew from the sound of his voice that he'd arched a brow in challenge.

"Am I to receive thanks for that, too?"

He meant the stockings. Her cheeks flushed. "Not at all," she whispered, although no one could overhear. "*That* you shouldn't have done."

"Why not?" The challenge laced his voice. "Don't you like them?"

"They're lovely, but it's far too scandalous, you buying me clothes."

"I didn't buy you clothes." He leaned in, lowering his face level with hers. "I bought you stockings."

"When you put it like that," she drawled dryly, "it's so much better."

His mouth quirked into a grin. "Are you wearing them tonight?"

Heaven help her, she was. She hadn't been able to resist, privately amused by the secret she kept beneath her skirts. She should have answered that it was none of his business, that a proper lady would never answer a question like that from a gentleman. But she'd enjoyed their flirtatious sparring, enjoyed how feminine and desirable he made her feel—

"I'll never tell."

"Well then." A teasing glint lit his eyes. "I'll just have to find out for myself."

Before she realized what he was doing, he knelt in front of her.

She gasped as he reached for her hem and smacked him lightly on the shoulder. "Stop that!"

"I spent good money on those stockings." His large hands slipped beneath her hem and reached for her shoes. "A sizeable part of the dukedom, in fact."

"You did not!"

"Two estates and a farm, I assure you." Clucking his tongue, he shook his head. "Might have to forget plans to send Pippa away for schooling now."

She couldn't stop the giggle that rose to her lips at the ludicrousness of that.

"A man needs to keep a close eye on his investments." Then he lowered his voice and murmured huskily, "A *very* close eye."

"Stop that," she repeated as he lifted her foot and removed her satin shoe, but this time, the order was forced out between lighthearted laughs. Then between squeals when he tickled her toes. "Stop that, too!"

"Just checking the quality of the knitting." His hand went to her other foot and did the same, this time tickling much longer until she was practically jumping on one foot to end the sweet torture.

"They're of exquisite quality, thank you very much." She slapped her hand against his shoulder. "They do not need to be inspected. And certainly *not* while I'm in them!"

"No?"

"No."

"Pity." He forlornly heaved out a sigh, then paused for a contemplative beat. "I'm also good at inspecting corsets."

That unexpected comment brought a new bubble of laughter to her lips, and then he joined in, once more tickling her feet and making her dance a small jig. Oh, after removing her shoes, those beautiful stockings would be ruined! But she couldn't make herself be angry at him, not when she hadn't laughed like this in so very long.

Neither had he, she was certain, based on the rusty sound of his laughter. For a little while tonight, at least, they could forget their shared grief over Elise, let go of the pain, and enjoy each other's company. A warm happiness blossomed inside her.

Still kneeling in front of her, Marcus tilted his head back to stare up the length of her.

Her heart stuttered at the astonishing sight of him, of this indomitable man kneeling at her feet. Never had she felt more feminine, more powerful in her entire life... *never*. And all because of him.

An inexplicable mix of excitement and comfort twirled through her as she reached down to cup his face between her hands, then bent over to kiss him.

Fifteen

MARCUS TILTED HIS FACE UP TO HERS AND WELCOMED her kiss, reveling in the spicy-sweet taste of her lips and the feathery warmth of her breath as it fanned across his cheeks. Her delicate fingers gently caressed his cheeks as she held his head still between her hands.

"Marcus," she whispered, an aching plea.

"Whatever you wish." With that murmur, he gave her permission to take all that she wanted from the kiss. And from him.

She smiled against his mouth, and that silken movement twined a low heat through him, only for it to turn to liquid flames when she took his bottom lip between hers and sucked. Each pull of her lips tugged in a straight line down to his cock, which began to ache, then flexed when she gingerly slipped the tip of her tongue between his lips.

He stayed perfectly still as he continued to kneel in front of her, to let her explore his mouth with little licks across his inner lip and teasing slides across his tongue, but the effort for restraint made him shake. Letting her kiss him like this without pulling her into his arms and returning the kiss as ravenously as he wanted to do was sweet torture, one that had his pulse spiking and his lungs squeezing in ragged fits. When her hands moved to rest on his shoulders, she could surely feel the tension beneath her fingertips, just as he could feel the yearning desire growing inside her.

Then, the kiss changed. Not the way her lips teased at his, not the way the tip of her tongue continued to make small forays into his mouth—no, he tasted hesitation and sadness.

When he reached a hand up to her face in silent concern, she lifted her head just far enough to slip from his fingertips.

Her gaze fixed on his mouth. "We might learn all our answers tonight," she whispered, brushing her fingertips over his bottom lip. "What happens when we do?"

"We won't," he assured her glumly. It wasn't the answer she was looking for, but it was the truth. "Not tonight."

"Then soon. But we will." She hesitated. "And then?"

His heartbeat skipped as he realized that she wasn't asking about matters of justice or how they would turn their information over to the authorities. She was asking about the two of them.

He simply had no idea what the future held, except that he couldn't bear the thought of no longer seeing her. She'd come to mean a great deal to him, and more than as a friend of his late sister, more than as a source for discovering the truth behind Elise's death. More than as a beautiful woman whose kisses and caresses affected him more deeply than any other woman's ever had.

During the past few weeks since they'd been working together to find answers, she'd given his life purpose.

"Then we worry about it later. For now, we should only worry about this evening." He slipped his hands beneath her skirt to encircle her legs and bring her against him as he looked up at her. "And this evening, there is nowhere else I would rather be than right here, with you."

He meant every word. Since he'd returned to England, he'd longed to be back in the field with his men, where he knew exactly who the enemy was and how to fight against him, where outcomes were certain and decisive.

Except when he was with Danielle.

She ran her fingers tenderly through the hair at his temple. That simple touch confirmed silently that she felt the same.

She kissed him again, and this time without any uncertainty. He seized her mouth with his in an eager, openmouthed kiss that left both of them shaking.

"Danielle," he murmured hotly against her mouth, longing to touch her intimately as his hands slid up the backs of her legs.

She answered with a sighing whimper and closed her eyes.

He caressed her calves, running his fingertips over the silky smoothness of the stockings. He smiled—the same stockings he'd given her. The masculine rush of pride and possession that she'd worn them tonight was impossible to tamp down, or the desire that rose inside him.

As she continued to bend over him, eagerly kissing him from above, his fingers teased at the lace hem of the stocking, tied to her thigh by a ribbon. He wiggled his fingers down inside her stocking and drew a surprised gasp from her lips, only for the sound to turn into a full-throated moan when he pulled loose the ribbon and pushed down the stocking, baring her entire leg to his hands.

"That's…very nice," she murmured as his hand traced invisible patterns up her leg, from ankle to thigh.

"No, it's heavenly." He punctuated that correction by doing the same to the other stocking. But this time, instead of touching her leg with his hand, he pushed her skirt up out of the way and dipped his head to repeat the caresses with his mouth, placing featherlight kisses against her bare skin.

By the time his lips reached her thigh, her breath came in quick little pants, and her fingertips dug into his shoulders. "So…is that."

He chuckled. She was a delicious mix of confidence and innocence.

"And this?" He nudged her gown and chemise higher, exposing the juncture of her thighs to his gaze. He sifted his fingers slowly through her feminine curls, then bit back a groan when she seductively mimicked that gesture by combing her fingers through the hair at his nape.

"Yes," she whispered and leaned against the stone wall behind her for support.

The musky scent of her sex filled his senses, and he knew before he slowly slid his hands up her inner thighs to caress his thumbs between her legs—

Sweet Lucifer, she was already wet.

"And this?" As he teased his thumbs over her folds,

he leaned back to watch the expressions flitting over her face. He would stop with a single word if she bade him. But he prayed to every saint and angel in heaven that she wouldn't. He wanted this moment with her too much to deny either of them the satisfaction it would bring.

"Yes." She shifted her legs farther apart to open herself to him. "Yes, Marcus."

Not an agreement this time but permission. He dipped his head between her legs. Her gasp of surprise melted into a whimper of desire, and her hands tightened on his head as he explored her with his mouth.

At first, he worshipped her with light and delicate kisses, but as the taste and scent of her engulfed his senses, his restraint dissolved. The worshipping changed into plundering, the light kisses into hard licks, pulling sucks, and deep plunges of his tongue as he attempted to discover every secret part of her.

"Marcus!" Her body shook so fiercely with desire that her hands grabbed at his shoulders to keep her balance.

He shoved her gown out of the way and hooked her left leg over his shoulder. As he teased her folds with his fingers, he stared up at her, thankful as hell for the mask he still wore. God help him if she ever saw his need for her on his face.

"Hang on tight, love," he whispered, flicking his thumb across the sensitive little nub buried at the top of her folds and eliciting a wiggle of her hips against his hand in response. "And don't let go."

This time when his mouth captured her, he slipped

a finger inside her tight warmth. She cried out in surprise, but her arms tightened around his neck and her leg clenched tightly across his back as she arched against him.

He sucked gently at the little point at the center of her femininity as his finger continued to tease inside her. Evidence of her need for release slicked his hand, the taste and feel of her exquisite. She was so close that he could feel her quivering against his lips, could feel all those little muscles inside her tightening around his finger as he continued to stroke inside her. One more pulling suck of his lips—

She broke with a cry. His hands clamped around her waist to keep her on her feet as release shuddered through her and left her sagging bonelessly against the wall. When her leg slipped to the ground, he rose up to catch her in his arms.

She stared at him in wonder, her lips slightly parted and a visible heat in her cheeks even in the shadows.

The sight of her, flushed and satisfied, made him long to make her come again, this time while he was buried inside her. He couldn't have that, not tonight. But he would never regret bringing her this pleasure. "Danielle, are you all right?"

"I'm wonderful." Her trembling fingers lightly caressed his cheek.

Yes, she certainly was.

"But *you* didn't…"

There was no use in pretending that he didn't know what she meant. Danielle might still be innocent, but she wasn't ignorant. There was also no denying the stone-hard bulge in his trousers.

"No," he rasped, "I didn't."

"You don't…want to?"

Sweet Lucifer. He bit back a groan of longing so fierce that it shook him to his core. He captured her face in his hands and kissed her heatedly enough to chase any doubt from her mind about exactly how much he wanted her.

"When you give your innocence," he rakishly drawled into her ear when he could finally bring himself to tear his mouth away from hers, "it won't be on some cold piece of ground tucked away shamefully in the bushes. And it sure as hell won't be behind masks."

He felt her swallow. Hard. "Where will we be, then?"

His heart stuttered at the promise implicit in her words that he would be the man she would share that moment with, at the realization that she wanted that, too.

Cannon fire boomed across the gardens, signaling the start of the fireworks before the evening's end. In unison, all the bands sent up a fanfare that sparked excitement through the park.

"We have to return to the box," he told her, thanking fate for this small reprieve from having to answer her question, because he had absolutely no idea what to say. "The fireworks will be starting soon, and we'll be missed."

She nodded. But neither of them could bring themselves to loosen their hold on the other.

"When this evening is over and we have whatever

answers we're going to find from Lady Hartsham about Elise," he murmured, "the two of us are going to have a long talk."

Another nod against his shoulder, but this time, she slipped away from his embrace. She retied her stockings, slipped on her shoes, and backed slowly toward the path. Then she was gone, dissolving into the darkness.

Sixteen

DANI HURRIED THROUGH THE DARK STRETCH OF gardens as quickly as she could without stumbling on the uneven path. She wound her way back toward the lanterns and buildings of the main section of the park more relieved to be out of the wilderness with every step she took.

Her heart pounded brutally hard, and she gulped in great lungfuls of air. But she didn't dare stop. She also didn't bother to glance behind her, because she knew Marcus wasn't following.

As a gentleman, he would wait before he returned to the box, to give several minutes' space between their two arrivals to cover up any whispers of impropriety that they'd returned at the same time. And to give him an opportunity to collect himself, so there was no evidence of what they'd been doing in the darkness.

Oh, heavens, what they'd done! She pressed her fist against her chest to keep down the rising flush—not of regret or humiliation. *Never* that, never with Marcus. How could she ever regret something so wonderful with a man so special?

No, she fought down her emotions because she wanted nothing more than to turn around, run straight back into his arms, and beg him to do that again. To give him the same exquisite bliss that he brought to her. And with that, possibly lose both Nightingale and herself.

A long talk, indeed.

She slowed her pace as the path spilled out into the area surrounding the Chinese pavilion. Her fingers grabbed at her mask and she tore it off, her hand falling to her side and the long ties dangling against her skirt. She dragged in several deep lungfuls of the cool night air until it tingled her chest from the inside. But there wasn't enough air in England to fight down the flaming heat lingering inside her that Marcus had ignited. A heat she knew only he could extinguish.

As she approached the rear of the gallery, a figure moved out of the darkness. Dani halted with a surprised gasp.

"There you are." Mrs. Slater stepped into the lamplight from the shadows where she'd been waiting. "And gone dangerously longer than twenty minutes, I daresay."

Thankful to hide her lack of breath under the pretense of being startled, Dani half panted out, "The line for the ices was exceedingly long." But her voice held no inflection to support that lie. She added dryly, "Pity that we were separated in the crowd."

"Indeed." Mrs. Slater looked past her toward the avenue and lowered her voice, "And His Grace?"

Playing along with their very thin charade, Dani drawled, "I have no idea what you mean."

Mrs. Slater's face tensed as she continued to hunt for Marcus. "I was certain you'd have come back together," she murmured. "This isn't at all…" Then, in a beat, she cut off her musing, and her distraction was gone, a smile in its place. She took Dani's hands and held her arms open wide, then raked an assessing gaze over her from head to toe and back again, looking for any sign in appearance that she'd engaged in anything less than proper. "Well, I hope you found Vauxhall amusing."

Amusing. Not at all a word she'd associate with Marcus. Intense, overwhelming, dedicated…

He needed her help to put his sister's ghost behind him, and in that, she'd not let him down. She linked her arm with Mrs. Slater's and led the woman toward the box door. She had answers yet to uncover this evening, and a niggling suspicion tingling at the backs of her knees told her that not all of them would come from Lady Hartsham.

"The gardens were quite diverting."

That was the understatement of the decade, yet Mrs. Slater's only reply was to slide her a look that Dani couldn't quite decipher.

The two women slipped inside the box, arm in arm, exactly as they had left it, with seemingly not a care in the world except to drink one last glass of punch before the night ended.

Inside the box, no one had seemed to notice—or care—that they had been gone, although the gentlemen craned their necks each time the door opened, most likely in hopes that Marcus had returned. They all wanted one last chance to worm their way into his good graces.

But among the women, excitement rose over the

impending fireworks. They were all in heated discussions about the best viewing spots and whether they would have a better view from the railing just outside the box or out among the crowd gathering in the alley, whether they should wear masks, and would the attendants know to bring them more punch if they left the box?

Dani couldn't stand the prattling lot of them. Too much had changed tonight for her to have patience for such trivial matters. So she slipped away from Mrs. Slater and made a beeline directly for Lady Hartsham near the railing.

"May I have a word?" She attempted to snare Beatrice's attention away from solving the problem of the band playing too loudly from the box next to theirs.

But the countess waved a hand to indicate that she needed a moment to resolve the problem and gestured for the uniformed attendant who had been serving them all evening. "If you would please go across the way, to that box right there and—"

"A word, please." Dani put her hand on the woman's arm.

"In a moment, Danielle." With a distracted smile, Beatrice patted Dani's hand. "The noise, you see. Why, it's too loud to even hold a polite conversation!"

"I need to speak to you about Elise Braddock Donnelly." Dani leaned in to keep from being overheard and affected a smile for the others, as if she were doing nothing more than giving suggestions for noise control. "And the night she was killed."

Beatrice froze, except for a telling widening of her eyes for a single beat of surprise.

Dani took her arm and pulled her to the side of the box, away from eavesdropping guests. Anyone who saw them speaking privately would assume they were making plans for the rest of the evening or arguing about the fireworks and band.

"Did you see Elise immediately before she died?" Dani pressed, determined to find answers for Marcus's sake. She owed him this for her role in Elise's death. Oh, she owed him so much more! "Did you speak to her in the days leading up to her death or send any messages to her?"

"I—I can't remember."

Yet even in the dim lamplight, Dani saw the blood drain from her face.

Beatrice laughed stiltedly. "I cannot even remember what we had last night for dinner, let alone what happened all those years ago."

Not all those years ago. "Less than two." Anger rose inside her that Beatrice gave what happened to Elise so little thought or consideration now. "Surely you'd remember if you'd spoken to her or met with her, given what happened."

"Elise died, and it was a terrible loss, someone that young…with a baby, no less." She took the mask that Dani still carried in her hand and fussed with the ribbons, her fingertips plucking at the sequins edging the satin mask. "But I can't remember if I saw her or not.

We were always running into each other, here or there, around Mayfair." She pulled off one of the sequins and frowned regretfully at what she'd done. "What does any of that matter now?"

"Because Elise was murdered."

Beatrice's gaze flew up to Dani's. Her fingers stilled against the satin mask.

"I think she started her own network to help women in need." Dani forced the words past the tightening knot of grief in her throat and glanced away just in time to see the door to the box open as Marcus returned. "I think she crossed the wrong people and put herself in danger, that someone killed her for it. But no one knows who she was with that night, where she was going, who she was attempting to help…"

When she looked back at Beatrice, an icy chill sank through her. There was no surprise on the woman's face. Only guilt.

"But you know, don't you?" she whispered, unable to hear her own voice over the coursing of blood in her ears and the music flooding the box. "You know what happened to her."

"I don't know."

"You were part of it." Her hand tightly gripped Beatrice's arm so the woman couldn't walk away. "Elise called on you, asked you to be part of her secret… She brought you into her new network when Nightingale didn't need you anymore."

Beatrice turned deathly pale, the stricken expression

on her face made more intense by the flickering wicks of the lamps. Her hands began to shake so badly that she couldn't grasp the sequins beneath her fingertips. "Yes," she admitted.

Betrayal pulsed through Dani at what Beatrice and Elise had done, that they'd both gone behind her back and were keeping such secrets from her.

Beatrice's eyes glistened. "But she didn't want you to know. She was afraid that you'd try to stop her."

Dani nodded stiffly. She would have done exactly that. But there was no time now for grief, no time to give in to the hurt of being deceived by her dearest friend and the countess, someone her family had always trusted. Now she had to focus on uncovering as many answers as possible for Marcus. "And the women she was helping?"

"They were the ones you'd turned down for Nightingale."

Guilt stabbed her, so fiercely that she winced. "The prostitutes?"

Beatrice gave a jerking nod. "I'd heard about girls from the Manchester mills who had been drugged and brought to London, to be forced into the brothels in Southwark. I told Elise about them, how frustrated I was that Nightingale wouldn't help them—I wanted to save them and send them back to their families." Her voice was low and raw, desperate, and pleading for understanding. "I had no idea that Elise would try to rescue them herself, or I never would have told her about them. I promise you that, Danielle. *Never.*"

"I know," she answered, believing her. Beatrice McTavish had never been one for acts of bravery.

"When I learned what she was doing, I tried to convince her to stop, but…"

Her stomach roiled, and she pressed her hand against her abdomen to fight down the sickening hollow forming in her belly. "But?"

"But there were more women waiting in the brothel who—" Beatrice glanced across the box, freezing in place as if she'd seen a ghost.

Dani turned to look.

William McTavish, Earl of Hartsham. Her husband. He stood in the corner, surrounded closely by several of the gentlemen as they finished off the last of the port.

As Beatrice stared at him, her expression hardened so suddenly that Dani's breath strangled in her throat. She glanced between the two, not understanding why Beatrice should suddenly grow so afraid. No…so bitterly *angry*. Because the earl hadn't looked their way, hadn't paid them any attention as he went on talking and laughing with the men—

"Do not ask me about this again, Danielle. What happened to Elise was horrible," Beatrice rasped out. She turned away, crumpling the mask in her fist. Then she took one more glance over her shoulder at her husband and warned, "Make certain the same doesn't happen to you."

That cool threat slithered down Dani's spine, chilling her to her soul. She knew the truth then. She *knew*…

She looked across the box and met Marcus's gaze, too stunned to hide the shock that surely radiated from her.

As he returned her stare, his face turned to stone.

Boom! The first of the fireworks exploded over the gardens in a burst of light and a shower of sparks. Cheers flew up from the crowds. *Boom boom!* The explosions shot off like artillery fire and lit up the night in shimmering waves to the loud oohs and aahs from the spectators.

Inside the box, the guests scurried for the best views. The women hurried toward the door, while many of the men vaulted the railing into the alley, hooting and cheering as they went, bottles of champagne clenched securely in their hands.

Keeping her gaze locked with Marcus's, Dani pushed her way through the crowd to his side. He took her arm and led her from the box, careful to keep her from being jostled and bumped in the stampede to watch the fireworks.

"You have answers," he murmured as he steered her toward the shadows of the rear stairs behind the box and away from the crowd. "Tell me."

She grabbed his arm and stopped him, her fingers digging into his sleeve. "It's Hartsham," she choked out. "He killed Elise… Marcus, it was him!"

He stiffened, but disbelief flickered in his eyes as he narrowed them on her. "Her husband? She told you that?"

"Not exactly." She fisted the kerseymere in her hands, desperate to hang onto him as an anchor in the storm engulfing her. "But it's him! What she said, *how* she said it—"

The board behind her head splintered with a deafening bang.

"Get down!" Marcus grabbed her and shoved both of them to the ground as a second bullet tore into the building right behind where she'd been standing. "They're shooting at us!"

She lifted her head to glance around in panic. The world swirled in a cacophony of noise and movement all around them, and she saw nothing but a blur of lights and flashes of fireworks. The sounds of the gunshots were drowned out by the booms of the fireworks and the noise of the band. No one in the crowd heard or saw—

He let out a curse and grabbed her wrist. "Run—now!"

Scrambling to his feet, he pulled her up with him and ran, keeping her between himself and the gallery to shield her. She struggled to race beside him to keep up with his long strides. When they reached the end of the building and lost what little protection it provided, he pulled her in the direction of the main gates, and they wove their way against the coming crowd as it pushed toward the Grand Walk.

She turned to glance over her shoulder—

Her wrist slipped out of his grasp, and she tripped. She fell forward. Her hands slammed against the compacted dirt and gravel. She felt the rip of her flesh as a piece of glass sliced into her palm, and a pained cry rose from her throat.

But then Marcus was beside her, picking her up in his arms and running with her through the crowds.

Her arms tightened around his neck, and she clung to him, burying her face against his neck as he carried her through the gates. All of her went numb with fear and fresh grief, but her hold on him never eased, not even when he placed her inside his carriage and slammed the door closed.

"Drive!" He pounded against the side of the compartment with his fist. "To the armory—go!"

When the coach jerked to a start, he pulled her onto his lap and wrapped his arms around her. He grabbed his great coat from the opposite bench and placed it over her shoulders to keep her warm, then cradled her close.

She shook against him, unable to stop the shudders wracking her body, unable to ease the clenching of her arms around his neck. Fear and betrayal overwhelmed her, and she could do nothing more than cling to him.

"It's all right. You're safe now." He lowered his mouth against her hair and assured her, "It's all over."

She squeezed shut her eyes. Oh, he was so very wrong! The worst was only beginning.

When they finally came to a stop, the city around them was dark and unfamiliar. Marcus helped her to the ground, her hand secure in his.

Ordering the driver to go home to Charlton Place, he grabbed a carriage lantern from one of the tigers, then pulled her toward a metal door in the outer brick wall surrounding the armory. It clanged so loudly when he shut it behind them that she startled, but he didn't stop, pulling her across the small courtyard to the armory building itself and then inside its thick walls, where the darkness was so intense that she couldn't see beyond the small circle of lantern light.

Silence, darkness…*safety*.

Letting go of his hand, she staggered forward a few feet, then collapsed onto her knees on the stone floor.

"Danielle!"

He knelt beside her and pulled her into his arms. He held her tightly against him as the sobs finally tore from her.

"You're safe." His hands stroked her back, but she couldn't stop the emotions that poured from her. "They didn't follow us. They can't get inside—"

"No." Her fingertips dug into his shoulders as she clung to him, desperate for an anchor as the world tumbled away beneath her. "No…"

"Are you hurt?" He released his hold on her to cup her face in his hands.

So much concern gripped his face that she squeezed her eyes shut. She couldn't bear it! Her chest felt like a gaping wound had been ripped into her, and every inch of her body flashed between punishing pain and blessed numbness.

"Beatrice, the earl…" she choked out in a rasp. Then the name that sliced through her like a knife—"*Elise*."

Marcus rocked her in his arms. "We know now—we have answers." His whisper emerged as a solemn promise.

"It's going to be all right. We'll have justice for her after all."

Dani vehemently shook her head. Oh, he didn't understand! The lies, the betrayal—so brutal that she shook from it.

She tried to push him away, but he refused to loosen his hold around her, even as they continued to sit there in the silence, surrounded by darkness so thick that she couldn't see the room around them. Only darkness, coldness, hardness...betrayal.

"They lied! All of them... They lied to me, nothing but lies and deception..." Dear God, she felt like such a fool! "And I trusted them, all of them, with so much... with so many secrets...with my life..." *With my heart.*

A sob caught in her throat as another tear that she couldn't stop fell down her cheek.

"You didn't know." He soothed his hands down her back. "You can't blame yourself."

She shook her head and pulled back just far enough to look into his face. Her hands tangled desperately in his waistcoat, and she could feel the pounding of his pulse beneath her fingers. So strong and certain... Dear God, she wished she could have that same surety and strength! She wanted to find a way to crawl beneath his skin, claim it, and never let go.

"I *trusted* them." Especially Elise. A woman whom she'd thought had been closer to her than a real sister—ashes! The pain of mistrust was blinding. All she'd risked during these past few years, all she'd worked so hard to accomplish, had only led to lies and betrayal. "How do I ever trust again?" She clenched and released her fists against his chest in frustration. "How can I ever believe in anyone again?"

"Believe in me." He touched his lips to hers, and the bittersweetness of that kiss ached on her lips. "You can believe in *me*, Danielle."

A ragged sigh tore from her, and she wilted against him.

He rested his forehead against hers, and his warm breath fanned over her skin as he reached up to caress her cheek. "You can trust in me, Danielle," he murmured huskily. "Now and always."

Her heart swelled at the promise in his words, at the comfort he was offering. She'd thought they were working together to find justice for Elise, but what was blossoming between them was so much more than that. So intense that it swirled around her in a growing warmth, tingling at her toes and fingertips.

She trembled at the enormity of what he was offering her. To be able to place herself in this man's care, without fear of harm—

"Yes," she whispered, then tilted her face up to bring her lips to his.

Seventeen

MARCUS GROANED AT HER WHISPER OF PERMISSION. Unable to resist, he seized her mouth with his and turned the touch of their lips into a blistering kiss, one that throbbed fiercely with how much he wanted her.

Dear God, the way she twisted his insides! Never had he ached for a woman as much as he did Danielle, and not just physically—every bit of him wanted nothing more than to heal the wounds she'd suffered, to make her happy, to keep her beside him, safe in his arms.

But when her hand began to play with the buttons on his waistcoat, the longing to keep her safe transformed into a new desire, and liquid fire spread through his veins.

"Danielle." Her name was a plea to let him claim more, and she obliged, parting her lips and letting his tongue plunge inside.

When she responded by closing her lips around him and sucking with an unschooled instinct, a hot shiver raced through him, all the way down to the tip of his hardening cock. His restraint snapped. He lowered her onto her back on the stone floor and followed down after her, covering her body with his. His mouth never broke contact with hers until she tore her lips away to gasp back the air he'd stolen.

"I want..." she whispered, her hands shaking so hard

that they fumbled to unfasten the buttons of his waist-coat. But she couldn't finish putting to words the desire he felt blossoming inside her.

"I know." He reached up to run his fingers through her tresses until her hair lay around her on the stone like pud-dled silk. "I will keep you safe here. I promise you that."

But she shook her head. Her hands on his shoulders stilled him as he lowered his head to place openmouthed kisses across the top swells of her breasts exposed above the neckline of her dress that had sagged down in their flight from Vauxhall.

"No, I want—I mean...I *need*..." Frustration filled her voice as it trailed off.

He rose up onto all fours over her as she lay under him in the flickering shadows at the edge of the lantern light, and he lost all sense of time and place at the sight of her, the world around them falling away until there was only Danielle. Not from how beautiful she was—and she *was* beautiful, with her hair all wild around her, her lips flushed from his kisses, her eyes gleaming in the shadows. But from how she'd captured his soul the way no other woman ever had. The way no other woman ever would.

He brushed his hand along the side of her body in a soothing caress. "You need what, darling?" He dipped his head to tease his lips reassuringly over hers. "Tell me. Whatever it is, you'll have it."

She placed her hand on his chest and curled her fingers possessively into his muscles. Her quiet admission shivered into him as she whispered, "I want you, Marcus."

"I want you, too." Sweet Lucifer, how much he wanted! All of her, tonight, tomorrow—and every day and night after that.

She cupped his face between her hands to bring him down to her.

He kissed her deeply, drawing a whimper from her lips that turned into a sigh of satisfaction when he trailed his mouth down her neck and nipped at the tender flesh of her throat. Her pulse beat out a fierce tattoo beneath his lips, then nearly exploded when he cupped her breast in his palm. For a moment, he wondered if she would change her mind, if she would come to her senses about what they were about to do and shove him away—

But she arched into his hand and deepened the kiss, parting her lips and allowing him to ravish her mouth the way he wanted to ravish her body. He could taste the nervousness in her but not an ounce of uncertainty.

Marcus wrapped his arms around her and rolled them over, bringing her up on top of him, straddled across his hips as he lay on his back beneath her. She stared down at him, her mouth forming a round O of surprise.

He grinned lazily at her and answered her unasked question, "So I can do this."

He rose up to reach behind her and swiftly unfastened the row of tiny buttons at her back. Her loosened bodice dropped low across her breasts. With a shy gasp, she reached a hand up to catch it.

"Because you're beautiful," he murmured, taking her

hand and gently pulling it away to place it on his chest. "Because I want to see you, Danielle. *All* of you."

She bit her bottom lip, yet she didn't stop him as he crooked a finger inside her drooping neckline and tugged, pulling the dark-blue satin down her front.

When she shrugged her arms out of the dress and let it fall down around her waist, he reached behind her again, this time to feel for the laces tying her short stays. His gaze remained locked with hers as he worked to pull free the lace zigzagging up her back, then carefully removed her corset and tossed it away, leaving her in nothing from the waist up but her thin chemise.

She closed her eyes. "I've never…"

"I know." He brushed her hair over her shoulder. Instead of dropping his hand away, he teased at the chemise's thin shoulder strap. "And you know that I would never purposefully hurt you."

She nodded. "Yes."

"That I care about you," he admitted sincerely. "That I only want to make you happy."

Another nod, this time with a curl of her lips in a nervous but happy smile.

"Then trust me, Danielle." He pulled the chemise down her arm, baring her right breast to his heated stare. When he grazed the already taut nipple with the pad of his thumb, she shivered. "And let me make you happy."

He leaned up and placed an affectionate kiss to her nipple. She stiffened for a moment, her fingers digging into his chest, then the tension eased out of her when his lips closed around her and suckled. With that silent permission, he tugged down the other shoulder strap to bare both breasts to his seeking lips.

"This," she forced out between quickening pants, "makes me happy."

He chuckled against her flesh. The sound formed goose bumps on her bare arms, like magic. Which made him wonder where else he could make her tingle with his touch.

Pulling her skirt up around her waist, he slipped his hand between her open thighs to caress her intimate folds as she straddled him.

"And that?" he murmured.

Her ragged mewls of desire answered him. If this was happiness, he wanted nothing more than to spend the rest of his days making her happy.

Good God, she was so supple and warm against his fingers as he stroked her intimately, her folds wet with arousal. When he flicked his fingertip against her sensitive little nib, she gasped, and her thighs clenched against his hips. With a soft exhalation, she relaxed and smiled, an expression of such joy and trust that it melted him.

Tonight would be wonderful for her, he would make certain of it. He would ensure that she found her pleasure first—

When she wiggled out of the chemise and pushed it down around her waist to bare all of herself to him from the waist up, he groaned at the hot yearning that little movement shot down his cock.

If he survived that long.

She stilled. "Is this...all right?"

More than all right. "Perfect," he rasped out huskily and felt the tension drain from her. "You are absolutely perfect." He suckled at her breast as he continued to tease his fingers between her legs. "In every way."

To make his point, he slipped a finger inside her tight warmth. She gasped at the sensation of having part of him inside her, then the sound turned into a throaty moan as he began to tantalizingly stroke in and out of her.

Unable to sit still, she began to move her hips over him to meet each thrust of his finger. He rewarded her by slipping a second finger inside her, stretching her feminine lips wider and filling her even more.

"Marcus." His name fell from her lips, half the sound a guttural cry of passion, the other half a begging plea for more. She grasped at his shoulders for leverage as she instinctively began to ride his hand, to claim the pleasure waiting for her.

"That's it, darling," he encouraged as he rested his other hand on her hip to guide her. "Take whatever you want."

Instead, she surprised him by raising her hips so she could reach between them and unfasten his trouser buttons. Yearning for her tight warmth, his hard cock sprang free, and he sucked in sharply as his sensitive tip grazed the smooth flesh of her inner thigh.

She leaned down over him to place a kiss to his neck as she shyly whispered, "I want you."

With a growl, he pulled her into his arms and rolled her onto her back. He nestled his hips between her wide-open thighs, clasped his length in his hand, and guided himself inside her.

———————————

Dani drew in a mouthful of air as he sank into her. There was no pain like she'd expected. But he filled her so completely that she was stretched uncomfortably wide, with his weight pressing down onto her pelvis.

But then he began to move in slow and exploring little plunges and retreats of his hips against hers. The stretching eased, and the discomfort faded until all she knew was the wonderful sensation of him gliding smoothly inside her.

"Marcus," she whispered and wrapped her arms around his shoulders to hold him close.

This wasn't at all how she'd thought this moment would be. Not in an old, empty building with only his coat beneath her to protect her from the hard, cold floor. Not with both of them still wearing their clothes, with Marcus fully dressed and the fabric of his trousers rubbing against the insides of her thighs with each plunge of his body into hers. And not any other night but her wedding night.

But even though tonight was none of those things, it was still simply wonderful! Because of Marcus. Because she lay in the embrace of a man whom she had loved since she was a girl, a man who had promised to protect her and make her happy. Tonight, he was doing just that.

There was no other man she wanted to give herself to, and no other place she wanted to be in all the world but right here in his arms.

Wanting to bring him even closer, she wrapped her legs around him.

He groaned at the way the new position opened her even further to him, and his movements grew more intense, more urgent. With every deep plunge, he gave a teasing swirl of his hips against her before retreating, which brushed against that sensitive little place down *there* and nearly drove her out of her mind.

She bit back a cry as a throbbing ache pulsed relentlessly between her legs at that place where their two bodies joined. He'd touched her there before...kissing her with his mouth, caressing her with his fingers. But this—oh, *this* was simply divine!

"I want you," she whispered, burying her face against his bare neck and drinking in the wonderful flavor of man and the musky scent of sex.

"I think you have me," he returned with a chuckle.

"I don't..." she explained between labored breaths, "mean...this way..."

"You have me, darling," he repeated. "In every way."

He punctuated that promise with a searing kiss that left her panting for more even as he never slowed his steady thrusts between her thighs.

Happiness burst through her, and she shuddered

from the enormity of it…and from his body inside hers, her desire for him winding impossibly tight, like a coiling spring.

This wasn't only sex, only the surrendering of body to body. It wasn't even making love, although she certainly loved him. There was no doubt inside her about how much. No, what they were doing was so much more. Tonight, they were healing old wounds and absolving whatever threads of grief and guilt yet remained from the past.

"I've wanted this for so very long…with you…" She panted out that confession, unable to keep it inside. The words were a benediction for the new trust they were forging tonight, a way forward into the future. "Only with you, Marcus. *Only* with you."

When she arched her back beneath him, to bring him as deep inside her as possible, a masculine groan tore from the back of his throat. He shoved his hand down between them, to that spot where their bodies joined, and teased—

He touched the aching center of her, and she jumped beneath him, her hips bucking up against his. Electricity sparked through her. With a begging whine of need, she clenched herself around him like a vise, including all the little muscles deep inside her that tightened around him as the first ripples of release bubbled up from deep within her. He touched her there again, this time rubbing her hard and fast.

Stars burst behind her eyes, as brightly as fireworks.

His name tore from her lips in an explosive cry as she broke around him, all of her releasing in a lightning strike of pleasure and joy that shot through her to her core. To her soul.

He stroked deep inside her one more time, his hips jerking before he yanked himself out of her and thrust his length between their two bodies. A groaning shudder gripped him, and he spilled himself against her belly. The fierce tension inside him dissolved, and he lay languid over her as he rested his forehead against her bare shoulder, as the shivers of passion that still lingered inside him now seeped into her.

Keeping her arms and legs wrapped around him, she protectively sheltered him in the cradle of her embrace. She clung to him, holding on tight and never wanting to let go.

Eighteen

MARCUS TIGHTENED HIS ARMS AROUND DANIELLE AS they lay together on the old settee. In front of them, the small fire that he'd built in the large hearth cast a flickering golden glow on her bare shoulders as she draped her naked body over his. He pulled his overcoat across her to keep her warm, the only cover in the place that could serve as a blanket. But her body was warm and supple as her arms and legs tangled with his, all of her relaxed from making love a second time.

That time had been here on the settee, after taking their time to properly undress and thoroughly savor each other. She'd come that second time not with a passionate cry of need but a sigh of satisfaction. He placed a kiss to her bare shoulder—*perfect*.

She laughed, the dulcet sound fading into the silence of the large room around them.

He lifted her chin to touch his lips to hers, unable to stop kissing her, even though he'd just spent hours doing exactly that. "What is it?"

With a smile like the cat who'd gotten into the cream, she traced her fingertip in an invisible pattern over his bare chest. "We were supposed to have had a long talk about how we keep throwing ourselves passionately into each other's arms." She lifted her head from his shoulder and looked at him, an expression of such happiness on her face that his gut ached at the sight. "We seem to have neglected that."

He arched a brow at their naked state. "Apparently."

"Now we don't have to have that talk after all."

No, now so much more than she realized. He'd ruined her tonight, unable to deny himself from finding happiness inside her. But then, he also had every intention of marrying her.

And *that* talk needed to wait a bit longer, until they were both fully prepared for it.

He stroked his hand between her thighs to distract her from any stray emotions that might have crossed his face. She whispered his name and shifted to spread her legs wider in wanton invitation.

He bit back a groan. If she kept that up, he'd have her on her back again. Already, he'd satiated himself with her more than he should have, knowing how sore she would be in the morning from losing her innocence, and on a stone floor, no less.

He placed a light kiss to her lips and slipped from her arms to sit on the edge of the settee. When she wrapped her arm around him from behind, his pulse spiked beneath her hand as she strummed it lightly over his chest.

"The fire's going out," he offered as an excuse for why he needed to put enough distance between them to tamp down his lust.

She trailed her hand down to his cock and purred with amused irony, "Oh, I don't think so."

With a strained chuckle, he grabbed her hand and placed a kiss to her palm. Then he snatched up his trousers from the pile of their clothes at his feet and stood before she could touch him again and once more send him reeling out of his mind. He chastised teasingly as he yanked on his trousers, "Insatiable."

"Thank you."

When he turned around with a quip on the tip of his tongue that she'd exhaust him to death before dawn at this rate, he halted. Her stare focused below his waist, and disappointment dulled the brightness of her eyes that he'd covered himself from her sight.

As he finished buttoning his fall, he grinned at her with masculine pride that she found him so desirable. God knew he certainly felt the same about her.

She tore her eyes away, letting her attention drift around them at the old building. "What is this place?"

"An old armory."

As he knelt in front of the fireplace to stir up the coals and toss in more wood, he followed her gaze in an attempt to see the building from her perspective. That is, what could be seen of it in the dark shadows at the edges of the octagonal central room. But the fire was bright enough to reflect off the metal weapons on the walls, to show how thick and sturdy the old place was, even now after so many decades of being abandoned.

He'd spent uncountable nights here since he'd purchased the place, not falling asleep until the first light of dawn had shone through the windows at the top of the tower, because he hadn't been able to face the ghosts haunting Charlton Place. On those nights, he'd been alone.

Tonight, though, Danielle was here, and for once, he didn't dread the darkness.

"But you have a key to this building. Why?"

Balancing on the balls of his feet, he jabbed the iron poker into the fire to stir up more light and warmth for her. He'd found his own comfort in this place, and now he wanted her to feel welcome here as well. And safe. "Because I own it."

When she said nothing to that, waiting for him to continue, he tossed in a few more pieces of old wood from the bin beside the large hearth and watched as the flames bit into them as he decided how much to tell her.

"I had just returned to London and was taking my business ventures and accounts back under my control. They'd been in the hands of accountants and other caretakers while I'd been away, and it was time for me to oversee them again." He'd also needed something to do to keep busy, and he'd hoped that conducting business would do that. Good Lord, how wrong he'd been! Managing the accounts had barely scratched the need growing inside him to have a sense of purpose, to make a real difference in the world, the way he had during the wars. "I saw that this building was for sale and bought it to turn it into a warehouse. Now that the wars are over, normal trade will resume with the continent—and the Americans—and London's docks will be bursting at the seams with incoming goods and no place to put them.

What better to do with an old building like this than turn it into a giant warehouse?"

"But you didn't turn it into a warehouse." She swung her legs over the side of the settee and sat up, one hand keeping the coat in place over her. With the other, she gestured at the weapons on the wall.

"No, I did not."

He frowned into the fire. Her curiosity wasn't at all satisfied; he could feel her bewilderment as tangibly as he could still taste the sweetness of her on his lips. But he wouldn't provide any more answers about how he used this place than that.

Instead, he purposefully misunderstood her comment and answered as he rose to his full height, "We're safe here for the night. This place was meant to withstand invading armies."

"And Vauxhall assassins?" she challenged. "They might roll in like a troupe of acrobats."

Gallows humor. Her attempt to lighten the seriousness of their situation, yet he heard a trace of fear lingering behind it.

He explained as he stepped up to the side table along the wall and patted his hand against the bricks, "The walls are ten feet thick and built to survive direct cannon fire at less than ten yards, and it's built on a foundation of solid Dartmoor granite so it can't be undermined." He reached for the bottle of brandy sitting on the table and pointed it at the central tower overhead that stretched four stories high, the roof impossible to see in the darkness. "The only windows are all the way up there and covered with bars made from the same iron that was forged for both the outer and inner doors." He poured the brandy into a glass. "No one gets in or out unless we want them to."

"Impressive. Next thing you'll be telling me is that you have a portcullis at the ready to drop."

He glanced at her over his shoulder. "Two."

She paused for a beat, as if trying to determine if he was bamming her or not. Then she commented, "So this place is a fortress, then."

"I suppose you could say that." He brought back the glass of brandy and held it out to her. "One fit for an old soldier."

She arched a brow. "Or a new duke."

As she took the glass from him, he answered that silently with a glower. Damn her sharp mind. It was one of the things he liked best about her. Until right then.

When she lifted the glass to take a sip, the firelight reflected in the crystal and shone onto her hand—

A cut on her palm. A long slice and still pink-raw.

He snatched away the glass just as it reached her lips and earned himself an irritated scowl. "What do you—"

"You're wounded." Concern spiked inside him. He took her hand and turned it over, exposing the cut to the firelight.

"It's nothing, really. It's not even bleeding anymore." She lightly closed her fingers into a fist to hide it. When he refused to let her pull her hand away, she lowered her shoulders in capitulation. "I fell as we were leaving the gardens and cut my palm."

When they were being shot at, she meant. Guilt pierced him that she'd been hurt tonight because of him—for Christ's sake, that she could have been killed. Ruefully, he placed a kiss to her knuckles, then eased open her fingers so he could examine the wound. "Why didn't you say something about this before now?"

"We were a bit busy." She smiled conspiratorially. "And then a bit busy again."

This time, he didn't find her attempt at humor at all amusing. The thought of anything happening to her chilled his blood. "You should have told me."

"It's only a little cut. It barely bled at all."

But her assurances did little to ease his concern. Or his guilt.

She pulled her hand away and deftly changed subjects. Right back to him. "So this warehouse that obviously isn't a warehouse—you come here to do…what exactly?"

He handed back the brandy. "To be alone." He strode over to his training equipment and snatched up one of the clean lengths of cloth that he used to wrap his hands whenever he punched at the bags.

"Then I've ruined it for you." She stared into the glass. "You've allowed a woman into your gentlemen's club."

"A very beautiful woman." He raked a hot, searing look over her, seeing right through the coat to the delectable curves he knew were hidden beneath. "If being alone with you is ruining it, then I'll gladly have it ruined."

In the firelight's glow, he could see the bright flush of

her cheeks and the slight upward curve of her lips. "Are you certain?"

"You're special." More than she realized. "And you're right. You're the first woman I've allowed through those doors. Most likely the first woman ever allowed through those doors."

That surprised her, and her gaze darted up to his. "Ever?"

"It's an armory." With a shrug, he splashed water from a pitcher into a bowl on an old side buffet that he used as a washstand after his training sessions, when he wanted to wash away the sweat and grime and memories of the past. "Military men usually don't want women around and underfoot, especially where arms and weaponry are concerned."

"Worried we'll use them against you?"

"Terrified." He ripped the length of cloth in two, then plunged half of it into the water to wet it. "No one else knows about this place, except for Merritt Rivers and Brandon Pearce." He wrung out the excess water. "I'd like to keep it that way."

"Of course." She paused, then asked, "Brandon Pearce...the Earl of Sandhurst?"

"Don't let him hear you call him that, or you'll find yourself dragged out for a duel, skirt or no." He brought the cloth over to the settee and sat on the edge of it beside her. "Those are fighting words as far as he's concerned."

"What is it with you former soldiers," she mused as she leaned back against the arm of the settee and extended her injured hand toward him, "that none of you are grateful for your titles? You should be honored to possess them and what they represent—England's appreciation of your heroism."

"It's not that we're ungrateful." He kept his face carefully inscrutable at discovering her wound to be much deeper and bloodier than she'd let on. "It's that we know what we're giving up by leaving the military."

She studied him over the glass as she rested it against her sensuous lips. "Bad food and people trying to kill you?"

He threw back, "A night at Vauxhall, you mean?"

Her lips curved in a smile against the rim of the glass.

Careful not to cause her pain, he used the wet cloth to wipe away the dried blood and clean the cut. Her hand was small and dainty, and his gut tightened with self-recrimination to know that it might very well be scarred forever from this.

"What was it like," she asked, most likely reading his emotions and attempting to distract him, "being in the army? What was it *truly* like?"

"Truly?" His brows drew together in a frown, but he never lifted his gaze from her palm. "Freezing cold when it wasn't boiling hot or pouring rain. Loud when it wasn't unbearably silent. Usually uncomfortable. Always filthy. Long stretches of boredom broken by moments of sheer terror."

"Well." She sharply sucked in a mouthful of air when he touched a sore spot. "All that and poor pay, too? I can't see why every man wouldn't choose that for his livelihood."

His lips twisted at her sarcasm. "Fortunately, it runs deeper than that for a career soldier."

"How so?"

"When you're in the military, you have a sense of purpose, of a larger fight so much bigger than yourself and whatever regiment or battle you've been placed in." He slid the wet cloth over her palm to wipe away the last traces of dirt and blood. "Every day, you wake up knowing that you are fighting for morality and liberty, for a cause so good and right that it seems that it can't be anything other than divinely guided." He dropped the wet cloth to the floor and reached for the dry length that he'd flung over his shoulder. "You work hard all day to move just a tiny sliver closer to the end, and when your head hits your pillow at night, you can sleep well knowing that you did everything you could that day to support your men and the cause you're fighting for."

"And now?"

"Former soldiers don't have that." He slowly wrapped the linen strip around her hand to protect the cut and let it heal. If she were lucky, the scar would be small and would fade with time. But it would never completely go away. "They've returned to a country they barely recognize, where they can't find work or support their families. The crown would rather renovate a palace or throw a party than give out the back pay that the men are owed or fund hospitals to care for them, and Parliament makes it even harder by putting into place laws to protect its own interests by driving up the price of corn until the same men who fought so hard to defend English liberty now have to beg for food in the streets in order to survive."

He tied off the end of the bandage. Then he lifted her hand to his mouth to place a kiss against the wound, his eyes fixed on hers.

"So when they see how their brothers in arms have been treated," he finished with somber sarcasm, "men who were just as heroic on the battlefield as those given peerages, why would any former officer not want one?"

She trembled, but he knew it wasn't because of the cut. Of all the civilians he knew, she would be the only one who understood what he was telling her, who would be just as outraged about the plight of former soldiers as he was.

"But you, even now as a duke, you're still fighting." She touched her hand to his face, and the bandage scratched softly against his cheek. Her voice grew somber. "Are you ever going to stop waging war and find peace, Marcus?"

Nineteen

FOR A LONG MOMENT, THEIR GAZES LOCKED, AND Dani held her breath, waiting for him to answer.

But the only reply she received was silence as he took the glass of brandy from her and tossed down what was left in a single swallow, then walked away to refill it.

Her chest tightened as the limits of their newfound trust were so clearly exposed. They'd shared their bodies intimately tonight, but there were still some places that were off-limits. Unfortunately, that included his heart.

She'd promised Claudia that she'd help Marcus to find a sense of purpose. But how on earth was she supposed to do that when he refused to talk about himself?

Wrapping the coat around herself, she slid off the settee to gather up her clothes. She hesitated when she reached for her stockings, and an unbidden heat stung at her eyes.

With a curse at herself for being so sentimental—and now emotional, as her sight blurred from the unshed tears—she snatched them up and tossed the lot of her clothes onto the settee. Her hands shook as she reached for her chemise, the neckline of which had been stretched out of shape from Marcus's hands in his eagerness to touch. She'd have to throw it away. There would be no explaining this to Alice when her maid—

"How do you stop waging war when it's all you've ever known?"

His deep voice twined around her spine. She paused as she slipped the cotton material over her head, her heart skittering at his sobering question that revealed a vulnerability and doubt she never would have suspected lurked within him. Needing a moment to absorb that, she let the material caress down her body and fall into place around her legs.

"You start by laying down your arms." The irony of that! Even as she said it, she let her gaze drift around her at the weapons affixed to the walls. "All of them." *And then you open your heart to me.*

"Not when you're in the middle of a fight." This time, his voice was much closer, but she ignored both it and the sharp pang of longing in her belly.

She slipped on her corset, only to curse herself when she realized that she'd need his help to lace it up. And again with the buttons of her dress. Undressing had been so much more fun. Then, he couldn't seem to come close enough to her, not even with bare skin against bare skin, not even when he'd been inside her...

But now, even as he stood just behind her and reached out to tie up her corset without being asked, he felt half a world away.

"This isn't that kind of a fight," she whispered. But she knew what he meant, and when he finished with her laces, she surrendered the argument—for now—and changed battle tactics by changing topics. "Lady Hartsham didn't seem to know about how Elise died. When I told her that she had been murdered, Beatrice was shocked by it."

"Are you certain?"

She nodded, having no doubts at all about that. "But not by the fact that Elise was running her own network and rescuing women by herself." Passing over the stockings, she reached for her dress. She couldn't have borne to have Marcus watch her as she put those on. "Beatrice said that she'd told Elise about the girls in the brothels, but she never expected your sister to try to rescue them on her own."

"You think she told you the truth?"

"About that? Yes." She pulled the dress on over her head and carefully twisted the satin into place. "Beatrice has never been able to hide her emotions. That was one of the reasons why I never gave her more responsibility inside Nightingale."

Not turning to face him, she waited with her back toward him for him to button her up, just as he'd done with her corset. He did, and she reflexively shivered at the inadvertent scrape of his knuckles against her back. She closed her eyes to keep herself collected. How would she ever be able to look at him again without thinking of the intimacies they'd shared tonight?

"But Elise gave her responsibility," he drawled, his mouth so close to her shoulder that his warm breath tickled at her ear.

"I don't think so, not based upon what Beatrice said."

He took her hips in his hands and turned her to face him. "What did she say, exactly?"

"She and Elise had been having discussions about the prostitutes, the women that Nightingale couldn't help because vanishing them would have been too dangerous. Beatrice knew that some of the women had been kidnapped from the mills in the north, brought to London, and sent into the brothels. She told Elise about them." She dropped her gaze to the floor, the stab of betrayal still fresh. "Apparently to complain about me and how overly cautious I was being, how there were women whom we'd turned our backs on."

His hands tightened on her waist. "So Elise set about attempting to save them by herself."

Dani blinked hard and nodded, only for it to turn into an uncertain shake of her head. "But from what Beatrice told me, she didn't know what Elise was doing and so didn't directly help. She warned Elise to leave the women alone, that it was too dangerous. She said she didn't know anything about the people Elise was working with."

"You believe her?"

"Beatrice has always been worried that we'd be discovered. Even when she had easy responsibilities within Nightingale—running messages, arranging money transfers, collecting clothing—half the time, she'd lose her nerve and not do them. I cannot imagine her doing the kinds of risky work that Elise must have been doing."

He took her chin and lifted her head until she had no choice but to look at him. "At Vauxhall, you said it was Hartsham. That you knew he'd killed Elise."

"I thought so, from the way Beatrice stared at him…"

Her shoulders sagged in frustration as her doubts rose to the surface, now that the heat of the moment was over. "But it's Beatrice! She's always overly dramatic, even at the most relaxed of times. She's always been worried that the earl will discover what she's been doing with Nightingale. Maybe…" She shook her head. "I don't know… Maybe that's why she looked at him like that."

"Because he'd finally found out?"

"Perhaps." She frowned, then shook her head. "No— as if she were terrified of him."

"Then possibly he already knows what she's been doing."

"Or worse, that he found out and might have hurt her over it." Her stomach sickened, and she placed her hand on her belly to press down the guilt churning there as she turned away from him.

"Or hurt Elise."

She'd already thought of that, too. After all, that had been her first gut reaction when Beatrice had looked at the earl, when she'd warned Dani that the same fate might happen to her. She'd said it so intensely, with so much anger and hatred… Lord Hartsham had played a part in Elise's death. Dani had been certain of it.

But she knew him, for heaven's sake! He was good friends with her father, had come over for dinner countless times before her parents left for the continent—that was how she'd gotten to know Beatrice, why she'd invited the countess into working with Nightingale. How could the same man who laughed so heartily at Harriett's stories and gave both women guidance in her father's absence be a coldhearted murderer?

"I know that it doesn't make sense," she whispered. "But I saw her reaction. She *knew* who had killed Elise. I didn't even have to mention Porter or Scepter—she just looked directly at Hartsham, and her face... Good God, Marcus!" The cold accusation she'd witnessed on Beatrice's face had ripped the air from Dani's lungs with its intensity. "But why? *Why* would Hartsham want to harm your sister for helping prostitutes when Beatrice apparently had nothing at all to do with it? What could be gained by murdering Elise?"

"I don't know. But I'm damned well going to find out."

Fingers of worry played along her spine. "What are you going to do?"

"Whatever I have to in order to learn the truth." He stepped away from her, grabbed up the iron poker, and jabbed at the fire, and not because the fire needed to be stirred. If she weren't here, would he have taken out his anger with the weapons on the walls? The flaring glow of the fire lit his face and dark eyes, making him resemble the devil himself come from the fires of hell for vengeance. "Starting with Hartsham's whereabouts the night that Elise was killed."

Dread swelled coldly inside her. Already, the man was undoubtedly forming battle plans in his head. "Marcus, whatever it is that you're planning—"

"I'm not planning anything."

"And I'm a blue goose." She picked up one of the

stockings. "We don't have any real proof that Hartsham was involved. All we have are his wife's nervousness and my instincts, and I wouldn't place a bet on those, let alone accuse him of murder. The man's a peer."

"So am I." He jabbed the fire and sent a shower of sparks rising into the chimney. "You keep forgetting that."

Never. He wore the authority of the dukedom and his generalship like a second skin. "You cannot confront him about this."

"I don't plan on directly confronting him."

"And *in*directly?" she threw over her shoulder, knowing him too well.

He rested the poker against the side of the fireplace and turned to face her, his eyes darting immediately to the stocking in her hand. "Need help with those? I'm very good with stockings."

Her body heated with wanton desire, despite her knowing that he was simply attempting to charm her into distraction. For a moment, she nearly let him. "I'm fine on my own, thank you."

"Pity."

Ignoring that, she propped her foot on the edge of the settee. She struggled to ignore his gaze on her leg as she set about pulling on the stocking, but she couldn't forget how wonderful it had been when he'd removed them in the garden's shadows. Her throat tightened. Baring bodies proved to be so much easier than baring secrets and souls.

She pulled up her skirt to tie off the stocking around

her thigh, and her fingers shook beneath his stare. But she steered the conversation back to topic. "We can't be certain of Hartsham's involvement one way or the other. I think we should try to pry more information from Beatrice. I'm certain she knows more than she's sharing."

She switched feet and slipped on the second stocking. She'd never imagined that a man's stare could be so inviting. Or so torturous.

"So I'll approach her again." She tied off the stocking. Being so fully dressed in front of him now felt odd, especially since he wore only his trousers, his chest remaining deliciously bare. "I'll question her again on who else Elise might have been working with...innkeepers, pub owners, other men like Porter—"

"The hell you will."

She dropped her foot to the floor and faced him. The hardness of his expression stunned her.

"I will not let you put yourself into danger again."

"I won't be." The stone-cold look on his face must have terrified new recruits in the field. But *not* her. She smiled to reassure him. "I won't do anything more than talk."

"Like how you talked to her tonight?" He raked his hands through his hair, although she suspected that he did it to keep himself from shaking her. "For God's sake, Danielle! Someone tried to kill you." When she began to argue, he cut her off. "They've made the connection between you, Elise, and the women at the brothels."

Her blood turned cold.

"Anyone who was there tonight, who had a part in Elise's death, might have realized you were digging for answers. Perhaps the same men who broke into Charlton Place. Surely they saw the same panic on Lady Hartsham's face that you saw." His expression turned grim as he stroked his knuckles across her cheek. "Or they saw yours when you looked at me."

For once, there was no comfort in his touch. "But why? I don't know anything for certain."

"They won't wait to take the chance that you will." Worry and grief warred on his brow as he stared a hard warning into her eyes. "They'll silence you the same way they silenced Elise."

She swallowed, hard. The sickening sensation returned to the pit of her stomach.

He took her shoulders in his hands. "I care about you, Danielle." He hesitated, as if he were going to add something more, but then changed his mind with a faint shake of his head. "I couldn't bear it if you were hurt."

His soft concern spun through her on a churning wave of confusion and joy. Marcus cared about her, and more than simply because they'd been intimate tonight. A man like him knew how to separate his emotions from such intimacies, even if she found doing so to be simply impossible.

He pulled her into his arms and buried his face in her hair. "Promise me that you won't go anywhere near Hartsham."

She shook her head against his shoulder. "Only if you make me the same promise."

"I promise that we'll go after Hartsham together."

He punctuated that dodge with a kiss that grew in heat and intention until she sagged against him. She should have demanded more, made him pledge his word on his honor as an officer and gentleman—

But at that moment, when she had no idea where fate and the future would take them, she was happy simply to be in his arms. More than happy. Arousal began to quiver faintly inside her, and she couldn't resist placing a kiss to his neck. Then another against his bare shoulder. The hard muscle flexed deliciously beneath her lips. Then lower...

His hand drifted up her back and unfastened the tiny buttons. One by one as she continued to feather kisses across his chest, the buttons slipped free until her bodice hung loose over her bosom.

She slid her mouth away from his and eyed him teasingly with suspicion. "What are you doing?"

Nudging the strap of her chemise out of the way, he placed openmouthed kisses along her bared shoulder. "Right now, kissing you."

She shivered at the heated promise in his husky voice, that he planned on doing a lot more than just that. "So you watched me dress this entire time—helped me with the laces and buttons, in fact—only to undress me again." Her breath hitched when his hand slid beneath her bodice to cover her breast. "Why?"

He lifted his head from her neck and stared down at her as if she were a bedlamite. "If you're going to answer your own question, there's no point in asking it."

She bit back a happy laugh as his fingers at her neckline tugged down her corset and chemise, once again stretching out the neckline.

"But to answer you, I'm checking your stockings. A man needs to keep a close eye on his investments." He placed a kiss to the top of her breast and murmured rakishly against her flesh, "A *very* close eye."

"But my stockings aren't—" She gasped as he slipped his hand inside her corset. "There."

"Oh?" He caressed her nipple, rubbing it until it drew up taut and aching beneath his fingers and stirred the same aching between her legs. "Then perhaps you should show me where to find them."

She murmured wantonly, "Lower…"

With a devilish grin against her breast, he complied and lowered his hand down her front to caress her between the legs. "Here?"

She closed her eyes and gave over to his touch with a soft moan. "Close enough."

Twenty

"You look terrible."

Marcus cracked open an eye and stared past his valet, who was in the middle of shaving him, at Pearce as his old friend strode unannounced into his bedroom. "Good to know." Gesturing for his valet to continue removing the last of the two-day stubble, he closed his eyes again. "Because I also feel terrible."

Good Lord, did he ever. Last night with Danielle had exercised muscles that hadn't been used in far too many months, leaving him stiff and sore in all kinds of delicious ways. Ways that also left him filled with apprehension. He'd made love to Danielle, but Hartsham's presence still lingered over them, turning whatever joy they should have had from last night's intimacies into tangled uncertainty that grew with the light of day, until they'd both remained in preoccupied silence when he returned her to her town house.

Never had he felt more happy yet uneasy in his life—and damnably worried that Danielle would continue to put herself in danger, especially now that she thought she might gain answers about Elise, and that next time, he wouldn't be there to save her.

"Rough night on the town, eh?"

"You have no idea," he grumbled from beneath the layer of lather.

"Oh, I bet I have some idea of it." Amusement laced Pearce's voice. "One involving a certain petticoat, I'd wager. Did she discover that you'd put guards on her?"

"Far worse than that."

"Oh?"

"I intend to marry her."

Stunned silence greeted that announcement and filled the room until the valet finished the last stroke of the blade over his chin and handed him a towel to wipe away whatever stray traces of lather still clung to his face. Then his man deposited the shaving implements onto a tray and excused himself from the room, leaving the two of them alone to talk privately.

Pearce leaned against the wall, his arms crossed casually over his chest. But there was nothing casual about the hard set of his face. "That's an unexpected turn of events. What happened? Last I'd heard, you were dead set against marriage, especially with that one."

"Well, you know how courtship goes. Flowers, gifts…." Marcus turned his head back and forth to check the closeness of the shave in the mirror and ran his hand over his face. "Being shot at in Vauxhall Gardens."

Immediately concerned, Pearce pushed himself away from the wall. "Was she hurt?"

More than he wanted to admit as the memory of her tears pierced him. He shook his head. "Just a cut on her hand from taking a fall as we got away." He bent over the basin on the washstand to splash cold water onto his face. He wished he could have rinsed away the guilt of putting her into danger as easily as he rinsed away the soap. "She found answers about Elise, and someone tried to kill her for it."

As he dried his face with the towel, then pulled on the shirt the valet had left out on the bed, he explained the events of last night—heavily censoring all details related to what happened after they'd arrived at the armory. Not only wouldn't Marcus share that with Pearce, he didn't want to embarrass himself by thinking too much about how incredible it felt to have her in his arms, her body wrapped around his and mewling sounds of pleasure rising on her flushed lips. Even now, he wanted nothing more than to rush to her town house, strip off her clothes, and make love to her until she surrendered, until she agreed to stop putting herself in danger. Until she agreed to marry him.

First, though, he had to make certain that no one would ever try to harm her again.

"And you believe her?" Pearce pressed. "That the Earl of Hartsham was somehow involved with your sister's death?"

Marcus had seen the look on Danielle's face when the countess confessed about Elise. Her shock had been absolute. "I do."

But a look wasn't evidence of guilt. He had to prove the earl's involvement, one way or the other. And if the man were guilty, not even those pot-bellied, self-serving,

arrogant nodcocks in the Lords would be able to save
him from hanging. Marcus would make certain of it.

"And where is Miss Williams now?"

Marcus rolled up his left sleeve. "At home."

"I'll ask Merritt to double her guard."

"Thank you." But even though he trusted Merritt and
his men to keep her safe, posting guards was only a temporary solution. He needed to put a permanent end to
this, and he'd do it by picking up the investigation right
where she left off at Vauxhall. With the Earl of Hartsham.

"Are you in love with her?"

Marcus halted as he reached for his other sleeve. That
was a damnably fine, if unexpected, question. One he
had no intention of answering.

"I'm going to marry her," he dodged, "just as soon
as she agrees." *If* she agreed. He'd negotiated terms of
engagement many times with opposing forces, but this
time, he had a sinking feeling that he was on the wrong
end of the sword.

"Well then, congratulations." Pearce took a few steps
away to perch on the arm of the settee, once more crossing his arms over his chest. But this time, the stare he leveled on Marcus held no amusement whatsoever. "But are
you in love with the woman?"

"That's none of your concern," he answered firmly in
that voice he'd used with subordinate officers when he
didn't want his orders to be questioned.

He fumbled with the sleeve as he rolled it up his forearm. *Love…* For God's sake, how could he bring himself

to love her when she insisted on placing herself in harm's way? When he might lose her, too, just as he did Elise?

He had to find a way to convince her to stop working with Nightingale. He wouldn't survive if anything happened to her.

"It is my business if we have to use her to uncover more answers." Pearce's voice held a low warning. "If she's still keeping secrets from you."

"She isn't." Marcus trusted her more than any other woman he'd ever known. "And we won't use her like that. Not again."

"We might not have a choice." Pearce frowned. "We found out where John Porter worked. He was on the payroll there two years ago."

Marcus's hand stilled in midroll on his sleeve. His gaze darted to Pearce. "Where?"

"Venus's Folly. A brothel in Covent Garden. Merritt's there right now, trying to dig up more information. Ever hear of it?"

He shook his head and continued to dress, tugging on his braces over his shoulders from where they'd dangled around his hips. "There must be dozens of brothels in Covent Garden, and all of them changing their name on a regular basis."

"This one's special. Apparently, it caters to influential gentlemen—those with titles, wealth, judgeships, connections—and provides all kinds of entertainments. *All* kinds. All you have to do is ask and pay well, and they'll make whatever arrangements you want. Virgins, whips, ropes…" Pearce bit out, his anger and disgust barely hidden, "Children."

Good God.

"You name it, they'll arrange it, even right in your own home to avoid all that bother of having to travel to the brothel in the first place." Pearce paused. "Or to cover up any other unusual predilections you might have, including beating the woman half to death before tupping her." His voice turned mocking. "They'll cater to all your needs, General, from orgies to tamer pursuits."

Pearce's words triggered a memory in the back of Marcus's mind. Tamer…*tame.*

He wheeled around to face Pearce, a possible connection between Hartsham and Elise rearing its head like a viper. "Hartsham offered to make arrangements for me with women if I wanted them. And not so tame ones, in fact."

Pearce's eyes narrowed. "You think he's connected to the brothel?"

He was damned well going to find out. "Where's Porter? I want to speak to him."

"You can't."

Christ! He was tired of being told what he couldn't do. "He's the only person who knows for certain what Elise was—"

"He's dead."

The news struck the air from his lungs with the force of a punch. "When?"

"About four months ago. He was attacked in an

alley, his throat slit. His tongue was cut out and nailed to the wall above his dead body." Pearce arched a brow. "Whoever did it wanted to make a point."

"Apparently." Marcus yanked on his waistcoat but didn't bother with the buttons. "A murder like that didn't draw anyone's attention?"

"He'd been in prison several times, arrested for all kinds of crimes, including smuggling. He wasn't exactly one of England's finest. Who would notice a man like that, except the men he worked with?"

Elise. Because she'd been purposefully looking for someone with connections to the brothel and the women she wanted to help. Someone with exactly that kind of background. His head swirled with all the secrets she'd kept from him, and he struggled to find a way to sort through them all. "Was there a wife, a lover, landlord— anyone who might have known what he'd been doing with Elise? Anyone else we can talk to?"

Pearce dourly shook his head. "Most likely John Porter wasn't even his real name."

A dead witness…a dead end. Marcus bit down a harsh curse. "Then our only lead is the earl." He rubbed at the knot of frustration forming at his nape. "But why would he be involved with a brothel? What could he gain from it?"

"Blackmail," Merritt Rivers answered as he strode into the room, dressed head to toe in black and his boot heels making no sound against the floor. He eerily reminded Marcus of those ghost stories adults told children to make them behave, those tales of black wraiths who flew through forests at night under cover of darkness. Dressed as he was, with what was surely a brace of pistols beneath his greatcoat and a dagger up both sleeves, he could certainly be someone's nightmare.

Merritt nodded his greetings to Pearce, then tugged off his black gloves as his gaze settled on Marcus. "While Pearce was tracking down what happened to John Porter, I investigated the brothel. Their clientele might have been compromised."

Marcus puzzled, "Compromised—how?"

"I believe that someone's keeping records of select gentlemen—and even some ladies—who have made use of their special services. A thorough list with names, dates, and services rendered."

"What makes you think that?"

"I spoke to several of the women and found a pattern." Tucking his gloves inside his coat, Merritt leaned against the wall. "After every special service"—he didn't bother hiding the distaste in his voice—"the women are questioned, either by a stranger who pays them well for their information or enticed from them by the next gentleman who pays for their skills. They need the money, and they don't want problems with the clients, so they share what they know, including everything that was done and said. And I mean *everything*. Some of it's depraved enough to destroy lives if word of what these men have done is ever revealed."

Merritt blew out a harsh breath as if attempting to

shed the tarnish that now clung to him from uncovering what the women had done. Marcus understood. He felt the same layer of grime adhering to him.

Merritt continued, "But it's a different man who approaches the women every time, never giving his real name. Those men are nothing but agents for hire themselves, reporting the information back to whoever engaged them. No one knows who's keeping the list or why."

"Scepter," Marcus said quietly, every inch of him prickling with apprehension.

"Unlikely." Pearce shook his head as he crossed to the side table to help himself to the brandy. "Blackmail isn't something a criminal organization would normally do. Too much time and resources spent for too little profit."

"Pearce is right." Merritt's expression turned impenetrable, the same as it did whenever he stepped into court as a barrister. "All the blackmail cases I've seen have been the work of individuals, not organizations."

"An individual with ties to Scepter, then." Marcus's mind churned as it attempted to make all the connections between the brothel, Elise, and Hartsham. "The Earl of Hartsham—is he on that list?"

"There's no way to know."

Pearce eyed Marcus over the rim of his glass as he took a large swallow. "You think that's why he killed your sister? Because she found out what kinds of depraved services the earl had been requesting through the brothel, and he was afraid she'd tell his wife?"

"No," he muttered thoughtfully. "Lady Hartsham

already knew about his involvement with the prostitutes. That's how she knew the names of the women to give to Elise for rescue. I doubt he cared if she knew what he did with those women, but removing them from the brothel is a completely different matter and most likely the reason she's so terrified of him." He picked up his cravat and hung it around his neck. "It's one thing for a wife to know that you're spending your time enjoying prostitutes. But it's another thing altogether if that wife is actively working behind your back with her friends to stop you from doing it."

"So he found out that Elise was interfering with the prostitutes," Pearce summarized. "And killed her for it."

The same thing would happen to Danielle, too, if she didn't stop.

Except—

"Why would Hartsham care if he lost his favorite light skirt?" Marcus asked, desperate to force together the pieces of the puzzle but still unable to make them fit. "He could easily replace her, and immediately, too. London's filled with women desperate enough to do just about anything for money."

"Then he was worried your sister would tell more people besides his wife about what he was doing with those women," Pearce corrected.

"Elise couldn't reveal that without giving away how she learned of it, which meant she'd be betraying the women and men she was working with." Marcus shook his head. They were finally getting answers, but none of them were adding up. "She would never have done that."

No, he'd come to learn through Danielle how unquestionably loyal the women associated with Nightingale were. They would never put one another in danger. After all, Elise had kept her work secret from Danielle, and she had most likely gone to her grave because of it.

He glanced with a frown between the two men. "But Miss Williams has nothing to do with brothels and had no idea Elise was running her own network. So why come after Danielle Williams, and why now, after two years?"

"He's not," Merritt answered, his eyes grim. "He's coming after you."

Marcus froze. Only his heart moved, with a fierce pounding reminiscent of every time he'd charged into battle. "No. Danielle was attacked in the alley long before we knew of Hartsham's involvement in—"

"*After* you'd returned from the continent and began to pursue answers about your sister's death. After you waltzed with her at the party and then called on her at her home." Merritt shook his head. "If Hartsham suspected that Miss Williams had any information about the murder, he would have attempted to kill her to keep you from discovering the truth."

Pearce set down the empty glass. "And shot at you last night at Vauxhall after you'd learned what Lady Hartsham had told her. You're being watched, very closely, and whoever is doing it is keeping track of what you know and when you learn it."

"That's probably why your town house was broken into," Merritt added. "He wanted to discover how much you knew and to go through Elise's possessions in case anything incriminating had been left behind."

"And why Porter was killed four months ago," Pearce finished. "Right when you returned to London."

A sickening knot formed in Marcus's gut that *he* was the one responsible for putting Danielle's life at risk, that his family had been threatened because of him. Claudia—dear God, Pippa—

Christ. His blood turned to ice. In seeking justice for Elise, he'd endangered all of them. If anything happened to them because of him, he would never forgive himself.

"So we're back to the original question, then." Pearce strode forward to join the other two men. "What could Hartsham gain from it?" Standing in a triangle, they faced each other the way they'd done countless times before to discuss strategy before every battle. "Murder is an awfully excessive step to take just to keep rumors of debauchery from coming to light, even extreme ones."

"Unless it wasn't the debauchery he wanted to hide but the blackmail itself," Merritt deduced. "We've assumed that Hartsham was being blackmailed—or had done things worthy of blackmail—and wanted to keep her silent. But what if we're wrong?"

Pearce pondered, "If he's not being blackmailed—"

"Then he's likely the one who's doing the blackmailing," Marcus finished.

With that, all the pieces fell into place, and the three men stared at one another, their expressions bleak from the enormity of what they'd just determined.

After several long moments, Merritt broke the silence. "We're going to need evidence. Someone inside the brothel has to be giving Hartsham information about the men who come into the place so he knows which prostitutes to question."

"Or because he personally invited them to partake," Marcus said grimly. "The way he did with me. After all, who better to have on your list to be blackmailed than a new duke and former general?"

"It's not the name that matters, not when half the men in Parliament are publicly keeping mistresses and the other half regularly visit the stews," Merritt reminded them. "It's what's done with the women. And if Elise had spirited away some of the prostitutes who were providing the information he was using to create his blackmail list, then—"

"Then he would have murdered her to keep her from interfering, to keep his witnesses where he could control them." Pearce pinned him with a hard look. "And be on the hunt to kill you now because he's still keeping that list. When you refused his offer to arrange a prostitute, you quashed his chance to manipulate you. That's when he tried to kill you."

Marcus muttered, "He'll keep trying until he's stopped."

"So we stop him," Merritt assured him.

"Well then." Marcus grabbed up his jacket from the back of the settee and yanked it on. "It's time we begin."

Marcus clenched a cheroot between his teeth. "Hartsham."

As he strode up to the earl in the billiards room of White's, the man froze, his glass of port raised halfway to his mouth. His eyes flared wide in surprise.

Good. Always best to keep the enemy off guard. Although what Marcus had planned for this enemy wasn't an attack. It was a full-out massacre.

"There you are." Marcus slapped him good-naturedly—if a bit too hard—on the back and jostled the dark liquid in his glass. "I've been hunting you."

Despite how his face turned pale, Hartsham gave a stilted laugh at Marcus's purposeful slip of the tongue. "Hunting *for* me, you mean, I hope." He continued the slow lift of the glass to his lips. His drink hand visibly shook, while his other hand clenched around the billiard cue. "Call in the pack of hounds and the beaters, then. You've found me."

In the perfect place, too, surrounded by witnesses whose presence would prevent Marcus from murdering the bastard right there. "Wanted to give you my apologies for last night, for leaving the gardens so quickly without any goodbyes." He smiled tightly around the cigar. "And my gratitude for hosting the supper in my honor." *That* was the God's truth. If not for last night, he would never have known who to blame for Elise's murder. "It was good of you to introduce me to all those gentlemen. Knowing them will make working in Parliament much easier."

"That was the point." Hartsham relaxed only slightly but gestured for the other men at the table to continue the game without him. "You'll find that success in Westminster is all about making connections."

"Which is why I regret the way the evening ended." Marcus flicked the ash from his cigar onto the floor and ignored the scowl of the club manager. The man should be grateful that he was smoking. If his hand wasn't holding the cigar, it would have been around the earl's throat, and it wouldn't be ashes he'd be spilling on the floor but blood. "I was hoping to have one last word with everyone before we all departed." He paused and pointed his cigar at Hartsham. "Including you."

The man nervously took another sip of port. "Oh?"

"Yes, until Miss Williams ruined my plans." Marcus bit back a frustrated curse. "Daft woman became all hysterical when the fireworks went off. Thought people were shooting off guns." His mouth twisted in irritation. "Can you imagine—being stupid enough to confuse fireworks with gunfire?"

God help him if Danielle ever discovered the lies he was telling about her. The woman would flay him alive.

"I tried to explain to her that the sounds are completely different. For Christ's sake, I've been shot at enough times to know the difference. But did she trust the word of a general? Absolutely not." He laughed at

Danielle's expense. "Damnably flighty chit wouldn't listen to a word of reason. Insisted that I take her home, crying and carrying on as if the devil himself had appeared right there on the Grand Alley. What choice did I have except to escort her out? I didn't want her to make a scene right there in your supper box. Her father would have blamed me for the embarrassment, and I certainly don't need the diplomatic corps as enemies. You understand."

"Of course." Hartsham smiled coldly.

"After I delivered her home, I came back, but everyone was already gone and the gardens were closing down." Marcus shook his head. "Damn female hysterics... She cried all the way to her front door." He screwed up his face in distaste. "Not at all how I wanted to spend my evening." In actuality, Danielle had been in his arms. *Exactly* how he'd wanted to spend it. "So my apologies to you and your guests."

Hartsham's shoulders eased down, and he set the cue aside. "None necessary. I know how weak and simpering women can be."

Marcus said nothing. The bastard knew very little about women, or he'd have realized long before now that Danielle Williams was one of the strongest, most resilient people he'd ever met, in a skirt or trousers.

"Lady Hartsham and I will host a dinner for you soon in our home." The offer was polite but distant. Marcus knew he hadn't yet won over the man's confidence. "You can make up for lost conversation time with my friends then."

And give the earl an opportunity to put another target on his back? *Hell no.*

But Marcus smiled at the glowing tip of his cigar as he watched a tendril of smoke curl into the air. "Actually, there is something you can do for me. Something…a bit delicate."

"Oh?" *That* pricked the earl's interest.

"I've been thinking about our conversation from last evening." He purposefully turned his back to the room, indicating that he wanted their conversation to remain private. "I want to take you up on your offer."

"I'm pleased. I can always use another like-minded ally in Parliament, especially with the regent behaving like a tyrant who—"

"No." Marcus eyed him carefully over the cigar as he took a puff. "I meant the other offer." He lowered his voice. "About making arrangements for me."

Hartsham stiffened, his gaze narrowing on Marcus critically for a beat. Then he smiled brightly. "After Miss Williams's hysterics, I don't blame you for wanting an evening with a woman who knows how to behave around a man."

The earl had no idea of the irony behind that comment. Or how much Marcus wanted to pulp him for it. "You understand me perfectly." He smiled slyly as he toyed with the cigar in his fingers. "You said less tame pursuits. Did you truly mean it?"

"Of course." Hartsham took a sip of port. "If we wanted boring, we'd stay home and bed our wives."

Pretending to be unconvinced, Marcus shook his

head. "If what you're suggesting is that I venture to a brothel, you're mistaken. I'm too well-known now, too recognizable. I wouldn't feel at all free to do the things I'd truly enjoy doing, knowing that someone might be watching through a peephole or listening at the door." He lifted a brow and glanced around to make certain no one was eavesdropping even now. "It's one thing to tie a naked woman to a bedpost and whip her when you're a soldier in Spain or France. It's altogether different when you're a duke in London."

Despite the bile that rose in his throat at having to say that, Marcus kept his face carefully even and watched closely for Hartsham's reaction. He wasn't disappointed when the earl slapped him on the back.

"No need to worry." Hartsham grinned. "Arrangements can be made to bring the girl right to your bedroom." When Marcus couldn't keep his expression from hardening at that idea, Hartsham added hastily, "Or to wherever you'd like."

"No girl. I want a woman. Someone very much experienced and not at all hesitant to carry out whatever I suggest, understand?" Someone who might have participated in blackmailing other peers and high-ranking officials. "And no pox-ridden wench in worsted wool either. I've come up in the world. I want a creature who's at home in silk and lace, educated, well-spoken…" A woman other gentlemen would have requested. "Not a common moll but a true courtesan."

Hartsham's eyes gleamed, reminding Marcus of a

crocodile that was watching his prey draw nearer the water's edge. "Where should I have this special woman delivered?"

Marcus thought a moment. "The Earl of Sandhurst's town house on St James's Square. Pearce still owes me for his last promotion." He flicked more ash onto the floor and smiled, apparently delighted at the idea of doing anything he pleased, wherever he pleased. Even something debauched in his best friend's town house. Good God, if English peers truly behaved like this with one another, he was ready to run back to France. "I'm sure he won't mind giving the place up to me for the night."

"Women can be sent to entertain him as well, if he's interested."

He feigned sudden suspicion. "How are you gaining access to all these women, exactly?"

"I have connections in Covent Garden, at a little place called Venus's Folly."

"With whom?"

"The right men." Hartsham finished off his port in one swallow, set the empty glass aside on a nearby table, and picked up his cue to return to the game. "England's changed since you've been gone, in all kinds of new and interesting ways." He arched a brow in subtle warning. "When it comes to these kinds of arrangements, Duke, it's best not to ask too many questions."

No...all the way to the gallows. "Then contact me when arrangements have been made. And, Hartsham, I expect absolute silence and confidentiality about this."

"Of course." Hartsham smiled. "You have my word as a gentleman."

Worthless. Marcus tossed what was left of the cigar into the fireplace and turned on his heel. He stalked through the club and straight out the door, keeping his gaze fixed straight ahead.

Outside, his carriage waited in front of the club. Aware of the view from the bay window for those men watching from the dining room, he kept his face inscrutable as the tiger opened the door for him and he stepped up into the dark compartment.

"Go!" he ordered the driver.

He closed the door and sat back against the squabs, staring out the window at the dark city as the carriage lurched to a start and rolled down St James's Street. He felt filthy and wanted nothing more than a hot bath to wash Hartsham away.

"It's done, then?"

Marcus swung his gaze to Clayton Elliott sitting on the opposite bench. "He's going to contact me when final arrangements have been made. He's working with the women at Venus's Folly. We were right about that."

And about the blackmail. Hartsham had snatched up the opportunity to compromise Marcus far too quickly otherwise.

"You think he believes you about Vauxhall?"

"I think he doesn't care as long as he has the chance to blackmail me and bring me under his control." He turned back toward the window and muttered, "A live duke under his power and doing his bidding is better than a dead one in the churchyard."

And one who still had no undisputable proof that Hartsham had murdered his sister.

"And Scepter?" Clayton asked.

"He didn't mention it, but I couldn't press for answers as hard as I would have liked." Not without giving everything away. He had to make the man trust him enough to deliver the woman. "We have to assume that he's involved with Scepter. We just don't know why or how."

Even Clayton hadn't been able to turn up much more information about them except that they were a ruthless organization haunting London's underworld. Like an octopus, their tentacles stretched into all kinds of illegal activity, including brothels, but their criminal activity had been unlike any the Home Office had ever seen. As if they weren't concerned with money but in stretching their net as far as possible and not at all fearing the authorities.

Marcus was beginning to think that John Porter's warning to Elise to avoid Scepter was simply that—a warning to steer clear.

It was Hartsham who'd murdered her to cover up the lists he was keeping. And the man who would pay dearly for it.

"Once the woman is delivered," Clayton assured him, "then we find out what she knows and follow her back to Hartsham. At that point, we'll have enough proof of wrongdoing that my men can search his properties for evidence of blackmail."

Marcus nodded. They would catch him in the act of extortion, and the last links to Elise's murder would fall into place. If the names on Hartsham's client list were the ones they both believed them to be, then the majority of peers in the Lords would find him guilty just to keep their own secrets from being revealed.

He would watch the bastard swing by his neck if it was the last thing he did.

"And Miss Williams?"

"She'll be told later," Marcus assured him. "Once it's all done." Once she was out of danger.

"If you do this without her," Clayton warned, like Pearce and Merritt knowing all that had happened since his return to London—*almost* all, "she'll be furious at you."

"Then she'll be furious." He turned back toward the window and muttered, "But she'll also be alive."

And he'd finally have justice for his sister.

One way or another.

Twenty-One

BALANCING HER CUP AND SAUCER IN ONE HAND, DANI smiled at the ladies gathered inside Lady Balfour's yellow drawing room the next afternoon and made her way toward the side buffet table where plates of biscuits, sandwiches, and cakes had been set out. She placed a biscuit on the edge of her saucer, right next to the other two she'd already taken when admonished by Lady Balfour that she wasn't eating enough.

Enough? She hadn't eaten at all. Heavens! How could she possibly think of food when all she could think about was Marcus?

He made her happy, certainly, more than she'd ever thought possible. When she was with him, she felt free to laugh and be herself in a way she'd never been able to do in the company of any other man. And being in his arms...oh, simply divine!

But all that happiness he brought her couldn't prevent the niggling doubt that whispered a warning from the back of her mind that all this was merely temporary. That once Hartsham was arrested and Elise's ghost could rest in peace, Marcus would no longer need her. That there would be no reason to spend time together, and whatever affections he held for her would undoubtedly fade.

When no one was looking, Dani carefully set all the biscuits back onto the tray.

Around her, the ladies of the Foundling Hospital's Women's Charity and Guidance Committee drank tea, nibbled on impossibly small sandwiches and tiny cakes, and spent more time gossiping than discussing the children they were there to help. Not one of them realized that Dani's entire world had changed.

Not even Claudia Braddock.

Marcus's sister currently stood on the other side of the room, surrounded by a group of women and chatting away about her engagement and plans for her wedding. So far, Dani had managed to dodge her this afternoon. Whenever she'd seemed about to approach, Dani skillfully maneuvered herself away to another group of ladies or to the sideboards for more tea or another untouched biscuit. Her diversions had worked, and Claudia hadn't been able to capture her alone, to corner her into a conversation about Marcus. Dani didn't think she could get through it without her expression giving away exactly what she and Marcus had done. Or her uncertainty over what would happen next.

But she only had a little while longer yet to keep on her toes. With the tea winding down and several of the ladies beginning to say their goodbyes, she would soon be able to slip away from Claudia completely with nothing more than a kiss on her cheek and a promise to call on her and Pippa soon.

Easier said than done, though. Even in the middle of

explaining how she wanted a wedding breakfast with a Venetian theme, Claudia's attention would wander across the room to Dani, and she'd frown in perplexed concern.

But Dani didn't have the heart to confess anything to Marcus's sister, certainly not her feelings for him, and plastered on a bright smile that belied the roiling knot of emotions inside her.

"Oh, isn't the food simply divine?" Mrs. Peterson reached past Dani for another biscuit. "I plan on asking Balfour's cook for all the recipes. Do you think she'd mind sharing? Oh, of course not! She'd be thrilled to be asked, I'm certain." She jabbed the biscuit in the air to punctuate her point as she scurried away to return to the group of ladies near the bay window who had been discussing hosting a garden party for the group's next event. "You really must have another one of these cinnamon bites!"

"Yes," a voice said from behind Dani. "You really must."

Claudia.

Forcing her brightest smile, Dani turned to face her. "Actually, I think I might ask for the recipes myself so that—"

"You've been avoiding me," Claudia accused in hushed tones so the two of them wouldn't be overheard. But the other ladies had gotten into a squabble over plans for the organization's next meeting and were too caught up in that to care what the two of them might be discussing. "As Marcus says, if the enemy won't march to you, then you have to march to the enemy."

Not letting her smile fade, she dropped her gaze to her teacup. "So I'm the enemy now."

Claudia's shoulders sagged. "That's not at all what I mean. The exact opposite, in fact. But you haven't been to Charlton Place since the dinner. We need you there, Danielle, and I don't mean just for the wedding planning." She tapped the edge of Dani's saucer to capture her attention. "Marcus needs you."

She couldn't stop the short laugh that fell from her lips. "Your brother doesn't need anyone."

"More than you realize." Claudia shook her head in bewilderment. "What on earth is going on between you two?"

"I don't know what you mean." But Dani's traitorous cheeks flushed hot, and she had to take a long sip of her now-cold tea to hide as much of her blush as possible.

"Oh, I think you do," Claudia muttered knowingly. "Since his return last winter, Marcus has been absolutely insufferable. He's barely home at all, and when he is, he's mostly sullen and grim, except when he's with you. Then he has a spark of life in him, as if he's back on the battlefield and ready to charge after victory for all he's worth. But when he isn't with you, he spends his time pacing in his study and sorting through Elise's things in her room, as if hunting for something he's lost." She bit her bottom lip. "I think that *you* are that something he's hunting."

Dani choked on her tea and squeaked out between coughs. "*Pardon*?"

"I'm not a nodcock, Danielle. I've seen the way that man looks at you, how his entire demeanor changes when you're near—how he spent every minute of that supper with Adam, your aunt, and me pretending that he wasn't completely captivated by you. And the way he looks at you whenever you're with Pippa…" She looked away as her voice trailed off, but not before Dani saw the glistening in her eyes. "I thought before that he needed a sense of purpose in his life. But I was wrong. What he needs is so much more than that."

"He needs time to find—"

"He needs *you.*"

Dani paused for one brutally painful beat, so desperately wishing that were true. Then she repeated, reality slicing at her belly, "He doesn't need anyone."

"He does. He's just too proud to admit it."

Her shoulders fell in exasperation. "You don't know that."

"I do. In your heart, you know you do, too." Claudia clasped Dani's hand. "Please—come visit us at Charlton Place." She paused meaningfully. "Better yet, find a way to be there permanently."

Her throat tightened with emotion. "Claudia, what you're implying—"

"Yes, I know. But if you're at Charlton Place, then maybe he'll be there, where he belongs, instead of haunting that old armory."

Dani's gaze flew up to hers. She whispered, "You know about the armory?"

"I bribed our coachman to find out where he'd been the night when he didn't return from Vauxhall. In the past, he would come home to tuck Pippa into bed, then go off again somewhere, usually not returning until dawn. But he always came home. Until the night he went for supper at Vauxhall." Claudia smiled conspiratorially, not at all surprised that Dani knew of the armory. "Until *you* were with him."

She didn't know whether to blush or turn pale.

"I was beginning to think that place was just like his heart—impenetrable...unless you know how to get inside." Claudia reached into her reticule and withdrew a key, then took Dani's hand to press it into her palm and close her fingers around it. "This is a key to the armory." Her eyes sparkled. "And you are the key to his heart. So unlock it, please. Bring him peace and save him from himself."

Dani folded her fingers protectively over the key. "It isn't that simple."

"But it is. I know my brother. He thinks that life should be run like an army, with clear choices between right and wrong, definitive answers to every problem, and the enemy always easy to identify. It frustrates him to no end that the world doesn't really work that way. So whatever you do, don't let him treat you like a soldier. Stand up to him. Don't let him order you about. And make him realize that he loves you, which the rest of us already know."

Dani stared at her, struck speechless. She'd greatly

underestimated Claudia Braddock's audacity. And her intuitiveness.

When a group of women called out for Claudia, chattering on about using the gardens at Charlton Place for their next luncheon, she kissed Dani's cheek and left to rejoin them.

"I can't do that," she breathed out after her, so softly that she was certain that Claudia couldn't hear as she walked away. How could she make him do that when all he wanted was to keep waging war? Even in matters of love.

She set down her unwanted tea on a nearby card table before her shaking hands could spill it. Then she squeezed shut her eyes for a moment's peace to gather herself.

"Danielle, are you all right?" Beatrice McTavish, Lady Hartsham, sidled up to her and gripped her elbow. Concern darkened the woman's face.

Dani obligingly smiled, pushing down the sharp bite of betrayal that sparked inside her from their last conversation at Vauxhall. Despite all that Beatrice had done by hiding information about Elise, the woman truly was sympathetic. "Only a bit of a headache. Too much tea and biscuits, I fear."

That lie did nothing to ease Beatrice's concern. "Are you sure? You left so suddenly the other night at Vauxhall, and without a parting word, too. Mrs. Slater said you'd suddenly taken ill and needed to leave. She gave us your apologies."

Oh, Dani could have kissed that woman! Apparently, she'd found a kindred spirit in Mrs. Slater.

Beatrice's mouth twisted, and nervously, she lowered her voice. "It was what I said about Elise, wasn't it? I upset you."

The woman had no idea how much.

"Nothing at all like that." *No, it involved murder, lies, and your husband…* Shifting the key to her other palm, Dani held up her injured hand with its bright pink scar across her palm, and chagrin twisted her face. "When the fireworks started, I foolishly rushed outside to view them, tripped, and cut my hand." *All the while being shot at and fleeing for my life…* "His Grace insisted that he escort me away to have it immediately tended to." *Only to spend the night ravishing me…* "It was quite the evening. Truly." *Truly.*

Beatrice frowned. "But His Grace claimed that you'd left because the fireworks had upset you. That you thought you'd heard gunfire. I told my husband that the duke must have been wrong, that you'd never be that silly."

"No." She forced a smile. "Never."

Beatrice let out a hard sigh of relief and smiled. "Thank goodness it wasn't anything I said. As I told you, it's been so long since Elise died, and I simply don't remember anything specific from that time, except how horribly shocked I was. How we *all* were, including Hartsham." Her hands fidgeted with her skirt. "If I gave you any other impression than that, I am sorry for the misunderstanding. That was not at all my intention."

"Of course not." Dani was certain it wasn't. As anxious as the woman was, she would never intentionally implicate her husband. But she'd given away enough that Dani knew for certain that the earl had played a part in Elise's death. The question now was…how much?

Beatrice glanced apprehensively at the rest of the group to make certain none of the ladies were paying the two of them any mind. "But I'm glad that you brought up Elise, actually."

Dani's pulse stuttered. "Oh?"

"I've heard about a girl," she whispered. "One from the brothels, who needs to be rescued."

Dani bit back a guilty groan. "Beatrice, please—"

"Her name is Jenny," Beatrice rushed out. "She was drugged and taken from her family in Manchester, right from the mill where she worked and with the blessing of the mill's owner, just a few days ago. She's going to be forced into prostitution at a brothel in Seven Dials called the House of Delights. She needs your help."

"We can't. Nightingale doesn't have—"

"Elise would have rescued her."

The accusation pierced Dani like a blade, and her wounded hand went to her chest to physically press down the swirling emotions aching inside her. Yes, exactly the kind of girl Elise would have rescued…only to die doing so. To take that kind of risk—she could never ask the other women in the network to put their lives in danger like that.

"We don't vanish women from the brothels. You

know that," she said as firmly as she could, only to sound incredibly weak to her own ears. "It's too dangerous. And if this is the same place where Elise was working to rescue the women, then…" Then it was also deadly.

"It isn't. Elise vanished girls from brothels far more dangerous than this one." Beatrice looked offended. "I would *never* ask you to do something like that. Elise shouldn't have done that either."

"And your husband?" She fought to keep the anger and bitterness from her voice. "What part is he playing in this?"

"None at all. I heard about the girl from Elaine Slater."

Unease pricked at the backs of her knees. "Mrs. Slater knows about Nightingale?"

"No. She knows that I still have acquaintances in the mills in Manchester and thought I could help. That's why she mentioned the girl to me. Her husband returned from his trip to the midlands and told her that he'd heard rumors about this girl. Elaine knows nothing about Nightingale."

Knowing that Hartsham had nothing to do with this didn't ease the sting of frustration and helplessness at what Beatrice was asking of her. "Nightingale personally removes every woman to make certain nothing goes wrong when she leaves, and we can't do that at a brothel. We simply don't have access to the women when they're behind those walls."

A desperate worry distorted Beatrice's features. "Not even if you send inside one of your hired men to fetch her out for you? Surely no one would notice a man like that entering the house and asking about a specific girl. Once she's away from the brothel, you can vanish her as usual." Her eyes turned pleading. "I can't do this myself, Danielle, or I would. I've never done a vanishing. I don't have access to the network or its resources—I wouldn't even know how to hire men like the ones you use. I need Nightingale's help."

Beatrice's plan might work. Dani could ask Jenkins to do it and pay him to be responsible for every aspect of the vanishing, from start to finish, from the time he removed the girl from the brothel until he took her out of London and back to Manchester. She'd never asked this of him before, but he'd been working with her long enough that she trusted him to accomplish it. And keep his silence.

But there were lines she'd sworn never to cross, and if she attempted to rescue this girl, she wouldn't simply be stepping over that line—she'd be obliterating it. The need to protect the network warred inside her with the desire to help, just as it did with every vanishing lately.

"I—I have to think about it," she dodged answering. "I want to help, but…"

"There isn't time. That's why I'm coming to you now." Beatrice grabbed her arm and held her tightly, not letting her walk away. "She's been auctioned off."

"Auctioned?" A sickening hollow began to burn in the pit of Dani's stomach. Selling virgins to the highest bidder…an all too common and depraved practice. Yet it still shocked her.

"For her virginity." Her expression darkened with disgust and helplessness. "She's scheduled to be delivered in only a few days. She *has* to be rescued before then."

In so little time? Impossible! "I can't hire someone that quickly." Or make proper arrangements for the girl's disappearance once she was out of the brothel. Every bit of this would be impromptu, and Dani had never allowed that to happen before. She'd always protected the people who had worked with her and the women they'd rescued by meticulously planning everything down to the last detail, planning that often took weeks. "Beatrice, what you're asking—"

"I know. But, Danielle, she's only twelve." She swiped a hand at her eyes. "The same age as my daughter. How do I look at Anne every day, knowing that there is another girl out there, just like her, who is going to be raped? As a mother, how can I not try to save her?" Her watery gaze fixed accusingly on Dani. "How can you not?"

Guilt seared through her. "I—I have to think about it," she repeated, far more softly this time.

Beatrice nodded faintly as disappointment clouded her face, and she turned away as if she couldn't bear to look at Dani. "I understand."

"No, you don't—I want to help, but that's all I can promise right now." She reached out to squeeze Beatrice's arm. "But I *will* contact you as soon as a decision has been made."

"Thank you." Beatrice glanced down at Dani's damaged hand, and her expression turned troubled. "Take care of yourself. I don't want you to be hurt."

Dani's heart tugged, believing her. "I will. I just—"

She stopped. *Her hand.* The warning about Marcus that had been niggling at the back of her mind now began to scream.

"Beatrice, you said that His Grace claimed that I'd been upset by the fireworks… When did you speak to him? Did you run into him out somewhere in Mayfair?"

"Heavens, no. You know how reclusive the man has become."

She was beginning to suspect that she didn't know him at all…

"He met up with Hartsham at the club the next afternoon."

Dani flashed numb, all the way to the tips of her fingers and toes, only for the sensation to be instantly replaced by something much harsher. By betrayal. Marcus had promised they'd go after Hartsham together.

His duplicity burned in her veins. "*He* met up with Hartsham?"

Beatrice nodded. "So he could apologize for leaving the gardens without giving his goodbyes. But it makes sense now."

"Yes, it does." In a very anger-inducing way.

"His Grace wanted to protect you."

"Apparently, even now," Dani bit out. And enough for Marcus to maneuver behind her back to catch Hartsham by himself. *I promise that we'll go after Hartsham together…* Oh, she'd been such a fool to believe him!

Beatrice frowned. "Pardon?"

"Nothing." She clenched the key in her hand as she turned to leave. "If you'll excuse me, I have a battle to wage."

Twenty-Two

"MISS! I INSIST! YOU SIMPLY CANNOT—" THE BUTLER'S voice was drowned out by the angry stomp of feet.

At the unexpected commotion in the hall, Marcus glanced up from the stack of correspondence on his desk that he was sorting through as a way to distract himself from the fact that Hartsham had yet to send word about the woman he'd asked for. Pippa was in the park with Mrs. Davenport, and Claudia was out at a charity event of some kind. For once, he had the house to himself.

Or had, until Danielle appeared in the doorway of his study, flushed of face and breathing hard enough that her breasts heaved beneath her bodice with every breath she took.

He leaned back in his chair. Well. *This* was certainly a distraction. Of the very best kind.

"Your Grace." The flummoxed butler peered over her shoulder into the room in apology. "I asked her to wait in the drawing room to be announced, but she—"

"Refused," Danielle finished, that single word silencing the man in midsentence.

Quashing a grin at her audacity, Marcus rose to his feet. He was happier to see her than he wanted to admit. Especially since he hadn't laid eyes on her since he'd returned her home two days ago, that morning after Vauxhall.

But he also didn't want her anywhere near Charlton Place. He didn't dare risk that Hartsham would find out how much she meant to him and use that against them.

She came forward into the room with the butler following at her heels like a terrier.

Marcus frowned. This was completely out of character for her. Something was wrong. "Danielle—"

"How dare you go behind my back!"

Definitely wrong.

Calmly, Marcus gestured to the butler to leave them, but as the man retreated into the hallway and closed the double doors behind him, he sent Marcus a worried glance—perhaps fearing for Marcus's safety. At the way both of her hands clenched into tiny fists at her sides, Marcus didn't blame the man for being wary.

"Are you all right?" he asked as he stepped around the desk to approach her.

Her eyes blazed. "I thought we were working together."

"We are." He removed her bonnet and tossed it onto one of the chairs in front of his desk, then took her shoulders in his hands. "Danielle," he repeated pointedly, "are you all right?"

"Yes, I am." But before he could lean in to bring his mouth to hers and give her the kiss he longed for, she interjected, "But we're not."

He flinched at her double meaning.

Their lips were so close that hers brushed his with

every word. "*Not* when you approach Hartsham by yourself."

So this was why she was here. The realization washed over him like ice water. He released her shoulders and stepped back.

"You said I could trust you." Emotion grated in her voice. She shook her head. "Lies, all of it."

He clenched his teeth. "That was *not* a lie."

"Well, it certainly wasn't trust! I offered to speak to Beatrice, to learn more before we went after Hartsham. You absolutely refused to let me, said it was too dangerous—"

"Because it was."

She arched a brow. "But not dangerous for *you* to approach Hartsham?"

"That isn't the same thing."

She folded her arms over her chest. "From where I'm standing, it's exactly the same."

"From where *I'm* standing, not at all. For one thing," he drawled, crossing the study to the cabinet in the corner where he kept his finest liquor, "the Home Office has given me its help." He needed a stiff drink. Apparently, so did she.

"Lovely." The anger inside her was palpable. "However, you had *my* help from the very beginning, yet you met with Hartsham without even telling me."

"Because I couldn't tell you."

She gave him a look of betrayal so dark that it shivered into him. "You kept this from me, after I told you everything about Nightingale, after I gave you Beatrice's name—Dear God, Marcus!" Her voice lowered to an anguished whisper. "After I made love to you."

Frustration twisted in his gut. He fought back the urge to dash back to her, grab her into his arms, and prove to her right there on the rug in front of the fire how much she meant to him.

"I never lied to you." He passed over the cognac for whiskey, preferring something with bite for this conversation. "But I sure as hell don't regret not telling you because it was the only way to ensure that you'd be safe." He splashed the golden liquid into the glass. "So if you want to believe that I've betrayed you in that, then so be it. But I would do it again in a heartbeat."

She pulsed visibly with anger. "You had no right to keep this from me."

"To keep you from being killed like Elise? *Every* right." He shoved the crystal stopper back onto the decanter. "And let's be very clear about one thing."

He crossed the room to her, coming to a stop directly in front of her and driving his gaze into hers so there would be no misunderstanding about this.

"Making love had absolutely nothing to do with Hartsham. We made love because we wanted to share that pleasure with each other. *No* other reason."

"I wish that were true." Her face flushed scarlet, but she held her ground and didn't turn away. "But the only reason we were together that night was because of Hartsham. You've only sought me out since your return to London because of Elise."

"Yes, I sought you out because of Elise. But that is not the only reason why I keep finding excuses to be in your presence." He swirled the whiskey in the glass to keep his hands busy so that he wouldn't reach for her. Although whether to shake sense into her or strip her bare, at that moment he couldn't have said. "Once we've caught Hartsham, I very much plan on asking to formally court you."

Her mouth fell open in a surprised O, as round as her eyes.

"Until then, however, you need to let me do what needs to be done to both find justice for Elise and to protect you." He held out the glass to her as a peace offering. "And trust me."

Her hand shook as she accepted the glass and raised it silently to her lips.

"I didn't tell you that I'd sought out Hartsham because you can't be anywhere near the trap we're setting for him," he explained.

She wiped her whiskey-wet lips with the back of her hand. "What trap?"

He took back the whiskey. "I've arranged for him to deliver a woman from the brothel to me, to Brandon Pearce's town house. Once she's there, Clayton Elliott will question her, and we'll gather enough information for Home Office agents to search Hartsham's properties for more evidence of blackmail, which will hopefully be enough to arrest him." Staring down into the glass, he couldn't look at her as he explained, "But Hartsham has to believe I'm in earnest about committing all kinds of debauched activities with this woman, the kind that he could use to blackmail me, or it won't work. The presence of a society lady like yourself would undermine all of that."

Worse. If Hartsham had spies watching her or the house, he would know that she came here to speak to him—*him*, not Claudia, whom his men would have known was away for the afternoon. Her presence here was already enough to scuttle their plan and convince Hartsham that Marcus had lied to him, that he was being herded into a snare. If the earl realized it, he would slip away before they could capture him.

Eagerness shone on her face. "I want to help with—"

"Absolutely not. You are to stay away from Hartsham and Charlton Place until it's all over, understand?" He cupped her face in his palm to punctuate his words as he added solemnly, "And I want you to stop working with Nightingale."

She smiled to reassure him, but he wasn't at all put at ease when she said, "There's no reason to pause the network's activities. Nightingale won't be in your way. Hartsham has nothing to do with us. Beatrice hasn't been involved for months, and whomever Elise was helping, that was two years ago and—"

He silenced her with a touch of his lips to hers. "Not pause," he corrected, caressing her jaw with his thumb to ease the sting of what he was asking of her. "Stop it completely."

A haunting look of betrayal crossed her beautiful face. She repeated his words back to him, "Absolutely not."

She backed away from him, and he felt the growing distance opening like a chasm between them. But there was no help for it. He *would* keep her safe. At all costs. Including Nightingale.

Not breaking eye contact, she gave a faint shake of her head. "I'm sorry, Marcus, but I won't do that."

"Damnation, Danielle!" Frustration burned in his gut that she so adamantly kept putting herself into harm's way. "Someone wants us dead, and we're not certain that Hartsham is working by himself. He might very well have connections to Scepter. Your work with Nightingale is causing problems for him—for *them*—and they want to end it by putting you into the ground, the same way they ended my sister." Her eyes glistened when he added hoarsely, "They'll succeed, too, unless you stop."

The blood drained from her face, taking with it that beautiful flush in her cheeks. "What you're asking me to do...I can't," she whispered. "I won't do—"

"Why?" he demanded. Concern swelled inside him so strongly that he pulsed with it, along with a growing sensation he wasn't at all used to—helplessness. "*Why* are you so set on endangering yourself? You're willing to sacrifice your reputation, your position—for God's sake, your *life*—"

"Because of Harriett!" she blurted out, the words coming in a tumbling, angry rush. "I'm doing this because of my aunt and all the women like her."

That stunned him, and he loosened his hold enough that she could pull her arm away and step back. She stared at him as if she couldn't believe herself what she'd just admitted to him.

He waited silently for an explanation, but then dreaded it when it finally came.

"The viscount used to beat her." The intensity of her whisper matched the fierceness of her cry only moments before. "Sometimes so badly that she couldn't get out of bed."

Emotions warred inside him, disbelief at what she was saying yet an overwhelming need to trust her. He treaded carefully by countering gently, "I knew Viscount Bromley. He was a good man."

"They all are." Bitterness dripped off her tongue. "In public. Around their friends and society acquaintances. Even in front of the servants. They never leave marks anywhere anyone might see, are always so careful to hide what they've done. Long-sleeved dresses and buttoned-up spencers can hide so very much…" She jabbed up her chin as the frustrated anger inside her grew visible. "Even if they make a mistake and in their anger strike a blow somewhere visible, the women will claim they were clumsy and knocked into a piece of furniture, tripped on a path, burned themselves while stirring up a fire…"

As the words strangled in her throat, he saw her swelling tears, and he ached for her. "Danielle—"

"That good man you knew beat Harriett to within an inch of her life."

When he froze at the harshness of that, she took the glass of whiskey from him and drank down a large swallow, one that left her coughing and the back of her hand pressed to her lips.

She blinked hard to gather herself before she continued. "He'd been beating her for years, since shortly after they'd married, but she couldn't leave him—she had no property or money of her own to live on," she rasped out between her fingers, her hand still pressing at her lips. "All that transferred to the viscount. As it does with all women, in all marriages." Her voice lowered to a rasping whisper, so intense that it twined around his spine with every word. "And the Church was culpable when they told her that her role as a wife was to be subjugated to her husband, to obey him in all things...when they told her that her husband wouldn't beat her if she were a better wife."

Her hand shook so badly that the remaining whiskey splashed in the glass. She had to close both hands around it to keep it still.

"Divorce was impossible," she continued quietly. "It takes an act of Parliament, which means money and connections, and what woman has enough of either of those to secure one? Even then, a man can divorce his wife on grounds of adultery, but a wife has to prove not only adultery but also cruelty. What woman wants to bring even more shame and anguish upon herself by publicly admitting that her husband not only committed adultery but also beat her?" She raised the glass to her lips for a comforting swallow. "How does a woman even prove grounds for cruelty at all when English law gives a husband the right to beat his wife?"

"There are no laws that make that legal," he interjected quietly. "Those men are not protected in the courts."

"There are no laws that make it *illegal* either." Her hand clenched the glass so tightly that her fingers turned white. "Show me a man anywhere in England who was sentenced to gaol for beating his wife. I dare you to, because I know you can't."

She set the glass onto the desk, then buried her shaking hands in her skirt. It ripped his heart in two that she wouldn't let herself reach for him and the comfort he could give her. That he knew she would push him away if he tried.

"Husbands are seldom arrested for wife beating, and if they are, then the judges always find in favor of the husband. They rule that it's the husband's right as a male guardian to beat a woman in his care if she deserves it." A bitter laugh at the brutal absurdity of that fell from her lips. "If she *deserves* it…as if any living creature deserves to be abused! As if women are nothing more than animals to be beaten into submission, until they either die or their spirit breaks completely. Good God! How do we continue to let this happen?" She gestured in frustration at him. "We wage war against French tyrants but let Englishmen reign unchecked within our own houses!"

Her slender shoulders sank under an invisible weight,

as if the mere thought of why she was doing all this was enough in itself to defeat her.

"Not just wives but daughters, sisters, aunts… So many women! We have no idea how many are suffering in silence and fear. Harriett was one. I suspect that Beatrice is another." She met his somber gaze, admitting, "I could be one, if I make the same mistake and choose the wrong man to marry. One who hides what he's really like or who changes after we're wed."

He slowly approached her and tilted up her chin with his fingers. The sight of glistening unshed tears of anger and frustration—and pain—stabbed into him.

"Is that why you haven't married yet," he asked gently, "because you're afraid you'll marry a man who will abuse you?"

"No. But that's always a risk, though, isn't it, in a world where men possess all the power and strength, where women have only what men grant them? Every woman who isn't a fool fears that even just a little when she walks down the aisle. How could she not?"

He held his face inscrutable as he murmured, "The man who marries you would never do that."

She squeezed shut her eyes. "Oh, how I wish I could believe that!"

"You can," he assured her, every word a promise. "Because that man is going to be me."

———

Her eyes flew open, and his determined expression nearly undid her. Suddenly, she couldn't breathe, couldn't speak—all she could do was gape at him while the world rose and plunged around her. He couldn't have actually said…

"*Pardon?*"

Chuckling at her reaction, he slipped his arms around her waist to tug her against him. His pulse pounded so furiously that she could feel it throbbing into her until she couldn't tell where his heartbeat ended and hers began.

"I love you." He said that as simply as if he were commenting upon the weather, completely unaware of the twisting emotions those words sparked inside her. His lips brushed against her temple. "Marry me, Danielle."

Her hands tightened on his shoulders as she struggled to find her voice to answer. Since she was a girl, she'd dreamt of hearing those words from him, let herself fantasize about what it would be like to have his love—

She'd not divulged the truth a few moments ago. *He* was the reason she'd not yet married. How could she pledge her life to another when she'd already fallen in love with him? But not once in all those years of fantasizing about this moment had she ever imagined this much pain and confusion. Because she knew the truth. He wanted more than marriage. He also wanted the end of Nightingale.

The ultimatum he was unwittingly giving her sliced through her chest like a blade and into her heart that even now pounded with foolish desire to agree, to accept his love, to be his wife…

She summoned every bit of her strength as she stepped out of his arms and whispered the soft challenge, "If you loved me, you wouldn't ask me to give up Nightingale." She blinked hard and fast. Damn those tears! "You would help me with it instead."

His face darkened, his jaw clenched hard. "I will *not* help you into an early grave. For God's sake, Danielle."

He started to reach for her, but she stepped back, remaining out of his reach. If he touched her, she wouldn't have the resolve to resist.

"How many women have you risked your reputation and your life to rescue?" When she began to protest that she hadn't put herself at risk, he cut her off. "How many?"

She proudly raised her chin. "Ninety-seven."

"And for every one of them you've rescued, there are more—ten, one hundred, one thousand—women you can't save. What about those women? Why not work to change the lives of *all* of them, not just the handful you're able to help?" This time when he reached for her, he clasped her arms in his hands so she couldn't retreat. "You can do more for those women by working to save all of them than you ever can risking your life to save one at a time. By speaking out and telling their stories. By using the network to hound MPs and peers to change the laws—to change England for all of them."

When he slipped his arm around her, the embrace was bittersweet, because what he was suggesting would be the end of all her work. The end of actively helping women escape danger. A slow death by Parliamentary committee.

"There are women who live in fear of being killed every day," she said, aghast at his suggestion, "and you're asking me to take part in petticoat politics?"

"I'm asking you," he corrected slowly and pointedly, reaching up to caress her cheek, "to save yourself by working to save all of them."

All of them... Horrible memories flooded back of the bruises, cuts, burns, and scars she'd seen on the women Nightingale had rescued. A few of the women refused to admit the truth behind how they'd gotten them, still loyal to their apologetic abusers even at the very end when they were fleeing for their lives. Especially those attacks that weren't physical, the ones that abused a woman's mind and soul, done to bring her into submission or just out of sheer cruelty. How could women like those not think she was turning her back on them if she did as he wanted?

Anguish sliced at her insides. "I can't give up Nightingale."

"Not give it up. Change its mission."

"I can't!"

He didn't understand how important Nightingale was to her, how he was pushing her into a corner and making her choose between him and the network. He didn't understand the weight that she carried on her shoulders even now, the remorse over not being able to rescue more women. How did he expect her to turn her back on them just so she could capture her own happiness? The guilt would eat her alive!

He countered, "You can't help them from your grave either."

"That won't happen." She blinked rapidly, and damn the tears that threatened at her lashes!

"You can't be certain of that unless you stop the vanishings." When she pulled out of his embrace and walked away, he pursued her. "I want to marry you, Danielle. I want to be the devoted husband you deserve." He took her shoulders and turned her to face him. "And I want you by my side when I carve out a new future for myself, whatever it will be. You're the only woman who can be that support for me, the only one who has the confidence to stand with me and the spine to stand up *to* me."

His tempting words engulfed her. How easy it would be to give in! With a single word of agreement to have the future she'd always wanted, to lift the burden of Nightingale from her shoulders...and with that word put her own selfish desires before the needs of women who lived every hour in fear for their lives.

Her heart was rending itself in two.

"We can't have that if you're risking your life with Nightingale. I won't live like that, in constant worry that you'll be harmed. Or worse." He cupped her face between his hands. With an anguished, tortured expression, he squeezed his eyes shut and lowered his head to rest his forehead against hers. "Having to bury you in the ground, to mourn at your grave site…" His voice was nothing more than a hoarse rasp. His mouth was so close to hers that his warm breath fanned achingly over her cheeks, so close that his lips brushed faintly against hers with each word he murmured. "Dear God…it would end me."

When he leaned in to kiss her, worry and fear flavored his kiss. Dear heavens, so strong that she could taste it! Guilt and desolation swept fiercely through her, and she shuddered within his arms, for once taking no solace in his strength.

"Marry me, Danielle," he murmured. "I promise that I will keep you safe. Always."

But at what cost?

So many women, all of them needing to be saved in one way or another. Women all over England with no place to go, no one to turn to for help…except her.

She'd die before she abandoned them.

"I can't give up Nightingale, Marcus," she choked out. "I won't." All her dreams of a future with him disappeared as a single tear escaped down her cheek. She pressed her fist against her chest to physically fight down the wretched anguish that consumed her as she admitted, barely loud enough to be a whisper—"Not even for you."

Twenty-Three

Two Unbearable Days Later

DANI STOPPED PACING TO STARE OUT HER BEDROOM window at the puddle-drenched street below, but she saw nothing through the drizzling rain except Marcus's face.

But then, hadn't she seen only that since she'd refused to marry him? Even here, safe within her home, she couldn't escape him, not when his image played constantly before her eyes.

She'd sleepwalked through the last two days...not eating, not sleeping, yet somehow managing not to break down in tears. When Harriett returned this morning from her trip to Brighton, Dani had managed to smile through a brief welcome before feigning a headache and spending the rest of her day alone in her room, staring out the window when she wasn't fretfully pacing the floor. The men were out there somewhere, unseen, guarding her and the house, keeping her safe...and making her wonder if she could find one of them and convince the man to tell her how Marcus was, if he was just as miserable as she was or if he had given up on her and moved on.

Stopping her pacing before she wore the rug threadbare, she sank onto her reading chair, clutching the throw pillow to her chest. She'd had not one word from Marcus since she'd left Charlton Place, somehow even then keeping the tears from falling, if only to save her foolish pride.

But she'd heard almost incessantly from Beatrice, hounding her to know whether Nightingale would rescue the girl. She didn't want to think about the girl and her plight, but every message the countess sent only served to remind her of the choice she'd been forced to make...women who needed her or the love of her life.

The anger and anguish inside her burned like fire. He loved her... How many years had she dreamt about hearing those words from him, of him loving her and wanting to marry her?

But what he was asking of her in exchange—

Ashes!

Claudia's words about her brother the night of the dinner rushed back to her. That he was lost, that his new life in London lacked meaning and he needed important activities to fill his life...

He needs to be rescued from himself. But how did she save a man who didn't want to be saved? Who fought her every step of the way, even in this, something she held so dear—

"Damn you." The desolate whisper tore from her, and the burning tears she'd been holding back for two days finally squeezed from her closed eyes. "Damn you, Marcus Braddock..." *For making me love you. For making me want you, now and for the rest of my life. For making me have to choose...*

Overwhelming longing to be with him quivered inside her. Not only a physical yearning, but also the desire to simply be near him. Quiet conversations in front of the fire punctuated by challenging debates, strolls through the park, nights at the opera…nights spent just lying in his arms, warm and happy, as she drifted off to sleep.

God help her, she wanted a life with him. *Craved* it with every ounce of her being.

But not at the price he required of her.

"Damn you, Marcus Braddock!" She angrily flung the pillow as hard as she could.

Hurtling across the room, the pillow hit the wall above the fireplace, fell down, and smacked the mantel. It caught the corner of the music box and tumbled it off the shelf. When the box hit the marble hearth, it shattered with a loud crash. Metal parts flew in every direction across the floor, and the wooden lid splintered into pieces.

Her heart stopped as all of her flashed numb for one terrible moment. She stared at the pieces on the floor as they blurred beneath her tears, unable to let herself dare to believe it. The self-recrimination came swift and brutal, ripping through her like a lightning strike.

Elise's music box… Oh good God, what had she done?

She dropped to the floor and crawled the few feet to the broken box. The wooden case lay on the rug with its lid ripped back on the little hinges and a large shard of wood gouged out of its side. The metal disc inside had been bent beyond repair, and the tiny mechanisms that made it play lay scattered in pieces across the floor like brass confetti. All the pieces blurred together from her tears, and her hands shook so hard that her fingers couldn't pick up the little brass key lying on the rug at her knees.

She covered her face with her hands as tears streamed down her face. Broken. Everything in her life—*broken*! The women she helped through Nightingale, her chance at a life with Marcus…Elise. Everything she touched seemed to shatter.

A cry tore from her. Dear God, would anything in her life ever be whole?

"What on earth was—" Harriett appeared in the doorway. "Danielle!"

"I broke it," she choked out, picking up the case with trembling hands and carefully setting it on her lap. Then, no louder than a breath, "I've destroyed everything…"

"Oh, my darling!" Harriett rushed to her, dropped to the floor beside her, and pulled her into her arms.

Her sobs came freely now, uncontrollable and wretched. One hand clutched at her aunt, the other protecting what was left of the shattered music box. She shook violently as the crying overwhelmed her.

"It's all right," Harriett whispered, her hand rubbing soothing circles over Dani's back. "It's only a music box."

Oh, so much more! Her aunt had no idea.

Harriett's arms tightened around her, cradling her. "We'll take it and have it fixed. It will be good as new, I promise."

"No," she shuddered out between gasps. "I've ruined it."

"Nonsense. Everything can be fixed." Harriett placed a kiss to Dani's forehead, then pulled back just far enough to smooth away the hot tears on her cheeks with her palm. "We just have to try."

"Not the music box." Squeezing her eyes shut, she shook her head. "Marcus…"

Harriett tensed, but she couldn't hide her surprise. "The duke? How is he…"

Broken. The word clawed at her, and she forced out through her tightening throat, "He wants to marry me."

"That's wonderful!" When Dani smothered an anguished sob, Harriett paused and frowned. "Isn't it?"

Unable to find her voice, she miserably shook her head.

"But—but Marcus Braddock is a good and honorable man, with a family you adore and the respect of the empire." Bewilderment passed over her aunt's face. "He formally proposed?"

"Yes." The most wonderful, most agonizing moment of her life.

"Then what you have isn't broken, my dear." Harriett smiled reassuringly as she cupped Dani's face between her hands. "He's offering you a wonderful marriage and a good life."

"No," Dani whispered, her lips trembling as she held back more tears. "He's demanding an unconditional surrender."

She clasped Harriett's hand, and through uncertain starts and stops, Dani told her about Nightingale. Oh, she'd sworn never to tell Harriett! But now that the words were finally coming, they were pouring out, and the burden she'd carried on her shoulders for the past four years began to lighten.

Harriett listened silently, although her emotions of shock and surprise were plainly visible on her face. She clutched tightly to Dani's hand with both of hers, and when Dani dared to tell her about Elise, her fingers tightened so fiercely that Dani winced. But that small pain was nothing compared to the desolation that was devouring her.

"All this time," Harriett whispered when Dani finished telling her, ending with how Marcus wanted her to shut down Nightingale and carefully avoiding many other details about what happened between them that she could never bring herself to tell her aunt. "All this time, you've been helping these women in secret, all because of me... I had no idea."

"You were never supposed to know. I couldn't tell you." She lowered her gaze guiltily to their joined hands. "I only wanted to protect you."

"Or risk that Nightingale might become fodder for one of my stories," Harriett admitted with exaggerated chagrin, teasing the way she did to try to ease the pain for both of them. "But I would have changed all the names, I assure you."

Despite her tears, Dani couldn't help the faint smile that curved at her lips. Just as Harriett surely hoped for. "Or risk that you would have wanted to help."

"That, too," she acknowledged with a self-knowing sigh. "But now I know, and I can help by—"

"No! You've already been hurt too much." Dani brushed her fingertips over the music box on her lap as grief rose inside her. "You shouldn't have to be exposed to that ever again."

"I *can* help," her aunt persisted, undaunted, "with you and Marcus."

Her shoulders sank in defeat. There was no help for the problem between them.

"Whatever spats you two have had, I'm certain that it can all be worked out. You just need to do what all women do—realize that it's ultimately the man's fault and find a way to forgive him." She took Dani's hand in hers and squeezed it reassuringly. "And never stop loving him."

"No," Dani admitted, finally accepting the truth. "It's no one's fault."

She wanted to save the women, and Marcus wanted to protect her. But in the end, what he was offering was still an ultimatum.

"Listen to me, my dear." With a reassuring touch, Harriett brushed the mussed curls off Dani's forehead. "I made a terrible mistake when I married Bromley. We didn't love each other, but my parents pressed for the match. He was conservative and terribly old-fashioned, and they thought his influence on me would keep me from being so capricious and spirited. Always dashing ahead without looking—without caring, if truth be told—because the journey was so much fun. And it worked. His control over my life stopped me from being so impulsive." Her faint smile at her youthful antics faded, and she frowned with distraction at the memory, her fingers stilling at Dani's temple. "And his fists took care of the rest."

Dani wrapped her arms around her aunt. This was why she'd never wanted to tell Harriett about the network. Some memories were best left forgotten.

"I married a man whom I knew was completely wrong for me," Harriett told her, "and I suffered because of it. I don't want the same for you."

"That won't happen to me." She prayed the resolve in her voice hid the hopelessness engulfing her. "I won't marry unless I have love."

"It seems to me that you won't marry even when you do." Aggravation was beginning to replace the sadness in her aunt's voice. "Marcus Braddock loves you, Danielle."

That soft accusation ached. "Love isn't enough."

"No." Harriett shifted back, and the look of concern on her aunt's face pierced her. "It's *everything*."

"Not everything." Dani stared down at the music box. She brushed her hand over the splintered edge, and a shard of wood scratched across her fingertip. "Not when I have to give up my work to be with him."

"I am having a very difficult time faulting a man who wants to keep my niece safe." She paused, and when she continued, she gave voice to the doubts swirling in Dani's head. And heart. "Perhaps he is correct. Perhaps it is time that you stopped the vanishings."

So many times she'd wished for exactly that! To be able to stop taking risks, both for herself and the women who helped her, to lift the burden from her shoulders—

How? *How* did she simply walk away from it all? She'd been doing this for so long now that she simply didn't know how to stop.

"I wish…" The anguished confession tore from her. "I wish I could, but…I can't. I can't abandon those women." Or all that Elise had sacrificed.

"No, darling, not abandon them, but do as Marcus suggested. Turn your efforts and the work of the network into a force for change in Parliament and the courts."

If only it were that easy! "What you're suggesting will take years to enact—if it ever happens at all. Those women don't have that kind of time." Her mind turned to the twelve-year-old girl who had been forced into the brothel, who was even now waiting to be raped by a man who was wealthy and powerful enough to pay for the privilege… A frustrated sob tore from her. "They don't have any time at all."

"Then you had better get started." The resilient and defiant woman Dani loved came through strong and clear in her aunt's voice. "Bring their stories into the light and give them a voice. By advocating in Westminster, you can speak for them and speak to them. I can't help but think how different it would have been if I had known that there were people out there fighting for me. Angels and saviors to keep me from losing hope and feeling all alone. Maybe I would have been strong enough to ask for help sooner."

Wearily, Dani shook her head. "It isn't that simple."

"I never said it would be simple." She took Dani's chin and lifted her face until she looked at her. "My dear, it will be the fight of your life!"

Harriett clasped her suddenly and tightly to her, so fiercely that she nearly stole away all the air Dani had managed to regain after her tears had stopped.

"And you will win it, I know it." Harriett's tearful voice trembled in Dani's ear. "Just as I know that Marcus will help you, that he will be by your side every step of the way. Oh, Danielle!" A plaintive longing filled her voice. "Let him love you."

For a long while, Dani didn't move as thoughts and emotions swirled through her, everything she yearned to possess mixed with grief over all that she would have to surrender. But there were possibilities, too, emerging slowly from the darkness into the light of a new dawn.

Then, exhaling a self-absolving breath, she whispered, "I will."

As Harriett hugged her, the burden she'd carried for the past four years lightened, the grief eased. It didn't disappear completely—she didn't think it ever would. But now it could be borne. Because now there existed hope and opportunities for change, a new war to be waged out in the open. One, if given enough time and support, she might just win.

Harriett released her. She climbed to her feet and helped Dani to hers. The two women embraced one more time before Harriett slipped away toward the door, leaving Dani still holding the music box in her hand.

"I'll call for a tray of hot chocolate and biscuits for us," Harriett told her over her shoulder. Her voice was light, yet Dani saw her hand snake up to swipe at her eyes. "And a hot bath for you, with lots of lavender and salts. That always does wonders to soothe away worries."

Dani bit her lip as Harriett left the room. No doubt she'd have the kitchens in a flurry in a matter of minutes, heating the milk for the chocolate and water for the bath. She didn't want any of it, yet she didn't stop her simply because doing all that would make her aunt feel better.

She set the music box back on the mantel and closed the sprung lid, then began to pick up the pieces of the mechanism that had been scattered across the rug. When she found the little brass key, she slipped it into the small keyhole in the back with a prayer that Harriett was correct and that they could have the music box repaired.

"No more," she whispered as she traced her fingertip over the twisted hinges and the lid that folded, skewed, over the bent plate. "Nothing more is going to break, not if I can help it."

Snatching up her wrap, she paused only to grab the iron key from the drawer in her dressing table before hurrying downstairs and through the house to the front door.

Harriett followed her into the entry hall, clearly alarmed at her behavior. "Danielle! Where are you going?"

"I have an errand to run." She wrapped the shawl around her shoulders. "I'll be back before the bathwater cools."

She raced out the door and down the front steps, the key to the armory clutched tightly in her hand.

Twenty-Four

MARCUS DROPPED HIS SHOULDER AND SLAMMED AN underhanded punch into the sawdust-filled bag. When it went flying into the air, he pivoted on his left foot and kicked a second bag. Then a third and a fourth—each bag hanging from the beams in a circle around him swung randomly and jangled on its chains. He spun and ducked as he kicked or punched each bag randomly, whichever one moved closest to him first, to send it swinging away and the next one arcing toward him. A group fight.

He welcomed it.

Sweat stung his eyes, trickled down his bare back, and soaked through his breeches, and his arms and legs burned from exertion. But even that wasn't enough to keep his mind off Hartsham and the torture he wanted to subject the man to for daring to harm the women Marcus loved.

Or his own torture at having lost Danielle.

With a vicious kick, he sent the nearest bag high into the air.

Christ! Why didn't she understand the danger she kept exposing herself to, or how the thought of her being harmed was enough to put him into his own grave? He wanted to marry her, wanted a life with her—wanted to claim the sense of purpose and the best qualities of himself that she brought out in him. But he couldn't serve properly in Parliament, focus his attentions on running the dukedom, or be a good father and husband if he was constantly worried that she'd be harmed.

Frustration over her rejection and helplessness to save her from herself churned inside him. Not even being here in the armory, working himself to exhaustion, helped ease the burning pain or lighten the black hollow in his chest.

When he stopped to catch his wind and dropped his aching arms to his sides, a tingle of awareness prickled at his nape. He reached a hand out to the last bag that still moved on its chain and stilled it.

Not looking over his shoulder, he called out, "Hasn't anyone told you that it's dangerous to sneak up on a man when he's surrounded by weapons?"

"Hasn't anyone told you that it's dangerous to cross a woman?"

He grimaced as he turned to face Danielle.

She stood in the doorway, leaning a shoulder casually against the doorframe, her bonnet dangling from her hand by its ties. But there was nothing at all casual about the intensity that radiated from her or the anger that simmered beneath her alluring surface.

Leveling a hard look at him, she shoved herself away from the door and came slowly toward him. Damn himself that his gaze dropped to watch the angry sway of her hips. He knew she was a fury, ready to launch the second battle in the war that had sprung up between them, but he couldn't stop the tantalizing spark of desire she flared inside him. One made even sharper by the heat in her flashing eyes.

She stopped in front of him, and the two of them stared at each other for a long moment. Two opponents sizing up the other before a fight.

As an excuse for why he let his eyes drift heatedly over her, he asked, "How is your hand?"

"Cut." She did the same, trailing over his chest and abdomen, all the way down to his bare feet before moving just as deliberately back up his body. When her gaze moved over his crotch, his cock jumped. Her eyes darted up to his. Although he saw the hitch of her breath, he didn't dare let himself believe that the flush of her cheeks was anything more than ongoing anger with him. "Yours?"

"Bruised." He untied the knots that held the long strips of cloth in place over his knuckles.

"Then maybe you should stop fighting."

He paused as he unwrapped the cloths. Her underlying meaning pierced more than the chastising tone of her voice. "Then maybe people should stop attacking me." *And the ones I love.*

Her mouth tightened, and the urge to kiss her until it turned supple and yielding seized him. If he did, then she really would grab up one of the weapons and use it on him.

She stepped past him to the bags. "So this is how you spend your time." She tilted back her head to glance up the length of chain toward the beams high above. "Pummeling innocent bags of sawdust and grain." She arched a brow but didn't dare to slide him a glance, not even when she placed her bonnet on the top of the bag, where it had been fashioned to look like a man's head. "Maybe I should try punching this. Maybe then I'd think I could control the people who trust me."

Before he could bite out a reply to that to tell her how very wrong she was, she drew her hand into a tight little fist and smacked it knuckles first into the bag, which didn't move. Not even to wiggle on its chain.

When she drew back a second time, preparing to punch the bag with all her might, he grabbed her hand by the wrist and stopped her before she could wound her good hand. "No."

She spun around to face him, her breathing coming fast and shallow in her anger. So fast that the top swells of her breasts rose and fell rapidly at the lace neckline of her yellow muslin dress. Her lips were slightly parted, and a surprised gasp fell from them when he pulled her fingers open and placed a kiss to her palm.

"Never punch with your thumb inside your fist. You'll break it when the punch lands." He refolded her fingers into a fist, her thumb curled over the outside, and jerked a nod toward the bag. "Go ahead, if you think hitting it will help."

She clenched both her fist and her jaw. "Or I could punch *you*."

"Go ahead," he repeated solemnly, "if you think it will help."

With a glare, she yanked her hand free and stepped away from him.

"I won't surrender, Marcus." Her angry voice reverberated through the room, echoing off the walls and metal weaponry. "Not to you, not to anyone."

"Thank God for that." He slid a heated glance over her and appreciatively arched a brow as he murmured, "Only a damn fool wants a submissive woman."

Her cheeks flushed, although by the way her eyes flared at his audacity, he couldn't have said whether from desire or anger. "It was wrong of you to couple your proposal with shutting down Nightingale."

He bit back a reminder that he hadn't asked for that at all. She'd swallowed enough of her pride to seek him out, and he wasn't in a hurry to drive her away. Dear God, how much he'd missed her!

Her chin raised slightly. "But I am willing to forgive you for it." Her mouth twisted in consternation. "And love you regardless."

Hope sparked inside him. He took a step toward her, only for her to retreat.

"But the next vanishing that Nightingale does will—"

"Hell no," he bit out. Her words came like an unexpected punch.

She coolly arched a brow.

"You're still planning on putting yourself into danger, even now. Even when you know how desperate a man Hartsham is." He bit back a curse that would have curled her toes. Knowing better than to reach for her, he raked frustrated fingers through his hair. "You won't stop until you're dead, will you?"

"You're a hypocrite," she chastised. "You don't want me to work with Nightingale because you think it's too dangerous, yet you're chasing after Hartsham."

"I can hold my own against Hartsham."

"Is that what this place is for? All of this, to arrest one man?" She waved her hand at the armory around her and the weapons that covered the walls. "Look at this place! This isn't for going after an earl who couldn't win at fist-icuffs if his life depended upon it. All these weapons, impenetrable walls—for heaven's sake, there's a spiked portcullis over the main door!" She jabbed an angry finger at the floor. "This place is for waging war."

"Yes, it is." He strode toward her, closing the distance between them.

But this time, she stood her ground. The anger pumped inside her so intensely that she visibly shook with it, and with something else that he could see boiling up inside her that was just as intense, just as hot.

"So that you can continue to take on the world, so you can continue to fight," she bit out the indictment. "You're so eager to strip from my life the purpose that Nightingale gives it, yet you'll go to lengths like this to find some kind of meaning for your own."

"Yes, damn it!" he snapped, so fiercely that it echoed through the building. "I want purpose in my life. But *not* at the cost of the ones I love."

She pushed her hand against his shoulder as he leaned

into her, now so close that he could feel the heat of her front on his bare chest. He could smell the lavender scent of her that engulfed his senses, sent his head swirling, and had his cock stiffening. Just one more step and his hips would be pressed to hers, her yielding body molded against his hardness.

"You think that just because you're a powerful general and a duke that you can do whatever you please, whenever you want—the rest of the world be damned." Her voice emerged as a throaty rasp, one that spiraled like liquid fire through him all the way down to his bare feet. "But you can't. *Not* with me."

Every muscle in his body tensed in aching desire to claim the defiant fire inside her.

"This isn't the army, Marcus." Her eyes blazed as she shoved again at his shoulder.

A rising need pulsated low in his gut. The same need he now felt radiating from her.

"And I am not your enemy."

"Is this the only reason you came here, Danielle?" he drawled, audaciously lowering his mouth close to hers. "To yell at me?"

"No. I'm here to negotiate terms of surrender."

"But you said you'd never surrender."

"Not me." Each word tickled sweetly over his lips. "*You.*"

He gave a short laugh. "I've never surrendered in my life."

"Then it's time you learned how."

When she pushed against his shoulder again, he reluctantly stepped back. The strips of cloth still dangled half-undone from his palms and wrists as he crossed his arms over his chest and fixed a look on her that had terrified new recruits but barely gave her pause before she mimicked his posture, crossed her own arms, and stared boldly back.

"I will marry you if you agree to meet certain conditions," she announced.

He would have laughed at her impudence if the subject weren't so very important. "And what would those be?"

"That once Hartsham is arrested, you agree to support me in the next war."

He didn't like these terms, not wanting Danielle putting herself into the fray at all. But he was willing to hear her out. "What war?"

"The one that Nightingale will wage in Parliament and in the courts against all those who abuse women. We'll do it openly, too, right out in the streets, for all to see and hear."

His pulse stuttered. She was changing the focus of the network, just as he'd asked. But both of them would pay a price for this. He in Parliament and she in her heart at giving up directly helping women in need. Yet he took hope in her concession and tossed out his own condition. "No more vanishings."

"One more."

"*No* more." A position on which he would never budge.

"One more," she repeated pointedly, clearly brooking no argument on this. "And then they will stop."

Her bright intensity had seeped into him, burning low in his gut, and he stalked toward her, steering her backward and into the shadows falling along the edge of the room where the afternoon sunlight didn't reach. "Who?"

"The woman you've arranged for Hartsham to deliver to you."

He stopped in midstep at that and scoured her with a look to judge if she was serious. Her spine remained ramrod straight, but she couldn't stop the flush in her cheeks from spreading down her neck to her breasts from the heat of his stare or how her breath now came in small pants.

"Once she cooperates and tells you what she knows about Hartsham and the brothel, her life will be in danger. She won't have anyone to protect her from Hartsham if he's somehow exonerated in the Lords. Or if anyone else from the brothel decides to take revenge against her and make an example of what happens to prostitutes who turn against the house manager. Including Scepter, if it turns out that they're involved."

The same way they did with John Porter, cutting out his tongue and pinning it to the wall as a reminder of what happens to those who talk about them.

"She won't be safe as long as she remains in England," Danielle continued. "I want to use Nightingale's network to take her out of the country to America and change her identity, to give her a fresh start somewhere she'll be safe. It's the least we can do for her."

He closed the remaining distance between them with a single step. "But she might be just as guilty in all this as Hartsham. She might be willingly giving him information for her own gain."

"Then consider it exile." Resilience and strength shone in her eyes. "After that, the vanishings will stop, and Nightingale's network closes down."

He cupped her face between his hands, even as the ends of the half-removed cloth strips still dangled around his forearms and tickled at the top swells of her breasts. "And our future together begins."

Her lips parted, trembling slightly at the enormity of what she was agreeing to. "Yes."

His mouth came down possessively against hers, sealing their negotiations with a blistering kiss.

For a single beat, she stood frozen within his embrace, her lips unmoving beneath his and her hand still against his shoulder. Then her mouth eagerly responded to his, and the hand on his shoulder that had been pushing him away now pulled him close in an aching need. She pressed herself against him, and the inarticulate noises that came from her throat weren't moans of pleasure or soft mewlings—they were fierce, frustrated sounds of need and desire, swelling up from deep inside her and matching his own yearning.

Her hands lost their purchase on his sweat-slickened shoulders, so her fingertips sank into the hard muscles of his back to maintain her fierce hold on him. When she thrust her hips forward against his, a throbbing ache consumed him. He pushed her backward and pinned her between his body and the wall.

With both hands planted against the bricks on either side of her, his hips pressing into hers to hold her in place, he kissed her relentlessly, hot and openmouthed, until she had to tear her lips away to pant for air. Even then he didn't lift his mouth from her, lowering his head to lick and suck at her throat while her pulse pounded deliciously against his lips. With a groan, he sank his teeth into her neck.

She cried out at the sensation of pleasure-pain that shot through her. Her hand at his shoulder slipped up to grab his hair and yanked his head back, curving his neck toward her as her mouth darted to bite at his throat the same way he'd done to hers. The bite shot all the way down to the tip of his cock, and he sucked in a mouthful of air through clenched teeth.

Regaining control of the kiss, he grabbed her wrists and pinned both of her arms over her head with one hand. Her back arched against the wall, and her bosom was thrust up temptingly toward him.

"Sweet Lucifer," he murmured, brushing his free hand down her front. "What you do to me, Danielle." He cupped her breast against his palm. "How you drive me mad."

"And you with me...you frustrating man," she panted out when he began to massage her through the layers of her clothing, hard enough to pucker her nipples into little points.

"Good. Because if this is frustration, then I want nothing more than to frustrate you for the rest of our lives."

To punctuate that promise, he swept a finger beneath her bodice between her skin and chemise and teased at her nipple.

He grinned in triumph when a mewl of mounting desire fell from her lips. "I want to spend every day with you, arguing and making up. Just like this."

He shoved his hand inside her dress and captured her breast, rubbing her nipple hard against his palm. The whimper on her lips dissolved into an aching moan of need.

"I won't stop helping those women," she rasped out obstinately, even as she arched her back to push herself against his hand. She shook with need and yearning, and her hips pressed into his, unwittingly caressing his hardening cock through their clothes. "Even if it means sacrificing everything."

Her words slapped him, stunning him just long enough for her to slip her hands from his grasp. But instead of pulling away, she wrapped her arms around his neck and tugged him down to her, to give him a scorching kiss that had her eagerly rising up onto tiptoes to meet his hungry mouth.

"Then we're even," he ground out hoarsely against her lips, his voice little more than a husky scratch. "Because I plan on doing the same for you, love."

He yanked at her bodice and the corset beneath, pulling it down far enough to bury his face in the swells of her breasts. The beast in him wanted to tear the dress from her back, to bare her to his hands and mouth, then simply devour her. But he'd settle for this maddeningly small taste of her and licked his tongue into the valley between her breasts.

But when she slipped her hand down between them to unbutton his breeches and free his cock from the tight material, his restraint vanished. He grabbed her hand to close it over him, then thrust his hips into her palm. Her fist tightened around him, drawing a plaintive groan from him as he stroked himself against her hand. Aching, yearning, hard—and growing impossibly harder. When she smeared the drop of moisture that had formed at his tip over his smooth head with her palm, he groaned with hard-won restraint and clenched his buttocks tightly to keep from spilling in her hand.

"Danielle," he rasped and grabbed at her skirt to yank it up around her waist.

Panting hard, he paused a moment to look down at her. Except for her stockings, she was beautifully exposed to his eyes…long stretches of bare thighs, feminine curls between her legs, and the folds below, already glistening wet from her desire for him.

She stared back at him, confident and bold beneath his lustful gaze, then stepped her legs apart in wanton invitation. She reached up to cup the back of his head in her hand and bring his mouth down to hers in a kiss so heated that he couldn't stop drops of his seed from trickling onto her fingers.

His hand dove between her legs and stroked her hard and fast, grinding the heel of his hand against her pelvic bone, just above where her sensitive nub lay buried. A hot shudder of desire pulsed through her. She darted the tip of her tongue out to wet her lips in sweet anticipation, and he groaned at the unwitting gesture of seduction. And permission.

He needed to be deep inside her, surrounded by her tight warmth and silky softness. Needed to hear her cry out in passion for him, to feel her writhe and shudder around him—

Sweet Jesus. He needed *her*. Every bit of her. Now and always.

His hands slid under her arse and lifted her into the air, her thighs clenching against his hips for support and her arms wrapping around his neck. Holding her in place against the wall, he stepped forward and impaled her with his cock.

She cried out in surprise and swift pleasure, but her body eagerly welcomed his, taking him deep inside her. Locking her ankles together at the small of his back, she clasped herself to him and held on for this desperate, wicked ride.

He planted his hands against the wall on either side of her shoulders for leverage and thrust into her, twisting his hips against her with each plunge to go as deep as possible. He drove into her. Each penetrating thrust brought a cry of satisfaction to her lips, each retreat a whimper of loss.

His hands grasped firmly at her buttocks. With every thrust and retreat, he yanked her up and down over his length in a galloping rhythm that soon had her bucking helplessly against him.

"Marcus..." The strained sound of her voice shivered through him, and her body clamped around his like iron bands...arms, legs, all the tiny muscles inside her bearing down around him—"Marcus!"

She came violently, screaming out as her release tore through her and slammed into him. The cry echoed through the brick building and filled him with an intense joy unlike any he'd ever known before.

He thrust into her once more, twice—then he held her pinned there against the wall as his cock jerked inside her and his seed gushed into her, so powerfully that he yelled.

She convulsed around him again as a second release consumed her, nearly as fierce as the first, then went limp in his arms. Only his body pressing against hers kept her from sinking bonelessly to the floor.

Carefully, he loosened his hold on her. She slid down his front and found her feet beneath her, but her knees were still too weak to support her and buckled. He caught her and encircled her in his arms, holding her close to him while she struggled to regain her breath.

He buried his face in her hair, which was still in its pins, in their desperation to make love not bothering to remove a stitch of clothing or a single pin. Never...*never* had he loved a woman the way he did her.

"Don't you see?" he murmured against her temple, tasting the faint flavor of perspiration that had sprouted there from the ferocity of their lovemaking. "We belong together, Danielle. In every way."

She continued to cling to him as residual shivers of release passed over her, as her breathing slowly deepened and her racing heartbeat calmed.

Then he steeled himself to do the one thing he'd sworn he would never do—put her into danger. "One last vanishing, then." He placed a kiss to her lips, still hot and trembling from his kisses. "But you'll do it with my help and the help of the Home Office." He tilted her chin up until she looked him in the eyes. He wanted no misunderstanding about this. "I'll be by your side every minute."

She stared at him for a long while, long enough that the flush of making love eased away from her cheeks. Long enough that he suspected she might change her mind and refuse him after all.

But then, with a capitulating sigh, she kissed him.

"Yes, Marcus, I accept your terms of surrender," she whispered, sending joy soaring through him. "I will marry you."

———————————

An hour later, Dani hurried up to her room and to the writing desk positioned beneath the window, where she took out a piece of the plain stationery that she used to send messages for Nightingale. Quickly, she scratched out a letter to Beatrice. As she wrote, the burden of Nightingale lifted, but the guilt remained as strong as ever. She knew now that it always would, along with grief that it had ended, but she also knew that she'd made the right decision.

> *I cannot rescue the girl you told me about—I am so very sorry. If you want to help her, you will need to do it yourself. Contact a man named William Jenkins through the innkeeper's wife at the Golden Bell Tavern at the Strand and Fleet Street and tell him that you are with the network. Pay him well, and he will smuggle the girl back to Manchester for you. With faith in you...*

She paused to read over the letter, then signed it,

Nightingale

Her hand trembled. It would be the last time she ever penned that name.

"Miss?" Her maid Alice hurried into the room, her face pale and worried. "The viscountess is downstairs, stirring up all kinds of fuss over hot chocolate and baths for you. Is there a problem?" She glanced over her shoulder and lowered her voice. "With Nightingale?"

"No." A twinge of sadness struck her as she blotted, folded, and sealed the envelope. "There will be no more problems with the charity."

Alice frowned, not understanding.

"Take this and deliver it to Lady Hartsham." She held up the note. "Then send word to the Golden Bell as you usually do to notify Mr. Jenkins to expect a message about a vanishing."

"Yes, miss."

"Take no risks, but hurry back," Dani called out as Alice scurried from the room. Her eyes fell onto the music box. "We have a vanishing to plan for."

The very last one she would ever do.

Twenty-Five

WRINGING HER GLOVED HANDS, DANI PACED THE length of the entry hall. Her long coat swished around her legs with every step of her laced-up half boots and made her flushed with heat, but she didn't dare remove her outer layers. She had to be ready to leave immediately, the carriage due for her at any moment—

The long case clock in the drawing room struck half past nine, and her shoulders sagged.

No, the carriage was past due.

She craned her neck to glance out the sidelight at the street. In the darkness, she couldn't see anything beyond the halo of light cast by the oil lamp hanging over the door. With a frustrated groan, she began to pace again.

Thank goodness Harriett had gone out tonight to a concert with Mrs. Peterson so she didn't need to explain her behavior. Not that she could have given an explanation anyway. Not until Hartsham had been arrested and she knew that all the people she loved would finally be safe.

Where on earth was Marcus?

He'd sent a note to her that morning to inform her that Hartsham had finally contacted him about the woman and to give her instructions about tonight. She was to wait at home. After the woman had arrived at nine o'clock and been placed securely under the Home Office's guard, Marcus would secretly leave Brandon Pearce's town house in Bedford Square and come for her in an unmarked carriage. He would take her to Bedford Square, where she would wait while Clayton Elliott finished questioning the woman and securing whatever statements they needed to act against Hartsham. Then, Dani would bring the full resources of Nightingale into play one last time to create a new identity for the woman, rush her out of London to the docks at Greenwich, and put her on the first ship bound for America. They would give her the chance at a new life. How she chose to live it was entirely left to her.

With that, their trap for Hartsham would be sprung. And not a moment too soon.

In his note, Marcus had warned her that if the situation at the town house with the woman grew complicated, he might have to send another man in his place to fetch her—his friend Merritt Rivers, who had served with him in France and had now staked out a notable career as a barrister, a man who by all reports could be trusted to protect her with his life. But she wanted Marcus at her side tonight. And every night for the rest of her life.

Oh, where *was* he?

Motion caught the corner of her eye through the door's sidelight. In the dark shadows of the street beyond the lamp's glow, a carriage stopped suddenly in front of the house. *Oh, thank God!* She flung open the door to rush from the house, only to halt in midstep at the threshold when the door of the hired hackney opened and a woman hurried to the ground, gathered up her skirts, and dashed up the front steps toward her.

"Miss Williams, thank goodness!"

The woman stepped into the lamplight beneath the small front portico. When she pushed back her hood to reveal her face, Dani finally recognized her.

"Mrs. Slater?" Dani took her arm and led her back inside the house. She couldn't help one last searching glance into the darkness for a second carriage but found none. "What are you doing here?" And dressed head to foot in gray and black worsted wool, no less, looking nothing like a prosperous mill owner's wife. The little hairs at Dani's nape prickled with unease. "What's wrong?"

"Oh, Danielle!" Mrs. Slater grabbed her arm and squeezed it tightly, not letting go. "We desperately need your help."

"We?"

"Beatrice and I—and the girl. We're in trouble."

The girl. The tingle at her nape shot like lightning down her spine. "How?"

Flustered and pale, Mrs. Slater rushed out the words. "We tried to rescue her on our own, but it all went so horribly wrong! Beatrice said that you could help us, that you'd done this sort of thing before."

Dread strangled in her throat. Dear God...had Beatrice told her about Nightingale? "You—you know about the girl at the brothel?"

Mrs. Slater nodded emphatically. "Beatrice told me

what she'd planned, and I couldn't let her do it by herself." Her fingers dug into Dani's arm, and she lowered
her voice, which vibrated with fear. "We went to the
brothel tonight."

"*You* two went to the brothel?" An icy dread spilled
through her. "By yourselves?"

"We had a man with us. The brother of one of my footmen. He agreed to go inside the house and sneak the girl
out while we waited in the carriage a few streets away."

Thank God that they were smart enough to do that.
"What happened?"

"Someone inside the house saw Martin leave with the
girl and alerted the men guarding the door. They chased
after him. And then they chased after us." She released
her hold on Dani's arm, one hand flying to her mouth
and the other to her chest. "I was so terrified! The team
was racing so fast over the cobblestones that I thought
we would be shaken apart. We nearly tipped over at the
corners."

"But you got away." Dani soothingly rubbed her hand
up and down the woman's arm to reassure her, although
she also did it to ease her own guilt. She hadn't simply
refused to help the girl; she'd told Beatrice to rescue her
herself. If she had known how the night would go, she
never would have written that!

"Barely." Mrs. Slater shook violently, unable to tamp
down the lingering terror and agitation from the chase.
"At one point, they nearly caught us. We had to leave
the carriage and run on foot. That was when Martin left

us." Her voice broke with disbelief as she explained, "He just ran…ran away into the darkness and left the three of us there alone on the street. At night. With those men still chasing after us and the girl crying—crying so loudly! And she wouldn't hush, no matter how much we begged…"

Dani hugged her and repeated forcefully, "But you got away. That's what matters."

"Yes." Mrs. Slater swiped a hand at her eyes. "We've managed to avoid them for now, but they're still out there searching for us. I know it!"

She placed her palm against Mrs. Slater's cheek to make the woman focus. "Where are Beatrice and the girl now?"

"At the warehouse in the Strand where we were supposed to have met up with Mr. Jenkins so he could take the girl out of London. But he wasn't there."

"Which warehouse?"

"The one near the Golden Bell. Mr. Jenkins suggested it in his message when he agreed to help us. But he wasn't there!"

"I know." When a fearful tear slid down the woman's cheek, Dani wiped it away. "But I'll take care of you. Everything will all be all right." Dear God, she hoped so! "You need to go back to the warehouse and wait with Beatrice. I'll send a message to the other men I know like Mr. Jenkins, to have one of them come to the warehouse and collect the girl from you."

"There isn't time! That's why Beatrice sent me here

to you." She grabbed Dani's hand and tugged at it. "You have to come with me."

"I can't—"

"We don't know what to do!" She wrung her hands in distress.

"If you wait at the warehouse, one of the men will come for you," Dani explained, purposefully making her voice calmer the more agitated Mrs. Slater became. "He'll know how to take care of everything."

"If we wait, those men will find us and kill us!" Her face twisted with fear. "You have to come with me and help us—*now*."

Mrs. Slater's panic flooded into Dani and warred with the uncertainty inside her. Beatrice and the girl needed her, but Marcus was coming for her at any moment. Looking for an answer of what to do, she glanced out the open door at the dark street, still empty except for the hired hackney that continued to wait by the footpath.

Mrs. Slater clutched at Dani's sleeve. "Please, Danielle! You're the only one who can save this girl."

As she bit her bottom lip, her gaze fell to the small travel bag waiting by the door. She'd filled it herself this afternoon, as she had with every other vanishing that Nightingale had ever committed. Two changes of clothes, a night rail, enough money for a few weeks' room and board, documents that established a new identity—everything the woman at Pearce's town house would need to escape and start a new life. Had Beatrice even thought far enough ahead to assemble this kind of escape kit for the girl? Did she know to hide with the girl at an inn under a false name if none of the men came to collect her from the warehouse tonight, an inn far enough away from the Golden Bell and the brothel that no one would see her and suspect who she really was?

Of course she didn't. Beatrice was scatterbrained under the best of circumstances, but tonight, when everything was going wrong around her, hiding in the darkness with a crying child, fearing for her life—

Dani's heart ripped. "Yes," she reluctantly agreed, ignoring the unease prickling at the backs of her knees and making her decision. "I'll help you as much as I can."

"Oh, thank God!" Mrs. Slater's face lit up with gratitude and relief, although Dani suspected more of her tears might yet fall. "Let's go now, and we'll—"

"Wait here. I have to collect a few things from my room that we'll need." She forcibly wrenched her arm away from the woman, who clung to it as if terrified that Dani would change her mind and run away, the same way their hired man had. "I'll be right back."

Calling out for Alice, she hurried up the stairs to her bedroom. She yanked open the doors to her armoire and looked hopefully inside, only for her chest to sink. What on earth did she have in her wardrobe that a twelve-year-old girl would fit into? So she snatched up a short cloak, an old spencer, and one of her bonnets. They would have to do. Somehow.

When Alice hurried into the room, Dani thrust everything into her arms before she could blurt out any questions. "Find a travel bag and put all this into it, along with soap, a flannel, woolen stockings—whatever a young girl might need for travel. Then hurry back."

Alice nodded sharply, bewildered but knowing from past experience that now was not the time to press for answers. "Yes, miss!" she called out as she ran from the room.

Dani sat at her writing desk and quickly scratched out a message to the innkeeper's wife at the Golden Bell, giving her a list of men who had worked for Dani in the past and asking her to have them come to the tavern as soon as they could to carry out the rest of the vanishing. If the girl was gone by the time they arrived, they would still get paid, but the man who arrived first would receive triple his pay. An excellent incentive for them to hurry to help. And if none of the men came to the tavern, then the girl would be hidden there in an attic room until tomorrow, until Dani could vanish her completely. Even if it meant driving her to Manchester herself.

When Alice returned with a small travel bag stuffed so full that it could barely close, Dani gave her the note. "The Golden Bell. Take one of the footmen with you. Go!"

Then Dani wrote out a second message, this one to Marcus when he finally came to collect her, explaining what had happened and where she'd gone. Only a brief delay, she assured him, not more than an hour to wait for Jenkins or one of the other men to arrive. Certainly nothing as dramatic as Beatrice and Mrs. Slater were making

their situation out to be. She believed that men from the
brothel had given chase, although most likely giving up
after only a few minutes. But Dani couldn't abandon
Beatrice. She promised to arrive at Pearce's town house
as soon as she could, and then they would continue the
night exactly as planned.

"I'm ready," she said as she came down the stairs, the
bag in one hand and the note in the other. "Let's depart."

With a relieved nod, Mrs. Slater hurried out of the
house to the waiting carriage.

Dani paused as she closed the door behind her to
leave the note on the brass knocker. Then she ran to join
Mrs. Slater in the carriage.

Marcus walked up to stand beside Clayton in the double
doorway of Pearce's dining room. The woman whom
Hartsham had arranged for him sat on a dining chair
pushed into the corner of the room while Pearce guarded
her. *Guarding her* being a very loose definition of what the
man was actually doing as he leaned against the fireplace
with a glass of port in one hand and gestured enthusiastically at her with the other as he described what Spain
and France had been like during the wars, peppering his
portrayals with several tales of his own personal misad-
ventures. Including the one about the flamenco dancer
who swung through his bedroom window on the end of
a rope.

The woman stared at him, wide-eyed and saying nothing, just as she'd done since he'd started his tales nearly half an hour ago.

But of course she did. She obviously thought he was a bedlamite.

"Has he gotten to the Battle of Toulouse yet?" Marcus drawled in a lowered voice so he wouldn't be overheard.

Across the room, Pearce laughed and gestured with the glass. "One newspaper said that horses were in blood up to their forelocks. Their *forelocks*! As if they were swimming in it!"

"Yes," Clayton answered dryly, his face impassive. "For the last five minutes, in fact." He slid a sideways gaze at Marcus. "We should probably question her soon before we're accused of torturing her by setting Pearce on her like this."

"Not until Danielle arrives." He took another uneasy glance over his shoulder toward the front door. Where the devil was she?

The woman's late arrival to the town house had not only put going after Danielle behind schedule, but it had also raised Marcus's wariness about the night's plans to the point that he'd been forced to send Merritt in his place instead of fetching her himself so he could be here at the town house in case anything went wrong. Danielle was in very capable hands with Merritt, he knew that, perhaps even more so than in his own if he were honest about it, given Merritt's fighting skills. Yet he wanted her by his side, where he knew she would be safe.

"Is that a good idea," Clayton countered quietly, "having a society lady here while we ask that woman about the kinds of things that Hartsham is using for blackmail? Will Miss Williams be able to tolerate it?"

"Without so much as a blink." Marcus smiled in private amusement. Clayton didn't know the kind of woman Danielle was, a society lady who had more spine and resilience than half the men in His Majesty's service. "Her presence here will make the woman more comfortable when we question her and hopefully make her willing to tell us more. She can reassure her that she'll be set free as soon as we have the information we need and that Hartsham won't be able to harm her."

After the way the woman arrived—late and scurrying up to the town house alone from a rented carriage, only to be met not by one man as expected when she walked into the drawing room but four—reassurances were definitely in order. But they had time. All night, in fact. Hartsham had encouraged him to feel free to do anything he wanted with the woman, so no suspicions would be raised if she made no attempt to meet up with Hartsham afterward to tell him what Marcus had done with her. By dawn, she would be so thoroughly hidden that no one would be able to find her.

But Marcus wanted this over as soon as possible so that Clayton's men could greet the earl when he rose for breakfast, search his properties before he knew to destroy or hide any evidence there, and place him under house arrest until a formal warrant could be issued. The trial and execution might yet take months, but with the earl closely under guard and his every move watched, he wouldn't be able to harm Marcus's family again. A family that now included Danielle.

The front door opened, and Merritt strode inside and down the hall toward them. Alone.

Marcus demanded, "Where's Danielle?"

"Gone." He grimly held out a folded note. "She left this for you. I took the liberty of reading it."

Marcus opened the note and scanned it. His blood turned to ice as he read what she'd done.

"Two of the men guarding the house followed after her, and one stayed behind in case she returns," Merritt informed him. "They won't let her out of their sight."

The words swam on the page before Marcus's eyes as his gut squeezed so tightly that he couldn't breathe. "She's been tricked," he rasped out. *Christ.* "It's a trap!" He threw the note at Clayton and charged toward the front door.

Pearce appeared in the dining room doorway. "What's wrong?"

"We've been found out. Somehow Hartsham learned what we'd planned, and he's lured Danielle away." Marcus jerked on his coat and gloves. "I'm going after her."

"I'm coming with you." Pearce strode over to the entry hall table, yanked open the drawer, and withdrew a brace of pistols. "Once a soldier—"

"Always a soldier," Merritt finished, reaching into his coat to hand one of his own pistols to Marcus, then slapped him on the back and headed with Pearce toward the door. "Let's go."

Gratitude tightened Marcus's throat. But there was no time for emotion. He ordered Clayton, "Stay here and question that woman." The glance he sent into the dining room was murderous. "And God help her if she lies." Or if one hair on Dani's head was harmed.

The three men raced outside into the rainy, black night.

From the doorway, Clayton stared after them for a moment, then signaled to one of his men standing watch outside the town house to come inside and guard the door. Then he walked into the dining room, pulled up a chair facing the woman, and sat down, noting how her eyes flickered with fear.

He gave her his best charming smile to put her at ease. "Good evening, ma'am. We haven't been introduced yet. I'm Clayton Elliott, Undersecretary for the Home Office." He offered her a cup of tea from the tray sitting on the table. "Shall we talk?"

Twenty-Six

"WE DON'T HAVE TIME FOR THIS," MRS. SLATER grumbled as Dani called up to the driver to stop so they could change carriages a second time.

"I insist. Beatrice will be fine for the extra time this will take us." She gathered up her skirts. "But none of us will be if the men from the brothel somehow managed to track you to my house and are following after us now."

She stepped down from the carriage. Tossing a coin to the driver, she took Mrs. Slater's arm and led the woman across the busy Covent Garden street where she waved down a hackney headed in the opposite direction. Anyone who might be following them in a carriage wouldn't be able to turn around on the crowded street and chase after them. "St Paul's Cathedral," she ordered the new driver and ducked as she entered the small compartment. "Hurry, please."

"But we're not going that far," Mrs. Slater challenged, her voice riddled through with growing exasperation as the horse started forward before they were properly seated.

"No, we're not." Dani watched out the window as the lights of the theatre district slipped past as the carriage rolled east. "We'll stop before then and walk to the warehouse, doubling back two or three streets to make certain we don't lead anyone to Beatrice and the girl."

"You've done this before, then."

"Countless times," she whispered into the darkness beyond the window. But for once when she thought about the women, the crushing burden didn't weigh down on her shoulders. The end was in sight, even if she had to travel through the dark night—and change carriages three times—to arrive there. "We'll put the girl under a hooded cloak and take her to the Golden Bell, where hopefully one of the men will be waiting to take her out of London."

"What men?" Panic edged Mrs. Slater's voice.

Dani glanced at her. Even through the shadows, Dani thought she saw Mrs. Slater grow pale. "The men I contacted about the girl."

Then the woman's face turned absolutely white. "You shouldn't have done that."

"It's all right. I've worked with them before. They can be trusted, for the right price." At least she prayed that they could. The memory of how Kimball had attacked her in that alley teased uneasily at the back of her mind. "We'll hand the girl over to them to smuggle out of London and back to Manchester and her family. Then you and Beatrice won't be caught up in this any longer."

Mrs. Slater turned her face toward the opposite window, her hands fidgeting nervously in her lap. "I hope so."

So did Dani.

When the carriage drew near to Fleet Street, she opened the window, popped out her head, and glanced down the street—*empty*. No one had followed them. She banged her fist on the wall of the carriage and called out to the driver to stop.

"Quickly," she ordered Mrs. Slater, nearly pushing the woman outside. She handed the full fare to the driver and ordered, "Drive on to St Paul's."

Then she grabbed her arm and pulled her into a nearby alley. No one was in the dark street to see them leave the carriage and disappear into the darkness, and anyone who might have been chasing farther behind would have followed the hackney onward to the east. They wouldn't realize they'd been tricked until the carriage reached St Paul's.

Dani led Mrs. Slater from one alley to another, their path further concealed by the thickening fog and drizzling rain. Within minutes, they were hidden in the rabbit warren of alleyways and streets snaking along the Thames. She motioned for Mrs. Slater to stay silent as they doubled back along the Strand to once more head toward Fleet Street. In the past four years, Dani had put down a wild goose chase through London so many times that doing so had become second nature to her. But it was also a skill she didn't intend to call upon again after tonight.

Finally, she pointed down one last dark alley. Mrs. Slater hesitated, then followed warily between the brick buildings to an old abandoned warehouse, the one she'd used often for Nightingale.

"Here?" Dani whispered to make certain Beatrice hadn't taken refuge in the wrong building.

Lingering in the shadows, Mrs. Slater nodded.

Dani pushed open the door, the lock long ago broken and never fixed by the owners who had abandoned the warehouse. The ground floor room was dark, but she'd been here enough times to know her way to the lantern hanging on a peg from the center pillar, the one she'd always kept operational and filled with oil for just such an emergency. She struck a light from the little tinder-box she'd stashed into her pelisse pocket and brought the lamp to life.

The dim light lit the large room just enough for Dani to see—*empty*. There was no sign of Beatrice and the girl. Dread squeezed her chest.

"Beatrice?" Her voice echoed through the dusty building as loud as cannon fire to her ears. *Please God, let them be here in hiding!* "Where are you?" She paused to listen. "Are you here?"

Heavy steps scuffed over the floor above, and she jumped, startled, her heart flying into her throat. Struggling to keep herself calm, she turned toward the set of narrow wooden stairs in the corner that led to the floors above. She lifted the lamp higher to cast as much light as possible, and from the black shadows, a man's form emerged as he slowly came down the stairs. Slender and slight of build, not at all the type of broad-shouldered and beefy man a brothel would hire as security—

Oh thank God… "Jenkins." She eased out a relieved sigh and smiled. "I knew you'd come as planned. I've always been able to count on you."

"Have you?"

The deep voice slithered down her spine. He stepped into the halo of lamplight and revealed his face—

"Lord Hartsham," she whispered fearfully. "What are you doing here?"

He moved down the final two steps to the stone floor. "Waiting for you."

All the tiny muscles in her belly tightened sickeningly in instant terror—

She'd been led into a trap.

She wheeled furiously on Mrs. Slater, who stood just inside the doorway where Dani had left her. The woman hadn't bothered to step farther into the warehouse, knowing all along that Beatrice and the girl weren't here.

"You," Dani forced out past the knot of betrayal squeezing in her throat. Everything fell sickeningly into place… why Mrs. Slater had told Beatrice about the girl, knowing that the countess would initially approach Dani for help with the vanishing, why Dani hadn't given a second thought to rushing off to help…because all the pieces fit. "You deceived me. You brought me here. To him!"

"I am sorry," Mrs. Slater said remorsefully, not leaving her post by the door. But at least she had the decency to wring her hands in guilt. "I regret that you were caught up in all this. But I cannot let you ruin my husband's future."

"Your husband?" Dani rasped out, barely able to breathe. "What does he have to do with this?"

"You interfered! You put his business ventures in jeopardy, all that he and I had risked so much to establish."

The woman's voice lowered into an accusing hiss. "If you would have just left well enough alone—but you wouldn't, would you? You let Hampton seduce you into believing that his sister was murdered, that you needed to find her killer." Her eyes glistened in the lamplight, but Dani knew it wasn't from remorse at leading her here to the enemy. It was the same dark gleam that had glinted in all the women Nightingale had rescued when they spoke of their abusers—hatred. "I knew that night at Vauxhall that you had to be dealt with."

A shiver of realization pulsed icily through her. "It was you that night who was keeping watch so closely, who knew exactly where Marcus and I were..." Closely enough to realize the exact moment when Dani discovered the truth about who had murdered Elise. Bile of betrayal rose in her throat. "It was *you* who signaled for us to be shot at."

"She did as I ordered," Hartsham answered for Mrs. Slater as he stalked slowly toward her.

Dani stepped back in fear, still holding the lantern up high, as if the light alone could protect her.

"Just as she was the one who hired that man from among her husband's dockworkers to break into Charlton Place, to make certain no evidence of Venus's Folly was left among Elise Donnelly's things. Just as she did in bringing you here tonight."

"Where's Beatrice?" Dani asked, worried about the countess. She didn't put it past Hartsham to have beaten information from her.

"She should be arriving home at any minute. She's spent the evening waiting for Jenkins to deliver the girl to her at an inn in Southwark after he retrieved her from the brothel, then pass the child along to another smuggler to take her out of London. Exactly as planned. She has no idea that any of this is happening."

Dani slowly retreated. With her right hand still tightly gripping the handle of the glass oil lamp, she pressed her left into her stomach to physically suppress the roiling inside. Oh, she was such a fool! Mrs. Slater's worry and agitation, her insistence that Beatrice had sent her to Dani for help—she'd believed all of it. But there had been no reason *not* to believe her, not when the woman knew all the details of how a vanishing worked, right down to the warehouse. *This* warehouse. The only way she could have known was if Hartsham had told her. And the only way Hartsham would have known...

Dear God. *Elise.* He knew about this warehouse only because John Porter must have led him here two years ago, because this must have been where she was to meet up with him. Dani swallowed hard to force down the rising bile—because this was where Hartsham murdered her before dumping her body in the park to make her death look like an accident.

Shaking uncontrollably as fear knotted her insides, she moved away from him with every step he advanced toward her. "You lured me here so you can kill me the same way that"—her words strangled in her tightening throat—"that you killed Elise."

"Not the same way," he corrected coldly, his hands tightening and releasing at his sides. As if he couldn't wait to get his hands around her throat. "Two women with broken necks would be too suspicious. And not at all as easy with you, I suspect. Elise Donnelly was so trusting, so easy to kill. All I had to do was walk up behind her, grab her head, and twist."

Her belly burned with terror and grief. "This is madness! You're killing innocent women just because we've dared to remove prostitutes from a brothel, just so you can keep committing blackmail. Why? You're an earl, for God's sake!" Her gaze swung between the earl and Mrs. Slater. "You don't need the money—either of you—not badly enough to commit murder."

"This isn't about money," Mrs. Slater interjected. "It's about power and the crown and all—"

"It was *never* about money," Hartsham interjected to silence her. He pulled a knife from his jacket sleeve, and Dani let out a terrified cry. "It was about using the women and girls to exchange favors with men in important positions, or resorting to stronger tactics when the men don't want to cooperate. Elise Donnelly got in the way when she began to smuggle the girls out of London and had to be removed." He gestured around the warehouse with the knife. "If you had just stayed silent, no one would have known about her connection to the brothel. But you talked to Hampton, told him about the prostitutes, convinced my wife to confide in you—you're the link in the chain between Mrs. Donnelly's murder and the brothel, and tonight, that chain will be broken."

"Your wife! She knows. When she finds out that I've been murdered, she'll tell the authorities everything."

"No, she won't. You've overestimated my little wife's spine. So easy to control her... All I have to do is threaten to take our daughter away from her, and she won't whisper one word."

Oh, Beatrice was so much stronger than he gave her credit for! Dani had come to witness that with her own eyes. Her rescue of the girl tonight proved it.

She shook her head. "And Marcus—he'll come after you," she warned in a desperate rasp, "and he won't stop until you're dead. If you kill me, he won't wait to have you tried before he kills you himself."

"Not if I kill him first." He tilted the knife back and forth, letting the lamplight reflect menacingly off the blade. "A man so driven out of his mind by finding the body of his beloved, her throat slit open from ear to ear, that no one will think his death anything but a suicide. A pistol shot to his head."

A sickening pain flashed through her, and she remained on her feet only through sheer will. "No one will believe that! Not from a man like Marcus." Not from a man whose adult life was baptized in the fires and blood of war. Standing her ground as he advanced again, she raked a disdainful glance over him and shook her head in disappointment. "Such a little man compared to someone like Marcus," she drawled with open disgust. "You can never begin to measure up to his greatness."

A growl of rage tore from his throat, and he lunged. Dani screamed—

The warehouse walls burst in around them as the shuttered windows and closed doors smashed open with an earsplitting shattering of wood and glass. Half a dozen men rushed inside, all of them with guns drawn and lanterns blazing, flooding the room with light and the jarring metallic sound of cocking pistols.

Hartsham grabbed Dani by the waist and yanked her back against him, raising the knife to her neck. The blade pressed into her throat, and she gasped with fear.

"Stay back, or I'll kill her!"

The men halted immediately in their steps, surrounding them on all sides. From the corner of her eye, Dani could see Mrs. Slater and the man in black who held her at knifepoint, then Brandon Pearce, who stood wide-legged with a gun in each hand pointed directly at Hartsham, and to his right—

"Marcus!" Her cry was silenced by the pressure of the knife biting into her throat and making her wince.

His expression coolly inscrutable, Marcus slowly raised his pistol and pointed it at Hartsham. Not one stray emotion crossed his face; not one tremble of uncertainty was visible anywhere in him. Steeliness glinted like ice in his eyes. He stared down the length of his arm to sight the barrel at Hartsham's head, every inch of him revealing the battle-tested general he was.

"Let her go," he ordered, his voice impossibly calm.

"No!" Hartsham held her close as he turned in a circle, his gaze darting around the warehouse to hunt desperately for a way to escape but finding none. "Get back, all of you! Or I will slit her throat right now!"

A man at the side of the room signaled to the men, who all took a step backward. Only Marcus remained where he was, standing as immovable as iron.

"Hurt her," Marcus warned in the same chillingly controlled voice, "and you're dead where you stand."

"I'm already dead!" Hartsham gave an unnatural laugh and yanked her roughly against him. "But I can make certain she dies, too."

With a fierce cry, Dani kicked her foot into Hartsham's knee. The blow threw him off balance, but the upward arc of the knife blade couldn't be stopped and clipped her neck. As the blade sliced her skin, she screamed and dropped the lamp. It smashed onto the stone floor at their feet in a burst of glass and flame.

Hartsham cursed and jumped back from the flames. Dani lunged out of his arms and fell onto her hands and knees, gasping for air as her hand flew to her throat.

Marcus dove over her, his shoulder lowered and slamming into Hartsham with the strength of a bull, sending him flying and then landing on the floor with a violent thud. A flurry of punches and kicks as the two men grappled—

Then Marcus shifted his weight back onto his left leg and kicked a swinging hard blow with his right. His heel caught the earl square in the chest, sending him crumpling to the floor. He pounced on top of Hartsham, throwing such hard punches that a groan of exertion came with every fist he plowed into Hartsham's face and abdomen. Each blow landed with a sickeningly dull thud that had the earl lying nearly lifeless on the stones, yet still the punches came from Marcus in great, ferocious swings.

A new fear shivered through her as she watched him—Marcus was going to beat the man to death.

She scrambled to her feet and ran to him, heedless of the blood that dripped from her neck or the flames that singed at her hem and ignoring Pearce as he rushed forward to stop her. She would *not* lose him to the darkness, not now that she'd finally found her way into his heart.

"Don't!" She grabbed his right shoulder to stop the punches, only for him to continue to strike with his left. "Please stop!"

Hartsham lay nearly unconscious beneath Marcus, his bloodied mouth moaning in pain and both eyes already swelling shut. Yet still Marcus punched mercilessly at him with all the strength he possessed, putting his full weight behind every blow.

"Marcus, stop!"

She crawled in front of him, wedging herself between him and Hartsham until he was compelled to stop and sit back on his heels. She grabbed at his hand and cried out at the sight of his knuckles, all bruised and bloodied.

When he tried to wrestle his hand away from her, to move her out of his way so he could continue to beat the man to death, she pressed herself into his arms and placed her palm against his face. She whispered, blinking hard to clear away her tears, "I won't let you kill him."

"The bastard deserves it," he growled, glancing past her to Hartsham as the earl writhed on the floor in an agonized attempt to crawl away.

"He deserves to hang even more." She brought his attention back to her by touching her lips to his. "Don't cheat Elise out of the justice she deserves by killing him here in the darkness. Let all his crimes be brought to light and dealt with in the open…no more shadows, no more secrets." She wrapped her arms around his neck and pressed her cheek against his to whisper in his ear, "You're a soldier, Marcus, not a murderer." A tear slipped down her face as she admitted, "And I love you for it."

His arms lifted loosely to her back. Then his embrace slowly tightened until he held her pressed against him, dragging in a deep and ragged breath as he nuzzled his mouth into her hair. Their hearts pounded in unison as they held each other, even as the other men came forward to grab Hartsham by the arms, yank him to his feet, and drag him to the side of the room.

"It's over," she murmured, clinging fiercely to him. All the grief and fear inside her lifted, and now there was only the sensation of Marcus's arms around her, his strength and love seeping into her and filling her up to her soul. "It's finally all over."

"And now?" Marcus asked sotto voce as he stood shoulder to shoulder with Clayton, who had arrived at the warehouse only a few moments ago and been quickly informed of what had occurred.

The two men surveyed the current state of the warehouse and the people within it. His men were awaiting orders, the same men who had followed Dani from her town house. Thanks to warnings by Marcus when they'd first been assigned to guard her, they knew to anticipate her carriage changes and doubling back of streets and hadn't lost sight of her when she and Mrs. Slater had made their way to the warehouse. Yet all that subterfuge had delayed her just enough that he, Pearce, and Merritt had arrived at the warehouse only moments behind.

Merritt still guarded Mrs. Slater, although he was only waiting for a signal from Clayton to put her into a carriage and take her to Newgate for safe keeping. There was much less certainty regarding what would happen to Hartsham, who currently sat on the floor, closely watched over by two of the men and waiting for Clayton to decide what to do about him next. Newgate wasn't an option. The man was still a peer, even if he couldn't plead privilege to avoid being tried for murder. But Marcus wanted to make certain the bastard wouldn't have another chance to harm Danielle or the rest of his family.

Now wrapped in his coat to keep her warm and cover the blood that had splattered on her dress, she stood on the far side of the warehouse, closely guarded by Pearce. A bandage marred her slender neck. Her uneasy gaze kept drifting back to Marcus, but he could offer her no more consolation until he finished confirming with Clayton what would happen next. Then he planned to scoop her into his arms, carry her home, and make love to her until the color returned to her face, the shaking stopped, and she once again felt safe.

"He'll be taken back to his town house and guarded while the property is searched. Then he'll be placed under house arrest, his every move watched," Clayton answered.

"When will he be officially charged?"

"That's a more difficult matter."

Dread swept through Marcus like an icy wind. "You think he won't be arrested?"

"He's a peer with accomplices. That makes all of this much more complicated." Clayton tugged at his gloves, his only outward sign of frustration. "It was Mrs. Slater who hired the men to break into your home and shoot at you at Vauxhall. She'll be the one arrested and tried for that, not him. As for the blackmail itself, if he's found guilty in the Lords, he can plead privilege to escape punishment." He paused as if afraid what he was about to say would cause Marcus to pummel the man a second time. "Even for his attack here on Miss Williams, since all would be considered first offenses."

"I'm beginning to like the aristocracy less and less," Marcus muttered.

Clayton slid him a sideways glance. "Yes, Your Grace."

Marcus's mouth twisted in vexation, but he ignored that bit of bait. "Regardless, he can't claim privilege in cases of murder, and he murdered Elise. He admitted it to Danielle."

"And that's the problem."

"How so?"

Clayton lowered his eyes to the scorched floor. "Whose murder do we arrest him for?"

"My sister's."

"Only if you're willing to destroy Miss Williams."

Marcus wheeled on him. "What do you mean?"

"Thanks to the woman at Pearce's town house, we have enough information to link Hartsham to John Porter's murder. He'll surely be found guilty for that. I suspect that half the men in Westminster are clients of Venus's Folly and willing to do whatever it takes to keep their proclivities hidden. Including sending him to the gallows to keep him silent." He lifted his eyes to stare somberly across the room at Danielle. "But your sister's murder is a different matter."

Marcus locked gazes with her as she stared back at the two men, careful not to let any stray emotions show on his face.

"We can only prove that he murdered Elise if you're willing to share with the world what happened here tonight, why Miss Williams left her home late at night to come to an abandoned warehouse in the Strand in pursuit of a young prostitute." He looked away from Danielle and added, "What she's been doing for the past four years and why nearly one hundred women have gone missing because of her."

His heart skipped. "You know about Nightingale?"

"There are few things that happen on English soil that the Home Office is unaware of." Clayton turned his back to the room as he explained, "There are wealthy and powerful men who would gladly see her life be destroyed in retribution for what she's done. I know you want justice, General, but you cannot link Hartsham to what Elise was doing with those prostitutes without also connecting your sister to Miss Williams. Everything she's done will come out, every last secret. Her life will be destroyed, along with her father's diplomatic career and whatever standing her aunt possesses at court and in society." He paused. "And the Braddocks by association, especially if you marry her. Claudia's marriage, Pippa's future…destroyed right along with her, just as soon as it all becomes public. Not even your reputation as one of England's greatest heroes will be able to mitigate that."

Across the room, Danielle frowned at the intensity with which Marcus continued to stare at her. His gut twisted, each breath now coming pained and labored. Despite the lamps that continued to light up the warehouse, he felt the darkness start to creep inside.

"We also don't know Hartsham's exact connection to Scepter or their endgame. Exposing his connection to your sister would destroy any chance we have of finding out." Clayton's gaze flicked darkly to Hartsham. "I don't think the earl is going to share information about them, even under interrogation."

Across the room, Merritt signaled to Clayton that he

was ready to escort Mrs. Slater to prison. He nodded and watched only long enough to see Merritt take the woman's arm to lead her from the building before folding his hands behind his back, his stance wide. The same posture Clayton had always assumed in the army when he was awaiting orders.

"The choice is yours on how to proceed," Clayton said quietly but with unquestioning resolve. "I'll do whatever you ask of me, General. So will every man here."

Danielle bit her lip in concern. Waving off Pearce's attempt to keep her in place, she started across the warehouse toward him.

The decision clawed at his heart, more fiercely with every step she took toward him...Elise or Danielle. Justice for his murdered sister or protection for the woman he loved. The same woman who had filled the emptiness in his soul and gave him purpose, who even now chased away the darkness that pushed in around him and threatened to suffocate him with what Clayton had revealed.

She loved him and trusted him. He would never betray her.

"There is no choice," he answered firmly. Then he stepped forward to greet her.

Just as her hands slid warmly into his, he saw Hartsham rise to his feet on the other side of the warehouse. He lunged at the nearby guard and wrestled the pistol out of the man's hand. He placed the muzzle at his temple.

"For Scepter!" he yelled, then pulled the trigger.

Twenty-Seven

One Month Later

"IF WE KEEP VERY QUIET AND STAY RIGHT HERE," Marcus murmured into Dani's hair as she snuggled against him on the settee in the library at Charlton Place, stealing a precious few moments to themselves, "maybe no one will notice for the rest of the evening that we're missing."

She laughed and tilted back her head to smile up at him. "And flee from our own engagement dinner? I don't think our families would like that very much."

"Our *family*," he corrected. "One family now. And they're going to have many opportunities for after-dinner conversations with us over the years. Tonight, I want you to myself a bit longer."

Hmm. She wasn't sure that her aunt and Claudia would agree with his logic, and certainly not poor Mr. Trousdale, who was currently alone with the two women. They were undoubtedly terrifying him with ongoing wedding plans that seemed to become more exotic and extravagant with each passing day. The last Dani had heard, Claudia was considering the theme of a Venetian masquerade in Hyde Park, complete with gondola rides on the Serpentine.

Dani's engagement dinner tonight was the complete opposite and very purposefully so. Given how overwhelming and perilous her life had been lately, she preferred a calm evening at home in which she and Marcus could finally—and formally—announce their engagement to their loved ones. Of course they wouldn't marry until after Claudia, and then in a small ceremony with only close friends and family in attendance. Despite Marcus's attempts to convince her to let him secure a special license so they could be married within the week, Dani stood firm. Claudia deserved this special time when she was the center of attention, and Dani didn't want to take one bit of that away from her.

He took her hand and laced his fingers through hers. "Besides, it's nice to have a private moment with you after dinner."

Thank God for that. This was the first time they'd had dinner together since that terrible night all those weeks ago, when Claudia had surprised the intruder in Elise's room. So much had happened since then that Dani could barely fathom it all. Her fingers tightened in his. She couldn't have gotten through these past few weeks without Marcus's strength to support her.

Although she still suffered nightmares over the last glimpse she'd had of him, Hartsham was dead and buried, his darkest secrets right along with him. Any attempt for more justice for his victims had been forced to stop. Under English law, neither a dead man nor his estate could be pursued for his crimes, and no one among the King's Counsel or on the Committee for Privileges saw a need to interfere with the earldom being passed to a younger brother and to Beatrice and her daughter inheriting the non-entailed properties, as set out in his will. When Brandon Pearce sent word of the government's decision, Marcus surprised her by accepting it without argument, his fight ending. He'd never told her why he'd let go of pursuing public justice for Elise, why he'd decided to allow everyone to continue to believe that she'd died from a fall from her horse.

In her heart, Dani was relieved, because now they could finally let go of the past and move on. Together.

The other lives Hartsham had worked to destroy were slowly being pieced back together. Venus's Folly closed without warning; the building where it had been located was abandoned. And then there was Mrs. Slater, the woman Dani had once trusted enough to consider bringing into Nightingale. In the end, she'd gotten away—of a sort. The carriage in which she was being transported to Newgate was attacked. Merritt Rivers, who had been escorting her and had gotten caught up in the attack, reported that the men who stopped their carriage took the woman against her will, with her fighting and screaming while they shoved her into a second carriage and drove off into the night. Merritt had been unable to put up a chase. Neither she nor her husband had been seen since that night, although Home Office agents were still scouring the country for them, convinced that Scepter was behind their disappearance. Dani knew they would never be found.

The same would have happened to the woman at the town house, too, if Clayton hadn't thought to spirit her away before he went to the warehouse, hiding her under guard in the last place Scepter would think to look for a prostitute—in the bedroom of the Right Reverend William Howley, Bishop of London.

So far, Scepter had left her and Marcus alone, but she feared that this wouldn't be the last they'd hear of them.

"I have something for you." He lifted her hand to his lips and kissed the backs of her fingers. "I've been waiting all evening for the right moment to give it to you."

"A gift?" Her chest panged with love at how wonderful he was. "You really shouldn't have." Truly…but she was also dying to know what it was.

"Not only should I do this, but I should have done it long before now." He reached into the small opening of the fob in his trousers. "If I wasn't such a nodcock, I would have done this the first evening I saw you again, right there in the garden at the party, looking so beautiful."

Her throat tightened with emotion, yet she managed to tease, "By the glow of Roman torchlight?"

His lips pulled into a lazy half grin that sent her pulse spiking the way it always did. Knowing better than to answer that, he took her hand and slipped a ring onto her finger. "For you, my love."

She stared at it, unable in her surprise to find her voice. Oh, it was simply beautiful…a gold band scattered with tiny pearls and delicate diamonds that glittered in the firelight.

"It was my mother's engagement ring," he said quietly. "She'd want you to have it."

"I can't accept this," she whispered, although she stroked a fingertip longingly over it. "It belongs to Claudia or Pippa…" And breaking her heart that such a beautiful symbol of love could never be hers.

"My birth mother's ring," he clarified. "Claudia and Pippa have enough special pieces from their own mothers. This ring is meant for the woman I marry. It belongs to you, my darling." He lifted her hand to place a kiss to the ring. "Now and always."

The words from the night he'd first made love to her, when he promised her his trust and devotion…*now and always*.

"Marcus," she breathed, blinking rapidly to clear away the tears. She couldn't put to words how beautiful it was and how special it made her feel. How deeply loved and cherished. So she slipped her arms around his neck and hugged him tightly to her instead, never wanting to let go.

"I also have a second gift. An early wedding gift of a sort," he murmured into her ear, "if you think you could bear it."

Another gift? But she couldn't imagine anything more wonderful than the gifts he'd already given her— this ring…and his love. "Yes?"

Releasing her, he stood to fetch a glass of port from the tray sitting on the mantel. He turned to face her, his gaze locking soberly with hers. Her heart pounded with sudden unease as she waited for him to speak.

"I contacted the prime minister last week," he informed her. "Told Liverpool that I was courting a secret reformer."

Knowing Marcus too well, she challenged, "You did not."

His eyes glinted mischievously over the rim of the crystal tumbler as he took a sip, and for a beat, she wondered if she were wrong and the dashing devil had done just that.

"Well," he admitted, "perhaps I didn't put it that way exactly. But I *did* tell him that you were interested in pursuing legislation that grants more rights to women over their property and in petitioning the courts to make certain that penalties for abusing women were enforced."

She swelled with pride and happiness, and with a sense of something so much bigger, so much more important, than she'd ever been a part of before.

"He said that he'd be willing to meet with you to discuss it."

Excitement bubbled in her chest. "This is marvelous!"

"*Only* to discuss it," he warned. "And probably only as a favor to me because he hopes to win me over to his side on the corn laws, which will never happen. Most likely nothing will come of it."

Yet she smiled, happiness blossoming inside her. "Most likely not. But it's a start." One she very much planned to build upon over the years to come.

When she thought of the grueling work ahead of her, instead of the burden that had weighed upon her for the past four years, she felt energized and excited. Ready to take on the world! And she wouldn't stop until real change was enacted to protect women. It would be her wedding gift in honor of Nightingale's memory—to honor all the women they'd saved, and especially the ones they couldn't.

She traced her fingertip lovingly over the ring. Grief panged in her chest and probably always would whenever she thought of the network and how it had once been. But when she'd told the women who had helped her that it was shutting down, most of them surprised her by volunteering to help with the new direction in which she wanted to focus her energies—not by helping women in secret but by attacking Parliament openly, sharing stories of battered women, and holding their abusers accountable.

A reformer, indeed. Lord Liverpool had no idea of the storm she planned on unleashing.

"You can't use the name Nightingale anymore," he murmured, raising the glass to his lips. "What will you call your new charity?"

She'd thought about that a great deal during the past few weeks. "Angel Wings," she answered. "To raise up those who can't do so on their own."

He returned to his seat beside her. "With that name, the men in Parliament might think that your organization will be insubstantial enough to frighten away."

"Then they are in for a rude awakening." When he held out the glass of port to her, she accepted it, then finished what was left in the glass with a single swallow. She smiled devilishly through her fingers as she wiped the drops of sweet liquid from her lips. "Because we're avenging angels, and God help those who stand in our way."

His eyes shone at her, full of pride and love. As he leaned over to kiss her, voices in the hall interrupted them. He stopped, his mouth poised less than an inch from hers, so close that she could feel the heat of his lips tickling over hers. She held her breath, achingly waiting for him to kiss her.

"He insisted that I pose for him, right there in the Louvre Palace!" Harriett related her story to poor Mr. Trousdale as the two passed outside the door on their way to the drawing room. "So I said, 'Antoine, I couldn't possibly pose *dans le nu* for you!' But he simply would *not* relent."

"Did Watteau paint you, then?" Mr. Trousdale asked, not yet having learned that it wasn't good to encourage Harriett in her stories.

"Well, I can never say, you understand, but I will admit that his *Quellnymphe* does look rather like me..."

Dani's lips curled into an exasperated but loving smile for her aunt.

"Didn't Watteau die before your aunt was born?" Marcus asked.

She patted his hand. "We never let the truth interfere with a good story."

"Of course not." He leaned in to touch his lips to hers.

Footsteps pounded down the hall toward the library. "*Nneeiigghhh-h-h!!!!*"

With a groan of frustration by Marcus and a laugh by Dani, he sat back just as Pippa came skipping into the room, galloping her stuffed horse through the air beside her. She launched herself into the air and landed on the settee between them with a neighing laugh.

"No galloping in the house," he scolded mildly, which went completely unheeded, as had every other admonishment he'd given her about not running indoors. "What are you doing awake at this hour? You should be upstairs in bed."

She trotted the horse across her lap, jumping invisible fences on her knees. "Brutus couldn't sleep."

"Oh?"

She nodded, not moving her attention from the horse as she danced it across her night rail and kicked her feet beneath her. Her pink slippers bounced in the air, her feet not touching the floor. "There are people in the house for dinner again."

Sadness panged in Dani's chest as she realized what the little girl meant. "It's all right, Penelope." She wrapped her arms around Pippa and cradled her close. "No one will break into the house tonight. You're safe here. Your Uncle Marcus has made certain of it."

The girl's slender shoulders relaxed, the only outward sign of her unease tonight as it faded beneath Dani's assurances. She neighed again and nodded the horse's head up and down in joint approval.

"So safe, in fact," Marcus added as he reached across the settee and took Dani's hand in his, "that Miss Williams is thinking of making Charlton Place her home, here with us." He squeezed her fingers. "What would you think, poppet, if I married Miss Williams and she came to live with us?"

A knot of emotion tightened in Dani's throat when the little girl's face twisted into an uncertain expression, only for the moment's fleeting panic to vanish when Pippa stuck out her bottom lip and demanded to know, "Would I have to let her ride Daisy?"

With his eyes gleaming mischievously, Marcus whispered into Pippa's ear with mock secrecy yet still loudly enough that Dani could hear, "I'm pretty certain that Miss Williams has her own pony and wouldn't need to ride yours."

"Then I think I'd like that!" Pippa answered with a resolute nod. Then she neighed again and translated for the stuffed horse's benefit, "So would Brutus."

Dani laughed. They hugged her between them, and Marcus leaned over his niece's head to finally bestow the lingering kiss he'd been attempting to give her since they sneaked into the library to be alone—the kiss her heart had been waiting to claim from the man she so dearly loved...*now and always.*

Epilogue

Three months later

"Good day, gentlemen," Marcus called out to the group of a half dozen former soldiers gathered in front of the old armory as he rode his horse through the opened outer gate and dismounted. "Thank you for meeting me here." He led his horse up beside theirs and tied it to one of the iron rings embedded in the ten-foot-tall brick fence encircling the outer yard. "My apologies regarding the horses. The mews aren't yet completed, but I didn't want to delay this moment any longer."

Around him, his old friends exchanged puzzled glances as they waited for him to explain why he'd asked them here. He grinned, certain they thought him mad for calling them all here, and today of all days—his last in London before he and Dani departed on their wedding trip to Italy, to visit her parents and spend much needed time alone together.

But he wanted this settled before he left.

"What moment would that be exactly, General?" Pearce called out from the back of the group.

Marcus smiled at him. Because of all the work involved with the armory and all the changes in his home life, Marcus hadn't seen Pearce much since he stood as